WRITE ME A MURDER ON JULES VERNE'S ISLAND

A <u>LIQUID COOL</u> COZY MURDER MYSTERY

Book Nine

AUSTIN DRAGON

WELL-TAILORED BOOKS

Published by Well-Tailored Books, California

Write Me a Murder on Jules Verne's Island
(Liquid Cool, Book 9)

978-1-946590-76-3 (paperback)
978-1-946590-72-5 (ebook)

http://www.austindragon.com

Book cover design by Leslie K.

Printed in the United States of America

CONTENTS

Introduction

Vacation!

We'd been planning it for more than a year, ever since I returned from my Lunar Colony Case. I'd never been to the Moon before, but that was no vacation. Giant killer isopods, running around in astronaut suits, laser-gun battles, almost getting sucked into space. Yeah, that wasn't a vacation. Besides I went there to work, not float around by the pool in gravity one-sixth that of Earth. Dot hadn't been on any vacation for years either. Cruz Jr.'s expanding vocabulary somehow included the word too lately. Kat couldn't really talk yet, so she was very low maintenance; she'd make her fun anywhere.

Dot and I learned another lesson as new parents. Vacations were damn expensive enough. Vacation with little kids? Now, we learned for ourselves why families so rarely did so. We both were making good money, but every time we looked at the total cost for our family outing our enthusiasm flew out the window via jetpack.

We ended up signing up with one of the many travel touring companies in Metropolis. It was owned by one of Dot's clients. They'd take care of everything—flight, accommodations, food, entertainment, and transportation. We were going to see ten countries in fourteen days. Sounded fun at first. We looked at our world map and circled all the countries in question. One vacation and we'd be able to cross off ten countries from our "visit every country on Earth" list at once. But as the departure date, neared our anxiety increased.

Then one day Cruz Jr. showed us a page he found on the family computer—Jules Verne's Island. He wanted to go to the Moon too, he wanted to walk on the bottom of the ocean, he wanted to see giant animals—and bring his sister too. I asked my employee/secretary/office manager—VP of Client Services, Punch Judy (it was hard for me to keep up with her job titles too) about it.

"Wasn't Jules Verne American?" I asked her.

"American?! *Mon dieu*! He's French! Cruz, how can you know everything but not that?"

"Was he a criminal?"

"No."

"Or a hovercar racer?"

"*C'est fou?*"

"I'm not crazy. Then I don't know him."

"He was a great, ancient, genius French writer of prophetic fiction! People hadn't even gotten to space yet, the submarine wasn't invented, and there were no illegal invisibility suits. Genius! They created a whole island and named it after him."

"What about the other island?" I asked. "H.G. Wells' Island. I hear it's better."

I was purposely winding her up and got the response I expected. "*Mange ta langue!* Sacrilege! That island is stupid! It's British. Nobody wants to go there!"

Telling me to eat my own tongue (I found out later that's what she said since I don't speak French) among other things, she went on for an hour. At first, I thought, *This Jules Verne's Island is for kids*, but Cruz Jr. kept after Dot and me, showing us all the fun things for mommies and daddies too. Then we saw the price. That ended the conversation.

The fateful day came, and the entire Cruz family was off to the Metropolis International and Interspace Airport bound for our fourteen-day, ten-country Asian vacation. So how did we get diverted to Jules Verne's Island anyway? Not for a real vacation, but to solve a murder!

My *Write Me a Murder* Case on a fantastical multi-amusement theme park and island resort named after one ancient sci-fi writer, occupied by a crazy bunch of current sci-fi writers—victim and suspects amongst them. I could've added this one to my From the Crazy Maniac Files, but those are single "crazy maniacs," good, bad, and in between.

It all happened in seventy-two hours. Me, my wife, my two kids, on a secluded island with a bunch of the scariest maniacs in the solar system—writers! And the most dangerous kind—fiction writers. The time when I needed a healthy array of weapons the most, I was gun-less (no omega-gun), Pony-less (no hovervehicle), and on vacation with the family. Why can't madness leave this detective alone long enough for me to have a decent vacation with my own family? Well, at least my kids got to have some fun.

PART ONE: DRAMA AT METRO INTERNATIONAL

I should have seen it for the omen it was. We left the Concrete Mama, our residential apartment megatower, early in the morning—me, my wife Dot, my son, and my daughter. The entire family loaded into a Let It Ride Enterprises hovervan bound for the airport. At four years old—or as he insisted, four and a half—Cruz Jr. was still a bundle of endless energy. He was too old for his favorite toy of terror—his hoverchair, but had found plenty of new ones, all seemingly related to cowboys and ninjas. Kat, on the other hand, was still in her adorable cute angel phase. Lots of smiling, giggling, wobbling around as a new walker, carrying her favorite stuffed pink cat wherever she went.

For a change, there was no rain at all in Metropolis. The summer season was here. The weather was absolutely beautiful, and at dawn the sun would come out to say hello, but it wasn't dawn yet. We'd be at the airport before it could arrive. The supercity of Metropolis, the largest on Earth with its fifty million residents was known for its ever-rain. Hovercars, mega-skyscrapers, and the rain. However, summer season would have to wait until next year. The family was on its way for its very first vacation ever.

The hovertraffic started twenty feet up. Our hovervan taxi rose into the sky lanes. All private hovercar traffic was funneled into designated virtual lanes, one above another. The only vehicles that could fly where they pleased were the police, firemen, garbage trucks, and megacorporate zeppelins floating through the air flashing their advertisements. The sky lanes, row above row, were usually chaotic, but we'd left early enough. The hovercar traffic wasn't too bad.

Dot held Kat in her arms. Our daughter had her face inches from the passenger window, staring out at all the hovercraft around us. I managed Cruz Jr., who wanted to see every hovercraft around us too, but, unlike Kat, was jumping all over the place to get what he was sure were better views.

"Stay with me," I said. "If the driver slams on the air-brakes, you're going to go crashing through the front windshield and you'll 'return to the surface.'"

He thought that was funny and then went back to ignoring me and jumping all around looking at the hovercars. Dot was uncharacteristically quiet. I put a hand on her shoulder. She looked at me and smiled.

"What are you thinking?" I asked.

"Our first family vacation."

"Yeah, it's great."

"I thought it would never get here."

"We'll be on the plane and off to ten countries in fourteen days."

"That's a lot to see. Do you think it's too much? I mean for the kids."

"No," I said. "We're going to have fun."

7

"We deserve it. I can't even remember my last vacation. Lots of trips for work, but no vacations."

"I promised you a vacation after my Moon trip and here we are."

"I want to go to the Moon, Daddy," Cruz Jr. said. He had stopped his rubbernecking at the hovercars.

"One day."

"Okay." That was all I had to say, and he was back to what he was doing.

We had a good hovertaxi driver. Let It Ride Enterprises was a transportation megacorp owned and run by my best friend Run-Time. The hovervan taxi was a gift from him for our first family vacation. The vehicle was plush, roomy, and had a nice floral smell, not too strong, just right. Let It Ride was high quality at all times. Our driver was making good time to Metro International.

Large hovercraft, like trucks and tankers, were in the bottommost virtual lanes. Buses and RV hovercraft were in the lanes above them. All personal and commercial hovercars were in the main virtual lanes above both. Hoverbikers (who everyone hated) zipped around wherever they wanted. The sun was peeking out from the horizon more and more.

Soon Metropolis International and Interspace Airport came into view. The last time I was there it was to go to the Lunar Colony. This time, thankfully, it would all be Earthbound. As we approached the massive, sprawling structure with the rings of hovertraffic around its many terminals and both air- and spacecraft departing and landing, it always reminded me of an invasion of extraterrestrial aliens. But the only extraterrestrials in our galaxy were humans from Up-Top.

We had arrived at the Asia Terminal. The hovervan landed in the passenger loading area and we began to pile out. My wife was known as China Doll by many, but women who knew her called her China; men called her Doll. We, her family, called her by her real name—Dot. She was more famous than me—second in command at Metropolis's premiere image and style salon, Eye Candy. As the consummate fashionista, even now every piece of her clothing, every accessory, and every piece of jewelry was the trendiest and most stylish. She was bundled up in a puffy jacket, a sheer head scarf, with her silky black hair tied back, black skintight pants, and neon blue heels

"Cruz, you have the diapers," she said to me pushing our daughter Kat in her hoverstroller.

My claim to fame was as president, CEO, COO, and detective-on-the-go of the Liquid Cool Detective Agency. Here, I was the diaper minder.

"It's in this bag," I replied.

As our hovertaxi driver helped us, I stood in awe of all our luggage. I didn't even want to count it. I'd be sick. How could four human beings have so much luggage? But our driver was already getting a large hovercart for us.

Cruz Jr. was at that strange age for me. He was too big to constantly carry or hold his hand, but he was still a little munchkin who loved using his ninja teleporting abilities—meaning disappearing when you weren't looking. He noticed me watching him and smiled.

"I got my eye on you," I said.

He laughed out loud.

"Stay with your mother and sister. And help your mother push Kat in her stroller."

"I can do it, Mommy," he said to Dot and ran over to push his sister's hoverstroller.

We had all our seemingly dozens of pieces of luggage stacked on a long hovercart. I generously tipped our driver, and we thanked him. He waited until we were all through the main doors of the terminal for check-in. Drivers had to stay close to their vehicle at all times. Drones ruthlessly monitored every inch of the terminals, and you'd get ticketed or towed if you weren't careful. I waved to him and the driver hopped into his hovervan taxi and was off into the sky. The family and I walked into the belly of the Metro International beast.

The smartest thing I did for our vacation was get us "premium check-in." You had to go through all kinds of background checks and pay a fee, but it was well worth it. We could bypass all the crazy, winding lines of people at the regular check-in counters. Why everyone didn't do it was beyond me.

What we couldn't bypass was security. We went through the scanning arches and luggage check-in as security personnel checked our tickets. Ordinarily, our luggage would be sent on its way, but neither Dot nor I believed in lost luggage. We kept our mountain of luggage with us and would pay the fee to physically watch it loaded onto our flight. The lines weren't that bad. We had gone through the entire thing in less than fifteen minutes and were headed to our departure gate.

"Please tell me you got the VIP waiting area upgrade," Dot said.

"Well, isn't the Cruz family VIPs?"

She smiled, reached over with her free hand and squeezed my chin. Kat laughed at us.

The VIP lounge was a secluded area away from the "mere mortals" of the departure gate. The seats were bigger and better, equipped with their own entertainment centers—music and TV. Lot of vending machines for cold and hot food and drinks. I even bought us all our own headphones. The screen was on a swivel arm. Dot found a movie as I situated both Cruz Jr. and Kat on one chair. Dot would watch them and I'd watch our mountain of luggage. We'd gotten to the airport and through everything a lot quicker than we thought. Better to be early than late, but we had an hour to go before boarding.

Everything around us seemed normal. The wife and kids were watching their movie. I watched our luggage and kept a roving eye on our surroundings. Inside the VIP waiting area was also an All-Vacationers Travel Hub—the fun, lively commercial area of travel agents. Their glass-walled office was filled with changing holo-screens of travel destinations and live bands of smiling performers. We made sure to sit as far away from them as possible, and they were why Dot had quickly grabbed the kids' attention with TV.

The purpose of the hub was to entice travelers with a sea of vacation offers. Deals offered were better than you could ever get on the Net, or so they said. Your bags were already packed, you were already regretting coming back to your day job—what better way to get you to buy a vacation add-on, or switch to a whole new travel itinerary altogether.

That's when I saw him. A clean-cut kid with blond hair wearing a light jacket and tie. He clearly was looking at me and seemed to be getting up the nerve to approach me. I didn't like it. I had no weapons to shoot anyone if needed.

The kid came out of the office and made a beeline to me. He smiled, then did a Japanese bow.

"Are you Mr. Cruz?"

"I am."

"Please, sir, may I speak with you?"

"Why? What did I do?"

"Oh, no. You have done nothing wrong, sir. May I simply speak with you privately?"

My wife and I glanced at each other, then looked at him suspiciously.

"It will only be a moment, sir, I assure you. I work for one of the companies that represents one of our travel destinations."

"Which one?" Dot asked him.

"Jules Verne's Island."

"We did want to go there," she said, "but it's far too expensive."

"Mr. Cruz, only a moment of your time. I'll even give a discount voucher for your time."

"Sure, I'll listen. But I don't want my luggage to get stolen."

"Oh, no, sir. I will take care of you."

The kid waved to someone and I saw a young security guard run to us. He told the guard to watch our luggage cart.

"Cruz, what have you done?" she asked. Of course, my wife stood from her chair and was suspiciously watching me, and so were my kids.

"Nothing," I replied.

I followed him into an office with clear glass walls all around. My wife and kids watched as we talked. The young man was a great salesman. He presented his case well, was prepared for all my objections, made me multiple offers I couldn't refuse, included bribes, and closed the deal.

We walked back out to the wife and kids.

"Cruz, what's going on?" she asked.

"Dot, Mr.—"

"Mr. Vec, ma'am," the young man said.

"Mr. Vec has an offer for us that I think we should consider."

"Cruz, we're on vacation and our flight will be boarding within the hour."

"Dot, I'm going to just come out and say it. The owners of the island want to change our vacation plans to Jules Verne's Island to take charge of a situation until police authorities arrive. We don't have to do anything but enjoy our vacation. The authorities will arrive, be off on their way, we'll still be there to enjoy all our vacation days to the fullest. We both want the Asian vacation, but ten countries and fourteen days with our avalanche of luggage and two kids—that means ten flights and ten more times at the airport. We both want simple, and this is it."

"All expenses paid, ma'am," Vec added.

"What's the situation, Cruz?"

I looked at Vec for a second. I turned to her. "There's been a murder on the island, or they think it is. It could be he just...expired."

The look on my wife's face was a cross between confusion, outrage, and incredulity.

"We wouldn't have to do anything. I wouldn't have to do anything," I told her.

"No!" Dot said.

"They don't have the personnel to properly manage the situation until the authorities arrive."

"No."

"The scene is sealed up. It's at a hotel. It's nothing dangerous."

"No."

"Actually, as a private detective, I'm not allowed to investigate a murder. Forget those books and movies. It's illegal."

"No."

"Every year this group of authors rents the entire island for the month. They have normal security, of course, but the island doesn't have its own police of any kind. They have to be called in from the mainland."

"No."

"My role would be to simply be there. That's it. It was on our list to one day visit, so here's our chance. A free vacation. Cruzie, Kat, can we say 'free!'"

"No."

"Since these authors have rented the island, no one else is there besides hotel and grounds staff. We'd have the entire island practically to ourselves. There are only five of these authors on the island and, they stay in their rooms most of the time."

"No."

"Yes, one of them might have murdered someone. The murdered man is an author too. But you see this is just a writer-on-writer thing, so there's no danger."

"No."

"So free vacation for us and the family. Then there are the perks. On-demand massage, spa, sauna, full gym, zero-gravity swimming pool."

Vec held up his tablet. As he pushed a button, the screen changed. The kids were watching closely too.

"Laser golf, holo-tennis courts, bike path encircling the island for running, biking, or hover-biking."

Vec displayed live-action demos on his tablet.

"Famous Jules Verne's amusement park all to ourselves," I said, "including steampunk-themed hoverchair transportation."

"Mommy, amusement park," Cruz Jr. said.

"Scuba diving, mini-floating islands for sunbathing, family hydrofoils for boating, para-sailing, and waterskiing."

Vec showed her on his tablet.

"And! The island has its own mini-mall. Of specific interest are its fashion stores featuring the latest styles from around the world."

Dot took the tablet from the man.

"Styles for adults and children—of all ages."

Vec and I stood quietly as Dot finished viewing images and demos on the tablet.

She looked at me.

"Yes."

I raised my hand in triumph. "Kids! Mommy said yes! We're going to have so much fun!"

She pointed the tablet at me.

"Cruz, we're on vacation! No working!"

"I can't work. I'm a private citizen. I'm not allowed to investigate the police's case. They'd put me in jail."

"Ma'am, all the owners want is his presence," Vec said. "This is beyond the scope of the island staff. The owners simply want peace of mind and will graciously compensate you for your wonderful time on the island. Mr. Cruz won't have to do a thing."

"Cruz, I am putting you on notice. No working cases! This is our vacation. Our first vacation as a family."

"Dot, I can't investigate a police case. I'm a private citizen. Private detectives can't go running around solving murder mysteries. That's all Movie-Town fakery. The one thing I can promise you is there will be no investigating by me on this vacation."

Welcome to my Liquid Cool Cozy Murder Mystery on Jules Verne's Island.

PART TWO: GETTING THERE

Thankfully, we'd kept our mountain of luggage with us, so our new change of vacation plans would work out smoothly. Cruz Jr. was jumping for joy that he'd get to see all the island's amusement worlds. Kat didn't know what was going on but was having a good time anyway. Dot was still suspicious, but Vec was not about to lose his "sale." Now, he was showing her all the many fashion, shoes, and accessory items she'd be able to touch, try on and take with her when we landed.

I'd been used to traveling on some fairly large aircraft and spacecraft. I'd never been on a one-level plane before. At least it was a hoverplane but it looked tiny to me. Vec told us we'd be able to hop on our flight fifteen minutes sooner, and that all the other passengers were already boarded. Dot and I didn't like being rushed, but when someone hands you a free, all-expenses trip to a luxurious island resort somewhere, you accept it with a smile.

The hoverplane had an unusual configuration.

"Daddy, it looks like a bird," Cruz Jr. remarked.

It did. A giant hawk-like construction, but all silver. Our luggage was loaded and we all walked up the steps.

"Does this seem like a small plane to you?" my wife asked me. "I've never been on a plane this small."

"We're only going to the Caribbean. This must be the size of planes for shorter trips," I said convincingly, though I thought we were boarding a toy plane too.

I quickly counted the number of passenger windows. At the top, Dot and I noticed two flight attendants wearing white fabric surgical face masks. We slowed down but they gestured us up.

"Everything is fine, please come on through," one of them said.

We stepped onto the plane and both flight attendants started spraying us with tiny metallic spray bottles. Cruz Jr. spoke for all of us.

"Yuck!"

Kat made a nasty face, which I'm sure looked like Dot's and mine.

"This is for your safety," the second one said.

"Our safety?" Dot asked.

"Yes."

"Do we get masks?" she asked.

"You don't need them, ma'am. You're safe."

"Safe? But we don't get masks. What about our safety?"

One of the masked flight attendants led us to our seats. It was then we realized that the plane was practically empty. The hoverplane had seats for under three hundred—rows of four connected seats in the middle and two connected seats on either side. A spattering of unmasked passengers were seated in different areas, no pattern.

"Where is everyone?" I asked.

"This is a special flight redirected by the company, sir, to get you and your party to the island as soon as possible. Then the plane will continue on from there."

"Is anyone else getting off at the island besides us?" Dot asked.

"No, ma'am. You're our special VIPs for the trip. You can have a seat wherever you wish."

Dot and I looked at each other and smiled. This was a bit overwhelming, in a good way, for us. We practically had an entire hoverplane to ourselves. Of course, Cruz Jr. was about to start running through the craft.

"J.R., sit!" Dot commanded before his feet could begin their jump to hyper-speed.

We picked almost dead center of the craft. Kat would be in the center of the four seats, I'd be on one side, Dot on the other. It made no sense to put Cruz Jr. in the center. He'd want to watch the entire taxiing and ascent into the sky from the window, then once the "seat belts on" light was off would be running around. Cruz ran to an empty window seat, fastened his own seat belt, and put his forehead on the window, looking out.

"How does he know how to fasten seat belts already?" I asked Dot.

"Cruz, it's the same seat belts as his hoverchair, when he had it."

"Oh."

"Cruz, I can't believe you talked me into this."

"It's the right thing to do. We both were feeling the same thing. Instead of hopping on and hopping off ten different planes in different countries, with two kids and a truckload of luggage, we get to really relax in one place that has everything we need. That's a vacation. The other trip would have been a marathon. We'd go, the days would fly by, we'd return and be more exhausted, wondering what kind of vacation was that."

"You're right. I want to live at the spa and shop in between."

"Exactly. The kids can play. I can sleep."

"Sleep? Is that a vacation?"

"Sleep is always a good vacation. Sleep on a vacation island. That's what I'll do, with one eye open to watch Cruz Control over there."

Cruz Jr. heard his nickname and turned his head to look at us.

"When do we go?" he asked.

"Ladies and gentlemen, this is special Flight 55 bound for Jules Verne's Island, then departing for the Bahamas Archipelago. Our flight crew will conduct final checks and we'll be departing from Metro International in about ten minutes. Total flight time will be about ninety minutes. Clear skies all the way. Please remain seated with your seat belts fastened until I give the visual and audio signals for you to move about the craft freely. Refreshments will be served and entertainment will be available. Enjoy the flight."

"Our feet will be on the ground on the island in less than two hours," I said to my wife. "If we did our multi-country trip, we'd still be in flight. Three hours from now, you'll be getting a massage at the island spa."

"Cruz, you don't need to keep selling me. We're here. It's not like I'm going to crash through the window."

"Yeah, that wouldn't be cool." I lifted Kat from her chair. "How are we supposed to strap a toddler in the chair?"

"Give her here."

Dot sat Kat in her lap and pulled out another strap from her chair, one side to the other, across Kat's belly. Our daughter looked at the strap and tried to pull it.

"Yeah, Kat, I don't know where that strap thing came from either."

"Daddy." We heard Cruz Jr. "Let her see."

Of course, we knew what he meant. Dot unfastened her and I was up from my seat with Kat in my arms to take her over to the seat with her brother. So now I was stuck with Kat in my lap looking out the window, Cruz Jr. leaning over to look out the window, and Dot sitting in the seat in front of us to look out the window. The hoverplane began to coast down the tarmac, no wheels. It climbed into the sky fast. Both kids were mesmerized. We were high up in the clouds before we knew it and still climbing. The sun was out. So beautiful. It looked like a postcard picture.

I was back in the center main row of seats, my seat inclined all the way back, and my eyes closed. The blur—also known as Cruz Jr.—ran past, down the aisle, in one direction. He was making his own fun. As long as we could hear him, things were fine. If he got quiet, that's when you had to see what he was doing. Knowing him, he'd be fiddling with the emergency exit. My last case I was almost sucked out into space. I wasn't about to get sucked out of a plane into the sky tens of thousands of feet above the surface of the Earth.

Dot had Kat in her arms. My wife was networking. I couldn't believe it. Before the plane landed, she'd know the names of everyone aboard, including the stewardesses. She'd have their business cards, they'd have hers, and she'd have more than a few as complimentary customers at Eye Candy. I chuckled to myself. I had no desire whatsoever to know any of the strangers on the plane or sign up any potential clients.

"Excuse me, sir?"

I opened my eyes. A well-dressed man was standing over me. I put my seat back in the upright position.

"Yes?"

"Your wife says you're a detective."

"I am."

The man sat down in the seat next to me. Cruz Jr. ran down the aisle in the other direction. I wanted to tell him to pull the emergency exit to suck me out of the plane.

"What do you do?" I asked.

"I'm a recruiter."

"For the military or law enforcement?"

"Not that kind of recruiter. Corporate. I'm the guy who hires people."

"Oh, talent acquisition."

"Yes."

"I've only hired one person and that's enough."

"I've hired thousands. The stories I could tell."

"I'm sure."

"How much does a detective charge?"

"Depends. I hear the case first. See if it's the kind of case I do, or can do. See if I could solve it successfully. Mainly make sure that it's not a matter better suited for the police."

"Assess first. Yes. Makes sense. I'm sure you have much better stories than me."

"Maybe. What does your megacorp do?"

"Funny you should ask. We're actually delivering a shipment to JV Isle."

"Is that slang for Jules Verne's Island?"

"It is, but you're not expected to know that. All businesses have their own verbal shorthand."

The man turned his arm over and touched part of his right jacket sleeve. A screen turned on and he began to scroll through a series of photos.

"Are those mannequins of famous people?"

"Puppets. My company makes the best, most realistic puppets in the world. String and autonomous."

"Autonomous?"

"Of all sizes." He gave me one of those self-satisfied cat-eats-the-canary smiles.

I hated puppets! I wanted this man away from me.

"With all those theme parks, isn't it dangerous?" I heard Dot ask one of the male passengers.

"Not at all. All these theme parks, including the exclusive island resort ones, have layers of security. Islands like the one you're going to have their own island security personnel separate from the island management and the standard security personnel. The two never interact. The island security is hidden from both visitors and island staff watches and records everything. An added layer of security. Peace of mind for the corporate owners of the island and for the insurance brokers."

Since Dot was networking, I had to do the same. I struck up a conversation with the two stewardesses and a gentleman who'd been to "JV Isle" at least twenty times before.

"What's the story about the surgical masks you two were wearing?" I asked the flight attendants.

"It's fine. You checked out," one said.

"*I* checked out?" I asked.

"A couple of flags came back on you, so we had to do a few more checks," she said. "That little quarantine incident at the Silicon Dunes Convention Center."

"That wasn't my fault."

"And you did visit the Moon recently."

"Up-Top has less germs than Earth. If they'd let me on their White Rock, I'm good enough to go anywhere."

"We still need to go through our own checks," she said.

"And I thought our fellow passengers here were the infected ones," I said, looking at the male one.

He laughed.

Of course they wanted me to tell them about both cases, which I did for awhile, but I wanted to know about the island.

"It's man-made?" I asked.

"Parts of it are real archipelago, but most are added man-made island," the man said. "Different sections, or worlds, for the enjoyment of visitors. One can spend time in one of those worlds without visiting another and be completely content."

"Twenty times you've been there?" I asked.

"At least. First time was thirty years ago during a big remodeling and re-launch."

"But the island right now is virtually empty?" I asked the flight attendants.

"Every year these writers rent the entire island for a few weeks."

"That must be a lot of money."

"These writers are some of the richest in the business."

"Sci-fi writers, you said?"

"Yes."

"I didn't think there was much money in writing sci-fi," I said. "Especially when we have hovercars and colonies on Mars. What's there to write about?"

"Quite a lot," the man said.

"But still, why would the island allow a bunch of writers to rent their entire island for that long, and lose all that business?"

"The tourist trade during this time of the year is brutal," the other attendant said. "It's their slowest time of the year, so I'm sure the writers made the island owners an offer they couldn't refuse."

"Steady income every year is always better than not knowing what will come in," the man added.

"I can relate to that," I said. "Do you have any virtual maps of the island?" I asked the attendants.

"Yes," one said and walked to her station at the front of the craft.

I felt a hand on my shoulder and glanced over to see that Dot had joined me, sitting to the left of me. In the seat next to her was Kat playing with her cat toy.

I returned my attention to the man and asked, "What can you tell me about the island?"

"What do you want to know?"

The attendant returned with a tablet.

"Can you project it, so we can all see?" I asked her.

She aimed it at a part of the craft wall above the windows and projected an image of Jules Verne's Island for us all to see. The island was huge.

"It's the largest man-made island in the Bahamas Archipelago," the man said.

"Tell me about the accommodations, different worlds, transportation, all the good stuff. Then when we're done with that, I want to hear about all the nasty rumors."

The attendants and man laughed.

"You want the juicy stuff?" an attendant said.

"The juiciest," I said.

Between the flight attendants, the man and others on the craft who joined us, we learned literally everything there was to know about Jules Verne's Island. Dot and I were receiving a crash course, and in the hour that passed we'd become certified experts. The only reason our group debrief had ended was because we had entered JV Isle airspace.

"I'll be right back," I told my wife as I left for one of the airplane's communication booths.

Whether audio or vid-phone, one could make whatever secure call one wanted to anywhere on the planet—off-world was extra, a lot extra. I didn't expect to reach him. Only leave a message with his office, but my best friend Run-Time was in.

He was the founder, President, CEO, and COO of Let It Ride Enterprises. He owned all the top car washes, hovercar body shops, hovercar rental shops, hovercycle rental shops, hovertaxicab, and hoverlimousine services in Metropolis and, thanks to me, even had off-world clients now. We'd been best friends since high school. He actually got his idea to wear hats from me. I wore my tan fedora, he wore his flat hats. Black, clean-cut, flat-hat, slim-fit business suit and slim tie, navy this time. His face was on the screen.

"Cruz!" he greeted. "You and the family are on the way to Asia."

"Change of plans. We've vacationing on Jules Verne's Island."

"JV Island. In the Caribbean. Very exclusive, Cruz. What friend got you that deal? You'll have to tell me so they can become my friend too."

"Since we'll be landing soon, can you do me a big favor?"

"Name it."

"Can you do one of those deep-background corporate financial and business interest searches of the island's ownership?"

"Cruz, aren't you on vacation?"

"I am, but I'd like to know about the island I'm taking my family to."

"Most people just look them up on the Net, Cruz. Never mind. At least try to enjoy some of your vacation. Call you on your mobile?"

"Yeah."

"I'll get you the info."

"Thanks, Run-Time."

"Say hello to Dot and the kids for me."

Anything and everything there was to know about JV Island, Run-Time would find out for me. He bought and sold companies for a living. I returned to my seat.

"Ladies and gentlemen, special Flight 55 has entered Jules Verne's Island airspace. We've begun our descent and will touch down shortly. We've turned on the seat belt signal, so please return to your seats if you haven't already done so. After landing, we will depart for our final destination, the Bahamas Archipelago, in thirty minutes. I hope you enjoyed your flight, and we look forward to serving you in the near future. And a special message to our special passengers, the Cruz family. Mr. Cruz, my son has a Liquid Cool T-shirt, and please do us the honor of signing an autograph before you disembark."

I could hear the low laughter in the hoverplane. Cruz Jr. got a kick out of the captain's words too. He'd glanced at us briefly, then returned his eagle-stare outside the window and was watching the craft descend. Dot, Kat, and I were in the main center rows.

"The captain didn't ask me for any autograph," Dot said to me.

"Don't even try it," I said. "I know you signed up every person in this craft as new Eye Candy customers, probably him too."

She laughed. "I did."

"That's what I thought. And you said no working."

"I'm not working. Networking is...networking."

"I'll remember you said that."

"Speaking of working," Dot began, "what was all that interrogating the flight attendants and that man about the island?"

"I was asking questions."

"Cruz, we are going to be on vacation."

"Yes, we are."

"It sounded like you were doing background research as if you're getting ready to investigate a case."

"I'm not, and I can't. We're getting a free vacation for my presence. I can't investigate any murder case. That's strictly a police matter. You know that."

"I'm not sure how I feel about a dead body on the island."

"I don't think you'll spend too much time thinking about it while soaking in a hot tub or shopping at the theme mall stores."

"Cruz, I'll be monitoring you. And I'll tell J.R. to do the same. No detective work. This is our family vacation. You're allowed not to work. It's only fun for a change."

"I told you, I will be having fun. I'll be sleeping."

"Sleeping?"

"Sleeping, with one eye open to watch Cruz Jr. They have great pools and beaches. How often do we get a chance to lay out in the sun in Metropolis?"

"Like never."

"Exactly. That's all the vacation I need. Pool and beach bum. I can't wait."

"Okay, but I'll still be monitoring you."

"You're concerned for no reason. We're here for a vacation, not to solve some great murder mystery."

PART THREE: THE ISLAND

I'd never been on a flight like that before. Since Dot had befriended most of the passengers on the craft, she had to personally say bye to everyone. For me, the two flight attendants and two pilots got my autograph, along with a few other passengers. Cruz Jr. even got to sit in the high-tech cockpit, in the pilot's chair no less, pretending to fly.

Finally, we disembarked from the hoverplane and officially set foot on Jules Verne's Island. In my mind, I pictured a big island with a bunch of gaudy amusement parks, but that's not what we saw. The island's landing field was constructed on a lower elevation jetty. Clear blue, cloudless skies, and a nice cool breeze.

Above was the main island itself. A giant mound of green. The hovervehicle that came for us looked like a steampunk submarine, only it could fly. It landed and a man in a hotel uniform exited. He waved to our hoverplane and in moments it was ascending to its final Bahamas Archipelago destination. We waved to the hoverplane too, even Kat.

"Mr. Cruz, and family," he said to us.

"Yes," I replied.

He greeted us with a Japanese bow.

"My name is Runner. I'll get your luggage aboard and get you to your accommodations immediately."

As he loaded our mountain of luggage into the hovernautilus, I could have sworn the number of our suitcases was growing.

"We have too much luggage," I said.

"We're a family of four, Cruz. What we have is normal."

I was about to say something snarky like "But half the luggage is yours," but my ma didn't raise no fool.

Runner slid open the passenger door for us and we all piled into the vehicle.

"What kind of hovercraft is this?" I asked.

"Unique to the island, sir. Our own hovernautilus. Based on actual schematics of our island's namesake."

"Can it submerge too?" Dot asked.

"Yes, it can, ma'am. A full submersible and it can sail like a yacht too."

When the hovernautilus vertically rose into the sky, we were able to see the full magnitude of the island. For a man-made island, it was not built to look futuristic but naturally created. A three-sided cove, ridged by mountains, and a single smaller island at the tip with a villa-style hotel and private bungalows. As we flew over the mountains the different worlds were visible for a moment.

"You have the five worlds, right?"

"Yes, sir. Moon World, Underwater World, Mysterious Island World, Center of the Earth World, and the largest, International World."

Dot was giddy. "We can still see the Asian countries we were going to," she said to me.

International World was an almost carbon copy of the best tourist sites and cities, though smaller, from around the globe. There had to be some kind of holographic or virtual reality trickery involved because the island was big, but not big enough to have all the countries of the planet.

I was interested in all the worlds, except Moon World. Been there, done that. And I didn't want to go back ever again. I liked normal gravity too much. Cruz Jr.? I already knew where he'd be wanting to go. He had his face pressed against the glass trying to get a better view of the worlds.

"Mr. Cruz, I'll let you and your family get settled. I can stop by in an hour. I'll give you a tour of the hotel grounds and the manager, Mr. Askey, can fill you on the situation."

"How many other guests are on the island?" I asked.

"Only five, sir."

"Five writers?" Dot asked.

"Usually there are eight to ten of them, but two regulars had to cancel and...well...the situation. Regardless, they always rent the island for themselves—their own writers' retreat."

"This is the slowest time of the year for the island?"

"Yes, sir. All destinations have slower months than others, no matter how popular they are. You and your family will have a great vacation."

"Leaving aside the situation."

"What are you talking about?" Cruz Jr. asked.

"Nothing, J.R." Dot replied. "Did you see the world you want to visit?"

"I want to ride giant animals, Mommy!"

"Daddy's going to take you to ride all the giant animals you want."

Cruz Jr. didn't need any ideas planted in his head. I wanted to jump out of the hovernautilus then and there.

The concierge guy led us to our vacation bungalow, pulling the hovercart with all our luggage. The section Runner led us to was the one with the larger two-story family bungalows. Cream colored, simple, ancient French architecture. Inside was clean and beautiful, a combination of hardwood floors and carpet. Cruz Jr. immediately ran around like a madman. Kat did her speed crawling trying to follow him.

"Kitchen, dining, living room, sitting room, enclosed patio on the first floor. All the bedrooms—master for adults and three separate bedrooms," Runner told us.

He showed us all the rooms on the ground floor, then took us up the carpeted steps to the second level.

"You have an open balcony on the second level too with a view of the mountains."

We didn't need to call them. Cruz Jr. appeared out of nowhere and began climbing the steps after us. Kat appeared soon after, looking at the steps for a moment to figure out how she was going to get up, then she stood up and reached out for Mommy. Dot walked back down and picked her up.

"You're with me," she said.

The master bedroom was huge. The other three bedrooms were smaller but still large. The balcony was like its own room. There in the distance were the mountains with several balloons floating in the air.

"Are people flying in those balloons?" Dot asked.

"No, they're for visual decoration purposes, but you can fly in any of the passenger balloons whenever you wish," Runner answered.

"I'll leave you all to get settled. Should I come back in about an hour?" he asked me.

"Sure, that's fine," I said.

"When you come to the office, we'll scan in your biometrics for the door."

We left the kids upstairs as we walked with him back downstairs. He bowed goodbye and left. Dot and I were left to get the hovercart of our luggage mountain upstairs. We got to the master bedroom to find Cruz Jr. jumping up and down on the bed and Kat seated on the ground, watching him and giggling.

"Cruzie, that's a bed, not a trampoline! Go find your own bed to jump on."

"I like this bed, Daddy. I'm staying here. Kat too."

My cyborg secretary would have loved the main JV hotel building. Designed like an old French chateaux, it was large but only three stories. In Metropolis, there were megatowers over three hundred stories. However, the island was built with exclusivity in mind, not volume.

Dot and I arrived entering through the main lobby with the kids. While Kat was snuggled in nicely in my wife's arms, Cruz Jr. was beyond such trivial activities as holding his father's hand. He was too big for that; he was too hyper for that. He ran through the entrance ahead of us and by the time we got in, we saw him climbing the steps to the second floor.

"Cruz Control, what's this in my hand?" I yelled at him.

He looked back and saw what I was holding in my outstretched hand. Then, he reversed course, reached the floor, and ran to me. He grabbed my hand with a big smile.

I had a leash in my hand, but not for dogs. It was for him. There weren't many things I'd give my wife's parents credit for, but the Hellspawn (my pet name for them) had come up with the perfect solution to my son's extreme hyperactivity. Put a leash on him. He, of course, hated it, but it gave us the perfect bargaining chip to get him to somewhat behave. Stay in sight of us, be as wild as you wanted without breaking stuff, no leash. Disappear, leash goes on.

All this time, the hotel's staff was quietly waiting for us from behind the main counter. Through the main entrance, with its auto-opening, extra-wide left and right sliding doors, was a small foyer. Past it was a threshold that indicated a barrier wall that came up from the ground or from the side, to a large semi-circle configured main lobby. At the back, along the curved wall was the main counter with the staff: two males and two females. The steps to the second floor and elevators were located at the beginning of a large hallway that must have led to the hotel's dining area and other accommodations. Floor, walls, ceilings were all in the same color scheme of white and ivories. Lots of art on the walls which I assumed were places in Neo-Paris I'd never seen, and never wanted to.

"Welcome to Jules Verne's Island, Mr. Cruz." The older man greeted me. He was impeccably dressed in a vintage cream suit and tie, white shirt and shoes. "This must be your beautiful wife."

"Yes, the big one," I said.

My wife, of course, gave me a look.

"I am Mr. Askey, the island's manager." He kissed my wife's hand. That annoying French custom, then my daughter's little hand. She giggled.

"Who might you be, mademoiselle?" he asked.

"Say my name is Kat," Dot said to her.

"*Enchanté*, Mademoiselle Kat," Mr. Askey said.

Cruz Jr. appeared in front of the man and lifted his hand up to him. "Me too," he said.

Askey laughed. He kissed my son's hand and Cruz Jr. smiled, satisfied.

"Let me introduce you to my staff," Askey said.

The other employees were standing by in front of the main counter now.

"This is my assistant manager, Ms. Modula. You've already met our main concierge, Mr. Runner. Ms. Strata is our second concierge."

Modula looked like she was in her late twenties, early thirties, same general age as Runner. She was slim with short brown hair. They were both dressed in light brown business attire.

"Only four staff on the island?" I asked.

"Our head chef, Mr. Stryper, is the other member of the staff on the island," Askey answered. "He's the acting manager of the island when I'm not here. He's been with the island longer than even me. I'm here the summer and fall months only. He's here the whole year round."

"This island is almost like a giant computer," I said.

"Yes, everything else is automated and this is the standard number, each year, when the island is rented by our special guests."

"The writers," I said.

"Yes. Every year for the last ten years. A group of them, the top sci-fi authors in the world, rent the island exclusively for their own personal retreat."

"How many writers?"

"The most has been a dozen, but usually around six of them, as was the case this year. Until the incident."

Askey and the hotel staff looked uncomfortable. They wanted to talk privately.

"Maybe Ms. Modula can give your beautiful wife and kids a tour of the main hotel while we talk, Mr. Cruz."

"That would be fine," Dot said.

I looked down at Cruz Jr. "Stay with Mommy and behave."

"What are you gonna talk about?" he asked me.

"Stuff. Go keep Mommy safe from bad guys."

"Okay, Daddy."

He let go of my hand and grabbed my wife's open hand.

"Mrs. Cruz, we'll start with the lunchroom, then the gym and spa facilities, then the pool and grounds," Ms. Modula said, leading the way.

"Yes, food," Cruz Jr. said.

"Yes, spa," Dot said.

"Mr. Runner, you can accompany them too," Askey said.

"Yes, Mr. Askey."

"Ah, Mr. Stryper is here," the island manager said.

A larger man appeared in the same brown business attire as the concierge staff, but he was definitely not slim. Seemed he liked to sample the food he cooked, and often. However, he looked professional and his black hair was perfectly groomed. We shook hands.

"Call me Chef," he said.

I watched the concierge staff lead my wife and kids away down the hallway. When they were gone, Mr. Askey quietly said to me, "Mr. Cruz, we have a terrible situation here, and it must have been divine providence that you were where you were when this happened."

"A murder," I said.

"Yes, Mr. Cruz, which means that we may also have a murderer on the island too."

This was my wife's and my vacation. Stuck on a secluded sci-fi island with a corpse, a murderer, and our kids. How did I get myself into these situations?

Mr. Askey led me down the hallway with the chef following. There was one locked door and I peeked through an open doorway next to it. It was the open restaurant and bar. The locked door biometrically opened for Askey. We stood in the main kitchen. It looked like many, many others I'd seen in the past, but my eyes locked on the door to the freezer.

"Yes, Mr. Cruz," Askey said. "We had no choice but to store the body in the back of the freezer."

"We do have three freezers," Stryper said, "so no food for current guests will be used from that one."

"One of the writers?" I said.

"Yes," Askey said. "Mr. Stellar, Rod Stellar."

"Only five other writers are on the island?"

"Yes. They are in their bungalows. We told them to stay in their rooms until they were summoned."

"They know about my arrival?"

"No, not yet. We only said we'd have someone arrive to take charge."

"Mr. Askey, I know what Mr. Vec at Metro International explained to me, but the more I think about it, it makes no sense. I may be a private investigator, but I'm still not the police. Civilians are not allowed to be involved in murder investigations."

"You're absolutely correct, Mr. Cruz. All that's needed is your presence. Nothing more."

"Where's the police, Mr. Askey? That's my real question."

"Mr. Cruz, Jules Verne's Island is a man-made resort. Somehow the corporate lawyers did not prepare for such a contingency. Accidents, death or injury from an accident, though the island's safety record has been nothing less than one hundred percent since its opening."

"I'm not worried," I said. "Go on."

"Yes, they prepared for accidents, death or injury from accidents, theft and assorted crimes, acts of nature, even suicide, but nothing for simple murder. The lawyers are fighting over it now, Mr. Cruz. The problem is that no one knows whose jurisdiction the murder investigation will fall under."

"Who might it be?"

"Your supercity of Metropolis, the UK, France, or China."

"China?"

"Yes, the island was a multi-nation, multi-megacorp project. We only need someone who can assume authority until the lawyers figure it out."

"Who legally owns the island?"

"A Mr. Derez. His family founded the island centuries ago. However, joint partnerships over the years with other countries and companies have caused the current confusion in this situation."

"Five writers on the island?"

"Yes."

"Five island staff, including you two?"

"Yes."

"Anyone else on the island at all, or scheduled to arrive?"

"No. The decision as to which authorities will run the police investigation should be arrived at any day now. You won't have to do a thing but enjoy a free vacation with your beautiful family."

"The freezer with the body is secured."

"Like Fort Knox," Stryper replied. "Locked and if opened, alarms will sound to alert the entire island."

The two men led me to a far end of the kitchen where a single freezer was closed with two big double-locks on the door. What really got my attention was a giant eye above the door.

"Anyone or anything that approaches the entrance is recorded directly to the Net."

"We're being watched now?" I asked.

"Probably," Askey said.

"Great," I said under my breath. "I'll stay out of the kitchen then."

"As you should," Stryper said.

"Who do you think killed him?" I asked.

The men were about to answer me.

"No! Don't answer me!"

They both were surprised.

"Ignore me. I was beginning to investigate. It's a nasty habit. I'm not allowed because it's a police homicide investigation. But more important than that, I'm not allowed because I'm on vacation with my family."

The men smiled.

"You should listen to your beautiful family, Mr. Cruz," Askey said. "You won't have to do a thing, I promise. The jurisdiction will be decided and the police will take over."

"You promise?" I asked.

"I promise, Mr. Cruz. This is Jules Verne's Island. We are a magical resort and living museum and amusement park for the entire family. If anyone asks you about a murder, say 'what murder?'"

He smiled, and so did Stryper.

That's exactly when I should have run, grabbed my family, and gotten us all onto the hovernautilus to get the heck out of there when we had the chance.

PART FOUR: THE SUSPECTS

Askey and the chef gave me a full tour of the luxury hotel, the accommodations, and the immediate grounds with its hover tennis courts, Olympic-sized pool, VR game rooms, and state-of-the art gym, equipped with exercise buddy robots. When that was done I returned to the bungalow, where I found Dot and the kids relaxing in the master bedroom area upstairs. I was glad that they were resting, because the bungalow interior would not be livable for my liking until it was cleaned CDC-style. The wife hadn't even gone shopping yet but had all these bags open around the room and was already planning how she would pack all the new things she was going to buy.

"Hey, hon. When are we cleaning the room?" I asked.

"Cruz, this is a five-star island resort. These are high-end bungalows cleaned by the best cleaning robots on the market. Even police and your favorite, CDC, use them to properly wash, scrub, decontaminate, disinfect, deodorize every inch of a place. I checked."

"You know how nasty hotels are?"

"Cruz, it's as clean as is possible without creating a real hermetically sealed room."

"But germs."

"Cruz, we like germs out here. J.R., Kat, and I. You can put on a bio-suit."

I gave her a smile. "I can wear my bio-suit again! Yeah! I can change diapers again. Nasty."

"Cruz, why are you here?"

"What's all this?" I asked, looking at all the stuff around her on the bed.

"Complimentary gifts from the island," Dot said sitting on the bed.

Cruz Jr. and Kat were each playing with new toys on the carpeted floor; he with a hovernautilus replica, she with a spongy crab toy. Dot had toiletries, candles, sunscreen lotions, all kinds of things, but all she was interested in was the shopping.

"Daddy, I want to ride animals," Cruz Jr. told me, running to me.

"Do you now?" I said with a hand on his shoulder.

"Oh, Cruz, let me show you what I got." She jumped up from the bed and walked to the dresser where there was another bag.

"What?"

Dot put a band device on my wrist.

"What's this?" I asked.

"You'll figure it out."

I watched two dots on the display screen; one was moving. I looked to my side. Cruz was creeping up to me. On the display screen, the flashing red dot was moving to the flashing white dot. I looked at Cruz Jr. again and he was on the bed jumping, while Kat sat playing with her sponge crab toy.

"Ah, he's the red dot. Kat's the white dot." I laughed. "That's what I'm talking about. Use today's technology to manage those crazy kids." I spun around just as Cruz Jr. was doing his ninja stalking run behind me. "Caught you!"

We decided to stay in for the day. Dot had to plan everything, so she was busy mapping out our itinerary for the week at the dining room table. The kids were playing with their toys. I was trying to take a nap on the big living room couch.

"Cruz, do you believe that story?" Dot asked me.

My eyes were still closed but I answered. "What story?"

"The story about which law enforcement has jurisdiction over the island. Lawyers wouldn't forget a thing like that."

"Contracts are so thick these days it must have slipped through somehow. Not our concern. We're on vacation. They'll figure it out."

"Did you go into the freezer?" she asked me.

My eyes opened. "Why would I do that?"

"Well, did you?"

"No. Of course not."

"I'm just checking."

"What freezer, Mommy?" Cruz Jr. asked.

"A big freezer in the hotel," she answered.

"What's in it, Daddy?" Cruz Jr. was now sitting next to me.

I looked at him. "Chicken."

Dot laughed. "J.R., ignore him. Nothing is in the freezer."

"Why did you want him to look in it then, Mommy?"

"Yes, Mommy, why?" I said.

"J.R., go play with your toys. Cruz, go back to sleep."

"That's what I was trying to do."

Later Dot and I were lying on the top of the covers of the bed taking a nap. From time to time, I looked at my band device to see where the red dot was. Most of the time, I could hear Cruz Jr. running around and making noise outside the room. Whenever he got quiet was when I checked the band device. Both the red and white dots were outside the bedroom. I looked to the side and Kat and the hovercrib were gone! What's going on? I thought.

I looked again at my device and the dots suddenly moved out of the bungalow and disappeared.

"What the—"

I jumped up from the bed. Dot was still sleeping. I heard commotion and ran outside the room, then down the steps. The front door was closed but a window was open! Outside I heard voices from more than one person, someone crying out, the sounds of water splashing. I peeked out, then immediately ducked back behind the curtain. I spun around to look around the bungalow, then dashed back upstairs to the master bedroom. Dot was still asleep, so I listened. I heard a sound. Nasty, I thought as I dropped to the ground to peek underneath the bed. There were Cruz Jr. and Kat! They started laughing.

"Isn't this great," I said as I grabbed for them. Kat was easy but Cruz Jr. tried to crawl away like an isopod. "So we're learning advanced criminal techniques early: locating body tracking

46

devices, planting body trackers on other things as a decoy, evasive maneuvers by hiding under beds. What did you put your trackers on, Cruz Jr.? I know it was you!"

Cruz Jr. just giggled. Kat just watched me smiling with big gums.

"What's going on?" Dot asked, half-asleep.

"Nothing, honey. You can sleep."

With both children in hand I walked back downstairs. I pulled the curtain back from the front of the bungalow and slide the bay window open. "So we know how to open locked windows too now." I peered out and standing six feet away was a big buff guy. He was dripping wet from head to toe. In one hand was Kat's hovercarriage. His other oversized hand was clenched in a fist.

"Hello sir," I said with a big smile.

"Your hovercarriage knocked me into the pool."

"Is that so?"

"That's so. I wasn't ready to jump into the pool at the time. I was about to eat a very delicious meal, but food isn't so delicious when it gets dumped into a pool."

"Looks like me and the kids are buying you lunch."

"That would have been a nice gesture, but the food is free. Seeing as I'm one of the people who rented the island with all the food we can eat and all the booze we can drink for two weeks."

"Is that so?"

"That's so. You're that private detective."

"Which author are you?"

"Rich Maxima."

"Ah, great. Can start putting suspect faces with names."

"Suspect?"

"Can I have my daughter's hovercrib back?"

He glared at me as if he wanted to throw it at me, but Cruz Jr. reached out for it through the window. Maxima stepped over and put in his hands.

"I'm not a suspect."

"If you say so, sir."

"Stop calling me sir. It sounds funny with you saying it."

"How did you know I'm a detective?"

"I saw you, your woman, and the brats land."

"The proper terms are wife and kids or children. And you know who I am?"

"I do, Detective. I researched you in the past as I was thinking of using one of your cases for a future novel, but changed my mind. I'd have to dumb down my work too much to make it work."

"Yeah, as opposed to writing about oversexed aliens all over the place."

He smirked. "You know who I am."

"Heard about you in passing from someone."

"I'm not a suspect."

"You said that already. Heard you then."

"I'll go get another sandwich. Hopefully your kids won't push me in a pool again."

"Hopefully, you won't be sneaking around our bungalow again, seeing as your author bungalows are clear on the other side of the hotel."

He gave me another smirk. I watched him walk away and disappear around the corner of another bungalow.

"Daddy, is that a bad guy?" Cruz Jr. asked me.

"Possibly. We'll see."

Dot's original plan was good, but unless we could inject the trackers under their skin subcutaneously Cruz Jr. would find them and put them on something else. But Dot was already on the job and called the main desk as soon as I told her what happened when she awoke. Mr. Runner showed up with another small bag. He told us that our son wasn't the first urchin to outsmart a tracker.

"What's that, Mommy?" Cruz Jr. asked trying to climb onto the dining room table.

"This, J.R., is called a body cam."

"You'll be like a policeman," I said.

"Body cam?" he asked.

Dot fitted him with the vest and snapped it locked right in the center of his back, where he wouldn't be able to reach it.

"Yes," I said. "This way you'll be safe wherever you go. Your mommy and I will be able to see wherever you are on the island."

"Really?" He wanted to see the tablet that went with it. He was fascinated with the display from his chest camera showing on the tablet screen.

"I have to go potty!" he declared and was about to run.

"Get that vest off that boy!" I said. "We don't want to see that."

Dot laughed as she took off his vest, but Cruz Jr. didn't run to the bathroom. He ran into the living room and leaped on the main couch and started jumping up and down. He was laughing himself silly, which started Kat laughing.

Dot and I looked at each other.

"He tricked us," Dot said to me.

"We're going to get you, Cruz Control!"

"We're getting you back for tricking us, J.R.!" Dot said to him.

"Since we are now being laughed at by our own kids, maybe we should go find our island-mates."

"You mean the writers on the island?" Dot asked.

"Yeah."

"Cruz, are you conducting an investigation?"

"No. We're on vacation. Don't you think we should meet them?"

"I guess." Dot made a face as she thought. "Aren't they suspects?"

"No," I said. "The island manager gave me all the details. It can't be the writers."

"Are you sure?"

"Yeah."

"Cruz, I know this is how you mess up those criminals. You tell them all kinds of lies mixed with truth, so they don't know which way is up, and you do all kinds of things behind the scenes to trick and trap them. Cruz, we're on vacation!"

"Dot! I'm not doing anything. I'm here in the room with you and the kids. Have I left the room?"

"No."

"So how can I be doing anything? And I brought you and the kids along to the main hotel to see our island-mates. You'll be watching me every step of the way."

"Kids, get your jackets. We need to keep an eye on Daddy at all times. He needs to understand we're on vacation."

"Daddy, I want to ride the animals."

"Yes, Cruzie, I'll take you to ride the animals after we meet our fellow guests on the island."

I don't know how they knew we'd be there, but when we entered the main hotel lobby they were all waiting there, clustered together as thick as thieves at reception. Five authors. Three males and two females. Mr. Askey greeted us and came out from behind the reception counter. He did the honors, introducing them to my wife and kids first.

"You all already know who I am," I said to them.

"Cruz, the famous detective," Marlan Overspeak said. He had silver hair down to his shoulders, thick beard and mustache. Deep tan. He reminded me of an African safari hunter.

"I prefer Metropolis private eye, Mr. Overspeak."

"Marlan. Everyone calls me Marlan, and so will you. Only my parents called me by my full name and I didn't like it. I didn't like it so much I left home at thirteen and never came back. When I became famous myself and had some money, they came around for some of it. Then they addressed me properly."

"Marlan it is. I can't call myself famous. Famous is kinda pretentious. You all are famous."

"The word is rich, Mr. Cruz." The woman was AC Vulcana. She was petite, smaller than all the other authors but her persona towered above all of them, with maybe the exception of Marlan. Her big ego could've been seen from miles away, as well as her indifference to those around her. But she was right. They were all successful and wealthy, so much so they could afford to rent out an entire island for themselves alone every year for the last ten years.

"So true. Well, I'm glad you're all together."

"Why is that?" she asked.

"The reason I wanted to see all of you was to talk. I didn't want any of you to get the wrong idea. I'm just a guest, special guest courtesy of the island. I'm not investigating anything so you can rest easy. In fact, we've already identified the murderer and informed the authorities."

The authors appeared surprised and looked at each other, then at Mr. Askey.

"Yes, Mr. Cruz is correct. I did call ahead to the corporate headquarters," he said.

"We did. My wife and I, and the kids will have our vacation and you all can continue with your retreat, despite the tragedy."

"Are you saying you've solved the murder already?" the other female author, Jean Code asked. "You only landed less than a couple of hours ago. You didn't do any investigating."

"And I'm not allowed to," I interjected. "This is an active homicide. Only the police can investigate."

"What do you mean you've already identified the murderer?" Jean asked.

"Just that," I said.

"Are you saying it's not one of us?" The author who asked was Dave Blackhat.

"Yes. You're all off the hook. We know who it is."

"Who did it then?" Jean was like a pit bull who wouldn't let go of the bone.

"The island's corporate headquarters knows it's none of you. We told them it's none of the writers," I said.

"How could you know anything? We didn't see you do any kind of investigation. You didn't interview anyone. Did you even visit the crime scene? Do you know where the crime scene is?" Jean asked.

"Mr. Cruz reasoned from my description of the events that the murderer had to have been from personnel or guests that left the island the night and morning before Mr. Stellar's body was discovered. All those persons are being held," Mr. Askey told them.

"That's what we had said ourselves," AC said, not taking her eyes off me. "So simple to deduce, a child could do it. Or a Metro private detective."

I maintained the smile on my face. Not sure why I'd gotten under her skin so quickly, but the feeling was mutual.

"We can all enjoy our vacation together as one happy island family," I said.

"You know who the murderer is," AC said.

"Yes, the murderer or murderers. We've been through all this."

"Not one of us?" Dave asked again.

"You're in the clear. You're cool."

"Mr. Cruz, I am not cool with you," AC said. "We've heard about you. I think you're lying. Everything you said."

"And Mr. Askey?" I asked.

"Him? He couldn't lie to save his life. If he's lying, so you are."

"Aren't you all writers?" I asked. "Shouldn't you be...writing something? Have a good day, ladies and gentlemen. My family and I are here for vacation, so we'll be off to it."

We left them all there in the lobby, and we could feel their glaring eyes burning holes in our backs.

I could feel the sun against my face, my eyes closed, and my mind clear. The tranquility of it all. Finally, our vacation was here. I opened my eyes to see clouds in the far distance. My hands gripped the rim of the passenger basket. I'd seen them before, but it was the first time I'd been in a real hot-air balloon. The giant balloon—designed as a globe of the planet Earth—hung above us.

My wife stood beside me in a similar contemplative state. She gazed out. The view of the entire island, the trees, brush, ocean. It was all breathtaking. Cruz Jr., in a rare state, was completely quiet. He was lying on his chest in the center of the glass-bottom basket with Kat. They were both mesmerized by the view from hundreds of feet up, floating in the air.

We could have stayed up there forever. Actually, it was the chef who suggested we skip the International World and do the balloon ride of the island. The balloon motor was set to do a continuous spiral around the island, and then back out again. None of us wanted to do anything else. Since we were in the Caribbean and not Metropolis, it would be sunny well into the night.

Floating slowly around the island also gave me a chance to study the terrain below. The island was shaped like a giant crescent moon. Between the tips of that crescent was the smaller island with the hotel and bungalows. That smaller island also had the landing field with two hovernautiluses and a full dock with hydrofoil craft and hydro-scooters. Inside the shore of the larger crescent island and most of the smaller island was lined with sandy white beach. Clusters of smaller islets dotted the ocean around the island, some rocky reefs, while others had their own beach.

The water sparkled and even from our height I could see schools of fish swimming below the surface. How could half a dozen writers rent such an island every year? I didn't think sci-fi writing brought in that kind of money, unless someone made a movie about it too. I checked—none of the writers' novels had even been movies.

Dot and I had to glance at the kids from time to time to visibly verify they were still there. They had never been in a hot-air balloon either, but we'd never seen both of them so quiet for so long. They were truly in awe of the whole thing. From their view, they were literally floating in the air with the clouds.

I reached into my jacket and pulled out my mini-binoculars.

"What are you doing?" Dot asked me suspiciously.

"Bird watching," I answered sarcastically. I studied the terrain with the aid of binoculars now. "I want to see what kind of fish those are in the ocean. I think I saw dolphins."

"Dolphins? Let me see!"

I handed the binoculars to her. She didn't see dolphins, but the fish she did see were plenty big.

"What do you see by the hotel and the bungalows?" I asked.

"Why?"

"Take a peek. Make sure no one's by our bungalow."

Dot was staring at something. "You need to take a look."

I took the binoculars from her and looked at the bungalows. I knew which one was ours. The numbers were on the roofs. I looked at the hotel. Nothing. I looked at the open space between the bungalows and the main hotel building. There stood three authors looking up at us with binoculars too. It was Blackhat, Maxima, and a waving AC Vulcana.

"Damn sci-fi writers," I said.

We were in the balloon so long that the kids had fallen asleep on the glass floor of the basket. They wanted to stay awake and see, but their eyes wouldn't let them. We'd also lost track of the time with the sun. It was actually nighttime, and if we didn't return we'd miss dinner.

The hot-air balloon may have looked vintage but it was equipped with a backup hoverengine in case of emergencies. The regular motor was quite advanced but simple to use. I'd planned to let Cruz Jr. land us, but he was asleep. We set down softly on the landing pad of the main hotel where Ms. Modula and Mr. Runner waited.

"How did you enjoy it?" she asked.

"We loved it," Dot replied.

I carried Cruz Jr. and Dot had Kat in her arms. The kids got their bearings but they had that sleepy-eyed look.

"Dinner still being served?" I asked.

"Oh yes, Mr. Cruz. The kitchen was waiting for your return."

As we stepped out of the basket, Ms. Modula led the way, while Runner attended to the balloon.

"What's on the menu tonight?" Dot asked.

"It's banquet style, Mrs. Cruz."

I stopped myself from convulsing. My wife shot me a disapproving look.

"I'm fine."

"Cruz, behave yourself," she said. "You're not a germophobe anymore."

"How can I be with two kids touching everything? I had no choice."

"Cruz, I'm about to start ignoring you."

Sure enough, we entered the dining area and it was buffet-style. Then it happened. I heard someone sneeze. Not a little sneeze. The kind of sneeze that was like when you were driving and the hovercar ahead of you cleans their windshield. The water sprays over their windshield, yours behind them, and anyone else around.

It was bungalow prowler, Rich Maxima. My eyes locked on him like a guided missile. With the same hand he used to cover his sneezing mouth hole, he wiped the front of his tank top. My mouth dropped open. Was that his version of properly washing and scrubbing his nasty hands? At this point I had set Cruz Jr. on the ground beside me.

"Daddy, what's wrong?"

"I'm on stakeout," I reflexively answered.

Maxima grabbed a clean plate from the stack with the same nasty hand, and I almost swallowed my tongue. He took a fork and chop sticks from the utensils table with the same nasty hand. Then he approached the food. The man was going to contaminate the entire island food supply for the night! Food my family was going to eat!

"Cruz!" I heard my wife scream.

I ran and tackled the man before he could spread his pestilence. How I got from where I was standing to where he was, I couldn't remember. But I did. The man was on the ground where he belonged. His plate and utensils on the floor around him.

Maxima rolled onto his back, beet-red, gritted teeth, and he slowly got to his feet with a growing menace and clenched fists.

"Please, gentlemen." Runner appeared between us.

"Why did you do that?" Maxima yelled at me.

"Go wash your hands!" I yelled.

"What?" Maxima was genuinely confused.

"You sneezed on your hands and you transferred that nastiness to the plates, the utensils, and were about to contaminate all the food. If I want to feed my family your germ spit nastiness, I'll have you spit in a cup and feed them from there. Go wash your hands, you dirty animal!"

I heard commotion behind me and turned. Cruz Jr. was laughing, my wife was laughing, Kat was giggling, Runner lost his battle to keep from laughing, and I realized that all the other writers were already seated with their food laughing. Maxima was even redder than before and blew past me for the restrooms.

"I want fresh plates and utensils," I told Runner.

"Yes, sir. Right away," Runner replied.

"You tell him," Jean Code said aloud, lifting her glass in a toast to me. "Hear, hear."

"Join us," Marlan's gravelly voice called out.

The family and I did. Once Runner had the chef bring out new dishes, the family and I got our food. Cruz Jr. was at that stage where he'd stack every choice of food mile-high on his plate, so I

58

told him he could have any three choices, but only three—and dessert wasn't a choice.

Runner brought a children's chair for Kat. She was at that stage where food was also a toy to eat or play with.

At the table, Marlan sat at the head. I was next to him, Kat in her chair, then Dot, then AC with Jean, Dave, and Maxima returned to sit at the other end of the table. Cruz Jr. sat next to Marlan too, opposite me. He seemed to like the idea that he had the whole other side of the table for himself, but he was too busy eating.

"May I?" AC asked my wife, reaching over with an index finger to the top of her shoulder.

"Sure, why not."

My wife always wore a colored neck scarf—today's was translucent white. Her neck, traps, and shoulders were all clearly cybernetic. She may have started to wear the neck scarf as a child to cover it, but as an adult it was part of her trademark style. AC tapped it and it sounded like padded metal.

"The sexy cyborg wife. How did it happen, if it's not too gruesome to say?" AC asked.

"Decapitation accident—"

"Dot," I interrupted her.

"What's decapitation, Mommy?" Cruz Jr. asked.

Marlan chuckled. "It's a type of accident to avoid," he said.

"Clearly, you've long recovered. We'll talk more and I'll get the gory details when your husband isn't around," AC said.

"Yes, please do," I said.

That was how I met my wife. I was a recovering germophobe, but my OCD tendencies were getting worse. My wife had a horrific hover-go-cart accident as a child. She wanted to win that race so bad, she flew her vehicle faster than she should have, went around a hairpin curb, the vehicle hopped up as it went under a bridge...her head, well we all know what the word decapitation means. Our phobias had been controlled and diminished but were re-emerging. For me, my OCD tendencies were becoming real OCD craziness. For Dot, her deathly fear of going under bridges now included doorways. My parents nagged me to see a counselor who sent me to a phobia support group. Dot's parents had done the same. No one knew who I was, but Dot was famous and did a lousy job with her disguise (she entered the room with a head scarf, big sunglasses, and a turtleneck top up to her chin). She sat next to me and we hit it off when our group of a hundred-plus was in our smaller breakout discussion groups. That's how I met my wife.

"Do you really know the chief of the Metropolis Police?" Dave asked.

"I sure do," I replied.

"I'm writing a sci-fi novel with the chief of police as the protagonist."

"Why would the chief of the Metropolis police, the largest supercity in the world with half a million police agents—" AC began.

"The word is police officers," I corrected.

"Police officers have anything to do with a little street detective who got lucky on a few cases?"

"I solved those cases with solid detective work. Blade Gunner. NeuroDancer."

"What ever happened to NeuroDancer? That whole situation is murky," Jean said.

"It's not murky. Read more slowly when you read so you can comprehend and retain information," I said. "Who else? The Jupiter Alien Case. The Android Zombies Case. I've had so many cases that many are still classified."

"Mr. Cruz, we've been told when you talk it's a rambling mess of lies, half-truths, and exaggerations," AC said.

"That's so you'll think I'm not too bright and won't notice me doing my thing, and you won't know when I'm closing in to make a citizen arrest or sic the police on you. I also use the tactic to make some think they can beat me in a shootout or a fist or martial arts fight. Most of the criminals I deal with are dummies but there are plenty of clever ones. So that's when the joking comes in. *Does he really not know what I'm up to or is he pretending?* they ask themselves. It drives them crazy. They try to be more clever than usual, extending way beyond their comfort zone, which just causes them to make mistake after mistake. The dangerous or psychotic ones, I just shoot them. I never play games with them and the police don't mind. It saves them a ton of paperwork. That's why they like me. Anything else I can answer for you?"

AC smiled. "No."

"Oh, I forgot to give you these." I reached into my jacket pocket and handed her a pair of plastic forensic gloves.

"What are these for?" AC asked.

"When you do that thing but don't want to leave any fingerprints."

She was about to throw them to the floor in annoyance.

"Don't do that," I said. "It's not like you can find them in the island store. Just throw them in your purse and forget about them."

Her mind was racing. Finally, she smirked and threw them in her purse.

"Women are smarter than men, you know, Mr. Cruz," she said.

"Yeah, NeuroDancer said the exact same thing to me. The ambulance took her to the morgue with a melon size blast to the forehead courtesy of me. She landed at exactly the same place as all the men who tried to do an O.K. Corral on me."

They watched me, wondering what to make of me, except for Marlan who found me an endless source of entertainment.

"O.K. Corral is a hip term that youth use nowadays. It means—"

"We know what it means!" Jean snapped, interrupting me.

"I didn't want to assume. You know some writers are hip, but others never leave their rooms and are oblivious to the real world."

"We would be the former," Jean said.

"Of course. How else could you all be murder suspects?"

They ignored me.

"We thought you all were dead or something up there in the balloon," Jean said to us.

"The kids had never been in a balloon before," Dot said. "With the glass floor, it was amazing. You're in hovercars all the time, but it's not the same at all. Up there you're floating in the sky."

"Don't ride in hovercars myself," Marlan said. "Fly my vintage hoverchopper. I have that same experience every time. When the kids are grown and gone, you both should get yourselves a matching pair."

"Assuming they're still together." Maxima just had to go there, stuffing his face at the end of the table.

Dot ignored him, but I wanted to throw something at him.

I looked at Cruz Jr. and said, pointing, "He's the bad guy."

Cruz Jr. laughed and watched Maxima for a bit as he continued to eat.

"I realize I don't even know much about the books you write," Dot said. "All I read is about fashion, clothes, and the latest hair and skin treatments. Tell me about what your write."

"The biz is a complete gutter of literary and literal hacks, wannabes and pseudo-celebrities," Marlan said.

"What dear Marlan really means to say is that he's no longer a top ten author, not even a top one hundred. No one buys his books anymore," AC said.

"What Marlan means to say is that the commercialism has corrupted the craft," Marlan said back.

"Yes, Marlan. That evil capitalism thing. However, it does allow you to rent big little islands and sit around most of the year without a care in the world."

Jean cleared her voice and focused her attention on Dot. "It's a bit different for all of us. I'm more of the workhorse writer, as I'm on staff three-fourths of the year working on a few TV series. When I was strictly a novelist I wrote mostly space operas—travel to distant planets and galaxies."

"Where everyone manages to look human and speak English," Maxima quipped.

"Says the man who writes racy sci-fi with space vampires and such," Jean said back to him. "Fiction is about relatability. What kind of story would it be if neither side could communicate with each other?"

"I did like those alternate history sci-fi novels you used to write, but you always managed to pick points in history no one cared about."

"Maybe I should have written the alternate history where you weren't born."

Maxima laughed at her.

"I write the more intellectual sci-fi by day," Marlan said. "It wins the awards. By night, I do other things. That pays the bills."

"Other things?" Dot asked.

"Don't let Marlan fool you. He's only a weekend author. He's really a megacorp executive. He could tell us exactly what he does for them, but then he'd have to kill us," AC said.

Dot looked at Dave Blackhat. "What about your books?"

"Children's market," he replied. "All my sci-fi is aimed at the kiddies. Friendly, fluffy, fun sci-fi, I call it."

"Would you believe he makes more money writing than all of us?" Jean Code said. "Even Marlan."

"Yes, Jean. It's a cruel universe," AC added.

"Well Jean already told you what I write about," Rich Maxima said. "Sci-fi monsters."

"I write in-depth futuristic dramas," AC Vulcana said. "I don't like the term sci-fi or science fiction. I prefer futuristic fiction. I explore the human condition through my work. The people we are, our dreams, the nightmares we create for ourselves, how we profess ourselves to be human but so often manage to be anything but. I do what Marlan does, but he's only a man. I do it better."

"You do it better only because I prefer to live life in the real neon jungle rather than holed up in my room 24-7. You've made progress with your agoraphobia," Marlan said.

"I never had that phobia. Only a severe aversion to humans in general."

"Funny, AC," Marlan said. "You write about the human condition but don't care much for actual humans.'"

"No stranger, Marlan, than presenting oneself as an ancient big-game safari hunter, anti-establishment type when you toil daily as a button-up, suit-wearing, Japanese-bowing automaton at some secret megacorp."

"Or that's what I want you to believe," he said to her.

Dot and I looked at each other.

"Aren't you all friends?" Dot asked them.

The authors smiled and chuckled.

"Mrs. Cruz, this is what friends do. We needle each other, insult each other. All in loving fun," AC said.

"Yes, honey," I said. "It's not like they killed anyone."

Every eye was on me. You could hear a pin drop in the entire dining hall.

"That's right, Mr. Cruz," AC said. "We didn't kill anyone. You said so yourself."

These writers. I saw the real reason why the hotel wanted me to "manage" the situation. I'd seen it in Askey's and Modula's faces especially. They were nervous around these writers. And none of them—from AC to Marlan—were stupid. They knew who I was.

They saw the hotel execs talking to me. They'd seen me checking out the hotel and grounds. Even if I adopted the best ninja teleporting tactics from my son, they would keep a watchful eye on me at all times. I had to devise a way to keep them off guard so I could question them. Maybe I could pretend I was a doofus and didn't know anything, but they'd see through that. So I'd go the other way. I'd pretend I was smarter than all of them combined. (Wait. I am smarter than all of them.)

I smiled. "Oh, of course. I'm sorry. I wasn't suggesting otherwise. We said it already. The murderer had to have been from personnel or guests that left the island the day before Mr. Stellar was discovered."

"Yes, you did say that," Jean said.

"And we said you and the hotel manager were lying," Rich said.

"What did Mr. Stellar write?" I asked.

"Rod wrote about humans pretending to be something they weren't," AC answered.

I smiled at her.

"But then you already knew that," she said to me.

"He also wrote about perceptions and realities appearing to be one way when they were something else," I said.

"Hey Dummy!" AC yelled at me.

She startled Dot and me. I suddenly felt something at my leg under the table. I glanced down and saw it—a dog. I hated dogs but it was a Golden Retriever, so it wasn't the most loathsome of dog species out there.

"Come away from the man, Dummy," AC said.

The dog disappeared under the table toward her.

My wife and I shot each other a look before I looked at AC again.

"Yes, Mr. Cruz. Perception versus reality. Like pretending to know nothing when you know all. We have access to the Net too. You make for quite interesting reading," AC said.

"I'll say it one more time," I said to them. "I'm here to vacation with my family. I'm not here for any kind of investigation."

"Man, just because Dummy sniffed your leg don't mean you should be one now. You're investigating, even now," Marlan said.

"No, I'm not," I said with a hint of indignation.

Marlan looked at my wife. "Is he investigating?"

"No." Her answer was emphatic—that wasn't the problem. The problem was she hesitated. That delay canceled out her answer.

I sighed heavily. "Honey, we have a long day tomorrow and for the rest of the week as we enjoy our *vacation*."

I stood up from the table, but they were all snickering and Dot was shaking her head from where she sat with her arms folded.

"What? What's wrong? We're going to enjoy our vacation."

"That's not what you said, Detective," Maxima said with a glare.

"What? That is what I said." I saw my wife's unhappy look. "What did I say then?"

AC did her unflattering imitation of my voice. "Honey, we have a long day tomorrow and for the rest of the week as we enjoy our *investigation*."

I rubbed the sides of my head with my heads. "I'm getting a headache," I said.

Finally, it got dark, sometime around nine-ish. I sat on the veranda of our bungalow reading, with a cup of silk coffee at my side. Kat was already asleep but I could hear Cruz Jr. still running around inside with his toys. Ordinarily, he'd be in bed too whether he wanted to or not, but it was his vacation too. Dot was watching TV. She was still not talking to me because of my Freudian slip, no matter how many times I told her I wasn't investigating an open homicide case.

"I can't believe you tricked me into taking our children to an island with a dead body in a freezer and a possible murderer on the loose," she'd said to me earlier.

I tried to remind her of our amazing hot-air balloon ride, but she wasn't falling for it.

There was a knock at the door. I jumped up from my chair and ran back inside like a rocket.

"No, Dot!" I yelled.

She was at the front door and about to open it.

"Step back. I'll open it."

"Cruz, I can open a door by myself."

"Weren't you the one yelling at me that a possible murderer was on the loose?"

She looked at the door.

"But you don't have a weapon," she said.

"Daddy!"

My wife and I stood there as we watched our four-year-old run to me from the kitchen with a butcher knife in his tiny hand. He handed it to me.

"Weapon," he said with a smile.

My wife and I were speechless. Another knock at the door snapped us out of it. Clearly, we'd have to have a long talk with our son. Dot stepped back and moved Cruz Jr. back. I held the butcher knife behind my back.

"Who is it?" I called out.

"Mr. Cruz, it's me, the manager."

I opened the door and there stood Mr. Askey, with both Modula and Runner. I wasn't fooled for a second by their fake smiles.

"What can we do for you, Mr. Askey?" I asked.

"May we speak inside, sir?" he asked.

I let them in, closed the door, and stepped over to my wife and son. They stood opposite us.

"Is that a knife behind your back, sir?" Runner asked.

"Oh, we were making sandwiches," I replied.

It was such a ridiculous answer but they seemed to believe it.

"Mr. Cruz, we have a problem," Askey said.

"What problem?"

"It's minor I assure you."

"Askey, does this have to do with the investigation?"

"It's minor, sir."

"You promised! I am not allowed to investigate an open homicide case."

"Unless."

Neither Dot nor I were happy.

"Unless what?" I asked.

"Unless the authorities authorize you to do so."

My wife's mouth dropped open and she looked at me. "You lying—"

"Dot, no cursing in front of Cruz Control," I said. "Mr. Askey, did you lie to me to get me to the island?"

"Sir, I promise I didn't."

"You promised me that you weren't going to have me involved in this, but here you are. Why would the police authorities authorize a civilian to work a homicide case? It's illegal. I could lose my license. You told me that I was to simply be a presence on the island until the legalities were sorted out and the proper authorities could arrive. That's what you told us."

"It's not us, Mr. Cruz," Ms. Modula said. "This comes straight from corporate headquarters."

"There's been a development," Askey said.

"Development?" Dot asked.

"What does that mean?" I asked.

"We don't know how. This...situation is now public," he said.

"Situation? You mean murder," I said. "What are you saying, Askey?"

"We need you to take a more active role, short of investigating, of course. This has become an issue of corporate damage control. We have to control the story before any lasting damage is done to the island's reputation or business model."

"What story, Askey?" I asked.

I'd been down this road before. I'd done it before myself many times. Someone had leaked the story to the media.

Askey reached into his jacket and took out his palm device. It was one of those extendable ones and he opened it up. He handed it to us after he tapped a button. It was the newsfeed.

Murder on Jules Verne's Island! Legendary author and TV producer, Rod Stellar, found dead on the exclusive and historic resort island. An international legal battle is preventing the arrival of police authorities, as proper jurisdiction of the island is in dispute. In a bombshell development, the island's owner revealed that he managed to dispatch famed Metropolis private detective, Cruz of the Liquid Cool Detective Agency to take charge of the situation in the meantime.

The story hadn't surprised me. It was only a matter of time before the media found out about it all—an island, a corpse, writers, me on the island. What I looked for was the date of the story. It was the same day at the airport when Mr. Vec pulled me aside with a "once in a lifetime proposal from the owners of the fabled Jules Verne's Island. The date of the news story was the same, but it was posted one hour *before* we had talked. I'd been setup from the start!

"That sneaky—"

My wife covered my mouth before the profanity started.

PART FIVE: THE INVESTIGATION BEGINS

"Cruz, I bet your parents told you the same thing mine did when growing up. If it sounds too good to be true, it is!" Dot said to me.

"Only mine didn't tell me in Mandarin Chinese."

"Cruz."

"I know."

"Free vacation. All you have to do is be on the island until the police can arrive. It was a setup from the start and you knew it!" Dot scolded.

"Well, you said yes too."

"Cruz, this is all on you."

"Why is it only my fault? It takes two to tango."

"All on you, Cruz."

"Well, I'm not investigating anything. We'll have our vacation. In fact, I'll pretend to be investigating so they won't bother us. Yes, that's it. We'll just ignore them. How about that?"

My wife and I were in the living room area. The kids were off playing with toys. I'd been pacing back and forth, annoyed. My wife stood there, leaning against a side wall, arms folded, miffed. We'd been set up good, but it was our own fault and we both knew it. Vec and the island didn't set us up. We wanted to be set up. Subconsciously, the prospect of running around all those countries with two small kids in tow was overwhelming. That would've been no vacation at all. They gave us an opportunity to be at one place and we pounced on it, even though we knew we were being used. We were okay with being used if it meant a free vacation, beach, sun, relaxing, and for Dot, shopping.

"What do you think?" I asked Dot again.

"I don't know. Will they let us stay if you don't do what they expect?"

"Forget them. They lied to us."

"We knew they lied, Cruz."

"Wasn't that hot-air balloon ride fun? The kids loved it."

"They did."

"We could have stayed up there all day. And we still haven't set foot in any of the other theme worlds. And you still haven't been to their shopping centers. I say we lie back to them. We're 'taking charge of the situation,' whatever that means, and we enjoy our vacation. String it out for as long as we can. Take it day by day."

"Cruz, are my kids on an island with a murderer?"

"No. That was the truth we did tell them, despite that AC Vulcana saying I was lying. We believe that the real murderer left with the last of the island guests as they departed the island. The writers rent the entire island free of any other guests so when that

73

time comes, once a year, everyone is shooed off except for the skeleton hotel crew."

"What do they do here by themselves? Only six, I mean, five of them."

"It's their retreat. I'm told they do team-building exercises, talk books, talk publishing. Honestly, I have no idea. Normal people would just rent a community room in a hotel somewhere, not an entire island. They're weird. They're writers."

"So none of these writers is the murderer?"

"No. Askey and the staff say they were accounted for."

"What about the staff?"

"Them too. It had to be one of the guests that left the island the night or morning before. But it's not our concern. The police will handle it. So what about my plan? Lie to them and enjoy our vacation with the kids."

"Cruz, I don't know about all this."

"Yes you do. You take Kat. I take Cruzie. And we do our thing."

"Do our thing? What does that mean? We're not staying together?"

"Dot, you want to go to the spa. I don't. You want to shop. I don't. Kat is an infant who wants to do infant things. Cruzie is a hyperactive terror who wants to ride animals. If you want to switch—"

"No, no, no. You keep J.R. Good plan. I like it."

"Then it's settled."

"Lie, then vacation."

"Lie, then enjoy our vacation for free!"

Having been on the Moon for real, the last place I wanted to go was the Moon, even a simulated one in an island's theme world attractions. But that's exactly where Cruz Jr. wanted me to take him first. I tried every trick I could to get him to change his mind. I reminded him he wanted to ride giant animals, but then that idiot Runner told him he could "rent" a giant animal and take it to the Moon theme world.

Runner was to be our driver. We'd be going to the Stables for Cruz Jr. to pick out his giant animal, then off to the Moon. Modula was going to be my wife's guide. Dot wasn't going to one of the theme worlds yet. She and Kat would be at the spa. Good for them. Soaking in gray mud all day and having strangers rubbing their hands into your back, not knowing where those hands had been. Good for them. We guys were off to the Moon.

However, as the hovernautilus rose in the air—already Cruz Jr. was getting hyper looking out the windows—I peered down to see Mr. Askey talking to my wife. From her body language, it was a serious conversation. What was the island staff up to now?

The Stables were more like a museum of fantastic creatures— real and fictional. When Cruz Jr. first saw the picture, he went crazy.

"That one, Daddy!"

The picture was of a dinosaur. My son wanted to ride a triceratops on the surface of the Moon. We "rented" it, but then I looked at Runner.

"How do we get the dinosaur there?" I asked him.

"He can ride it there," Runner said.

"Yeah!" Cruz Jr. yelled. "Up, Daddy!"

Cruz Jr. first tried to scale up the side of the very realistic-looking dinosaur—thirty feet long on four legs, ten feet high, bony ridged head with its two horns. Then he tried to jump in place to its back, then he started to do running jumps.

"Here you go, young man," Runner said. He pulled down a rope ladder and Cruz Jr. scurried up it and was seated on its back close to the head. My son was a bona fide dinosaur rider now.

My son laughed as he pulled the reins. "Giddee-up, cowboy!"

The dinosaur started walking forward.

"Wait a minute," I said, nervously.

"Mr. Cruz, he'll be fine," Runner assured me. "The dinosaur will take him to the Moon World with no problems. There's a moving walkway that will get them there quickly. He'll meet us there."

"But to leave him alone. He's only four."

Runner pointed to the tablet in my hand that I'd forgotten. My son had his body-cam, so I was viewing his path forward. Runner tapped the screen and we had an aerial view of my son from about fifteen feet in the air.

"How are you doing that?" I looked up and saw a small dome-shaped drone following alongside him.

"All unaccompanied children have drones assigned to them, so parents can keep an eye on them at all times," Runner said.

"Great."

"JV Island always aims to please its clients. Shall we go?"

"Sure, if we have to," I said grudgingly.

"You don't want to visit the Moon attraction?"

"I was on the real Moon already."

Runner and I hopped back into the hovernautilus.

"The Lunar Colony? When?"

"At the end of last year."

"I've never been. Must have been amazing."

"That's one word for it."

"Vacation or work?"

"Work."

"I envy you, Mr. Cruz. You get to visit the world and off-world. What a life."

"I'm happy with my feet on Earth and in my own home city of Metropolis. I'm only going to this Moon World because of the little one. Is there anything I can do while he's exploring?"

"All our attractions are adjacent to the beach—"

"Beach? So I can sit on the beach by the water?"

"Yes, you can, sir."

My smile had returned. "Let's go."

It took us no time to get to the site. I hopped off onto the beautiful cool sand of the beach and headed to the hover-lounge chairs. I threw myself onto one of them, lay back, and gazed out across the ocean with its blue waters. The sky looked like a postcard with the clouds posing for my viewing enjoyment.

"Excuse me, Mr. Cruz."

I turned to see Runner standing beside me. I'd forgot about him already.

"Will you be needing anything else?"

"Mr. Runner, I'm as good as a mice on ice. Maybe a beverage or two, but I'm quite content."

"Yes, sir. I'll have one of the drones drop off a couple of bottles immediately. Use your tablet to call the hotel when you're ready for pickup."

"Thank you, Runner."

"You're welcome, sir."

He waved goodbye and walked back to his hovercraft. I settled back in my chair. Before I closed my eyes I looked at the screen. Cruz Jr. was racing along the surface of Moon World on his triceratops.

I had fallen completely asleep when my alarm band woke me. Dot and I had learned the hard way that too much fun for Cruz Jr. was a nightmare for us. He'd be so wound up he wouldn't sleep at night. You had to allow only a limited time of fun and then give him a couple of hours to calm down. Cruz Jr. was having fun all right. He'd learned how to make his dinosaur run at top speed, jump over moon craters, and race up lunar hills. I had to get him out of there. He'd been in there three hours and was showing no signs of slowing down.

The island was actually two levels. The upper level was at the sea-level. But the theme attractions were underground, each in its own geodesic dome. Having been on the real thing, Moon World was still quite impressive. It looked like the real surface of the moon, except for the lower gravity, which still unnerved me. A grown man weighing less than thirty pounds. I'd be staying on Earth, thank you.

I decided not to call Runner. I picked up Cruz Jr. at Moon World and allowed him to ride his dinosaur back to the Stables, as I walked alongside and let him tell me all about what he did. He could barely contain his exuberance as he recounted what he did a mile a minute.

We dropped off his dinosaur at the Stables—all we had to do was leave it at the perimeter. Robot arms popped out of the ground and lifted it away. Cruz Jr. watched until they were all gone from sight.

From there we walked through the jungle back to the hotel islet. It was well past lunchtime but neither of us minded. Cruz Jr., smiling from ear to ear, continued to tell me all he did in Moon World with his dinosaur. From everything he said it sounded like he was there three months rather than three hours.

"When we see, Mommy, tell her all about it," I told him.

"Yes, Daddy. I want to ride dinosaurs all the time!" he declared.

"I'm sure you do."

We finally neared the hotel and bungalow area. As Cruz Jr. told his stories, I was carefully observing the terrain around us—the layout of things, how far away things were from each other, etc. I'd made notes in my tablet as we walked.

"Mommy!"

I looked up as Cruz Jr. ran like a cheetah to my wife standing in the distance. Kat was toddling next to her, holding my wife's hand. Dot looked like she had begun her shopping as she was wearing a new white and blue kimono-style dress. Cruz Jr. ran to her and received a big hug from my wife. He hugged her and then hugged his sister.

"Cruz, you two were gone awhile," she said when I reached them.

"Hey Kat," I said and lifted her up into my arms. "What were you and your mother doing?"

"Kat and I had a ladies' night out at the spa, the mall, and then the beach."

"Ladies' night? But it's daytime," I said.

"You know what I mean, Cruz. We had some fun. Isn't that right, Kat?"

The main crescent island was connected to the center islet by a bridge. On the other end I could see Askey and his two staffers, Modula and Runner.

"What do they want?" I asked.

Dot glanced back then looked back at me.

"There's been a new development," she said.

"What new development? Dot, are you now involved in their plot?"

"Me? I'm not involved in any plot."

"Then what development?"

"Um. You need to see something."

"Dot, you were the one who said we were on vacation."

"We are on vacation."

"Then why are you talking about developments? Cruzie and I had a great second vacation day and you want to spoil it."

"I'm not spoiling anything. But...let's talk."

I looked at my daughter. "Kat, help me out here. What is your mother up to?"

The plan was supposed to be lie and enjoy our vacation. Dot had unilaterally modified the plan. I just didn't know how Askey and company had coaxed her into doing it.

Cruz Jr. and I hadn't eaten lunch yet so we were treated to a special meal, and this time we were allowed in the smaller but more luxurious staff lunchroom. We sat and the chef arrived with a large covered silver plate. He set it down before us and opened it. I wasn't usually a big French cuisine guy, but our eyes widened in anticipation at the plates of food before us. The chef rattled off all the names, none of which I knew, but I did know lamb chops. And cognac Dijon cream sauce. Pasta, greens, sauces, beverages. Cruz Jr. and I dug in.

Askey, Modula, and Runner sat at the same table. Dot sat with Kat opposite them.

"What's going on, hon?" I asked.

My son and I were done, though he wanted another plate of food, but then the chef brought the chocolate mousse desserts. I'd definitely need a nap after all this.

"Maybe you should eat your dessert first," Dot said.

I put down my fork. "I'll eat my dessert after you tell me what's going on."

I looked directly at the island manager. "Askey, why did you and your conspirators lure me and my family to this island? The truth, now!"

Askey cleared his voice.

"When are the police arriving?" I asked. "The day."

"We're truly sorry, Mr. Cruz. We were following directions from corporate headquarters. They wanted you here as an insurance policy."

"What does that mean?"

"Crisis management said that if we could say that soon after the murder, we had you on the island, it would mitigate any bad publicity."

"When will the police be here?" I asked again.

"Any day now," Ms. Modula said to reassure me, but I wasn't in the believing mood.

"What is it you expect me to do? Exactly."

"We're not breaking our promise, Mr. Cruz," Askey said. "Nothing at all. Corporate headquarters only wants your presence on the island. Without you, this murder had the potential to embroil the island in a huge scandal. You can understand that, sir. We're doing what any corporate entity would do."

"Askey, let me be blunt. I've never heard of a murder investigation with a body on site being held up because of issues of legal jurisdiction. In such cases, *all* the authorities show up and they sort it out later."

"The island was being sold," Askey said.

"Sold?"

"Yes. That's the issue."

"The new owners don't want the liability."

"So it's not because different companies are fighting for jurisdiction. It's because no one wants to take on jurisdiction."

"Correct."

I looked at my wife. "How do we get involved in these things all the time?"

"I don't know," she said.

"Askey, this is our second day. I'll give you two more days," I said.

The three hotel personnel looked at each other nervously.

"But your vacation is for ten days," Modula reminded me.

"You told me that the authorities already identified the suspects in the murder as staff and guests who left the island the night and morning before the body was found. You told me that they were all being held for questioning. Now you tell me that the police investigation hasn't even begun."

"That's not true, sir," Askey said nervously.

"Are those tourists and staff being held for questioning by authorities, yes or no?"

"Well—" Askey said, stammering.

"Yes or no?"

"I'm not certain what actions have been taken to date."

"That means no, Askey."

"Cruz, we can stay longer," Dot said to me.

"Dot, what did they bribe you with?"

"Bribe?"

I stared at her without saying a word.

"We've been talking about, maybe, Eye Candy providing a line of its products to the island."

The bribe! My wife, the consummate businesswoman!

"Two days, Askey. Tell your corporate headquarters two more days and if the police aren't here, we're gone. We're all playing a game with each other. My family is enjoying their vacation. You're following your boss's directions. But that doesn't change the facts: there's a dead body in the hotel freezer and a murderer out there. The police need to be here, not me, to take charge. If it were just me, that would be one thing. But I have my family here, Askey."

"I completely understand, sir," Askey said. "Two days is more than fair."

What I didn't mention to any of them, including Dot, was on the way back from Moon World I had stopped to make a vid-call. Cruz Jr. was more than preoccupied with riding his triceratops and we were nearing the Stables.

"Cruz Control, before we drop off your dinosaur take it for one more spin around that hill there."

"Yes, Daddy!"

He had his dinosaur running along at double-speed. He really thought he was some kind of cowboy with his "giddee-ups." I waited until his drone followed him before I stepped under a cluster of trees to make my call.

"Cruz!"

My business associate, Phishy. His big head covered the entire screen of my vid-phone display so I couldn't see which off-white-colored, long-sleeved shirt with colored fish all over it he was wearing, always with a dark vest. Some called him a street hustler, my wife called him a slider, "sliding from one hustle to another," but nothing violent, dangerous, or too criminal.

Our working relation had come a long way from our first days. He wasn't just a business associate, he was a friend. He helped me run my informal network of street informers—the lifeblood of confidential intel for me. He was also a licensed gun dealer in Metropolis and had equipped me with my tools of the trade—my guns.

"How are you enjoying your vacation?" he asked me.

"The family is happy, so I'm happy. Look. My son is riding a dinosaur."

I lifted my mobile and turned it so Phishy could see. My son had learned to make the triceratops robot do donuts—walking in a complete one hundred eighty-degree circle, round and round.

"When can I come to ride dinosaurs too, Cruz?"

I moved the screen back to in front of me. "We can talk about that later. I have a job for you."

"Job? You can always count on me, Cruz."

"I know I can, Phishy."

"What do you need?"

"I need you to ship me a few things asap."

"Is everything okay there?"

"Maybe. Maybe not. I'm not sure. The job is just in case."

"You're not a famous detective for nothing, Cruz. You have a sixth sense about these things."

"I hope I'm wrong."

"If you feel something's not right, Cruz, then something isn't right."

"Get something to write with."

"Cruz, I can write on my screen."

"I hate when you do that. It looks like you're writing on my face."

"I'm not writing on your face. I'm writing on the screen, Cruz. These are modern times. You got to use the technology of the times."

"I couldn't disagree more. Get ready to write. I have a list and I'd like to get them by tomorrow. And let's hurry up before Cruz Jr. returns on his dinosaur and wants to ask me a million questions about what we're talking about. I don't want his mother to know we're talking."

"Why, Cruz? Is it illegal?"

"No, Phishy, it's not illegal. We're on vacation and I don't want to worry any of them. I want them to enjoy a rare vacation which the universe seems to be conspiring to ruin for us. Get ready to write."

"Two days is more than fair," Askey told us last night. The police would arrive on the island in two days or less? Of course, I didn't believe him. However, from a family standpoint, we'd continue on with our vacation as if he were being truthful.

Yesterday was spa and shopping for the girls and beach and dinosaur riding on the Moon for the boys. It was early morning for us, but I had the whole day planned. Our first vacation day was in the clouds as a family. Today, we'd be exploring the ocean depths in a hovernautilus sub—in Jules Verne's Underwater World. The kids couldn't get to the sub fast enough. They didn't even want to eat breakfast.

"Let's go, Daddy. Mommy, let's go." Cruz Jr. was pulling both Dot and me by a hand to try to get us to walk faster from the hotel to the sub docks.

Runner was our guide again, and he had the craft waiting for us.

"The nautilus craft will take us there automatically?" Dot asked.

"Yes, Mrs. Cruz. All our theme worlds are automated, but staff are always monitoring remotely. Will you all be spending the day there?"

"Yes, we will," I replied.

Kat was especially quiet cuddled up in my wife's arms. She was in one of those moods where she wanted to be a baby and not an adult. She wanted to be carried rather than walk, but her head was bobbing all around to look at everyone and everything.

"Mr. Cruz!" I heard Ms. Modula's voice.

She ran up behind us with a small suitcase-sized package in her hand.

"Morning mail?" I asked.

"Yes, sir. From a person named Phishy." She handed it to me.

"Great," I said. "Because of the change in plans, Dot and I didn't have the needed equipment for tomorrow's exploring—Center of the Earth World."

"What?" Cruz Jr. asked. "We go there tomorrow, Daddy?"

"Cruz Control, focus on today. We're going to the bottom of the sea to see big fish and squid monsters."

"Squid monsters!" Cruz Jr. burst out, giddy. He began running to the nautilus sub.

"J.R., stay with us!" Dot yelled after him.

"It's fine, Mrs. Cruz," Runner reassured. "There's no danger. He can board the craft. It's been prepared for the family."

"Thanks, Mr. Runner."

"Enjoy your day," he said.

"We will," we told him.

Up the walkway from the dock to the entrance of the craft—Dot had Kat in her arms, I had my package. It was an aquatic jet without wings. We could hear Cruz Jr. running wild inside. As soon as we all entered, the walkway automatically pulled away and the door closed. All the lights were on, but they weren't needed. The craft design was mostly glass. The front third had the swivel seats on a faux wooden section, but every other part was the clear iron-strength glass. We were in a virtually invisible seacraft.

As the nautilus automatically sailed away from the dock, slow and smooth, it began to submerge. Now, Kat wanted to walk. She wobbled over to one side where already we could see the aquatic life of the ocean. Cruz Jr. joined her for a moment, but he was running around from spot to spot. He wanted to see squids.

"We're not at the Underwater World yet," I told him. "You'll know when we're there. Then you'll see your monsters."

I sat on my chair next to Dot.

"What's in the package, Cruz?" she asked.

"Oh, nothing. I just had Phishy send me a few things I thought might be useful for the vacation. We have Center of the Earth tomorrow. If the police show up, then we can do the Mysterious Island next, though Cruz Jr. already got to ride a dinosaur, then we'll do the International World, even though we've had our hot-air balloon ride."

"Are we really going to leave if the police don't show up the day after tomorrow?"

"We have to make them think we're serious or they won't take us seriously. Dot, the police should be here."

"Yes, you're right."

"There's a body on the island and they need to be doing their job."

"Yes, you're right."

"Think about it. We're enjoying a vacation and someone's lying in a walk-in freezer. That's just wrong, Dot."

"Yes, you're right. Get the body out of here."

"And catch the bad guy, so we can enjoy our vacation."

"What is humankind coming to? Enjoying vacations on islands with bodies in walk-in freezers."

"Exactly."

"I would say it's a murder mystery."

"Dot, there is no such thing when it comes to a private street detective."

"Yes, Cruz. You're not allowed to investigate homicides."

"I'd lose my private investigator license."

"You keep saying that."

"Because it's true. Weren't you the one who was scolding me because you thought I wanted to break the law and investigate?"

"I wasn't scolding you."

"There, Daddy, we're there!" Cruz Jr. yelled.

The ride was smoother than we expected. I'd been in a submersible before in my Electric Sheep Massacre Case, but it was anything but smooth and the water was dark as night, not crystal clear. The nautilus seemed to be cutting through the water like a knife. There was a big sign: TO THE BOTTOM OF THE SEA. Into the darkness of an underwater cave.

Kat screamed.

"Kat, it's okay," Dot said.

The lights of the nautilus came on but very dim. Kat ran back to us and Dot picked her up. It appeared we were now in the underwater cave and the exterior lights of the nautilus flicked on.

Cruz Jr. screamed this time, but we all were startled at the figure that flew past and above the craft.

"What's that, Daddy?" he yelled, running forward, not taking his eye off it.

"That is a giant manta," Dot said.

"Giant manta, Mommy?"

"Yes."

He laughed to himself.

I pointed behind him. "You'd better watch or you'll miss something."

He spun around and ran back to the clear, open rear of the craft. "Squid monster!"

No squids, but plenty of colorful fish, giant fish, and when we saw our first shark, Dot got to her feet and joined Cruz Jr. at the glass. Dot loved sharks. So I minded Kat and Dot watched the running madman known as Cruz Jr.

Like the first day, the entire family was in awe of the sights around us. The craft first patrolled near the surface and then without warning dove, and for a moment Dot and I looked at each other. Were we really going down twenty thousand leagues to the bottom of the sea? Well, not quite. But Cruz Jr. got to see his giant squid monster. It swam alongside the craft with one giant eye looking in. Kat was amazed and scared at the same time, running to Dot, then stopping to look at it. Cruz Jr. was a giggling mess and had his face pressed against the glass to look at it; he was in heaven.

"Daddy, I want one! I want one!" he yelled, smiling.

My son wanted a squid monster. Yeah, we'd just capture it and keep it in the family bathtub. Dot and I knew it was another robot—lifelike in every way. Earthers didn't like humanoid robots—so as not to take human jobs—but synthetic wildlife robots were what made amusement parks so great these days. Dot took plenty of pictures of his squid monster for him on her mobile. We really didn't need to because another of the perks of visiting JV Island was that cameras on the craft and from drones were silently and constantly taking photos. All you had to do was pick the ones you wanted—and pay for it.

Kat had joined her brother at the main glass to stare at all the diverse sea wildlife—real and robotic. Dot and I lounged back in our chairs, taking in all the wonderful sights but relaxing, holding hands.

"If all we have is these three days, I'd be happy," she said.

She was so right. If we'd gone on our multi-country Asia trip, we wouldn't be doing much vacationing because we'd be so exhausted by now.

"I could stay down here all day," Dot said.

"We'll stay as long as we like," I said. "Because once we get back it begins."

"Begins?" Dot looked at me. "What begins?"

"The case."

"Case? What case?"

"The reason they tricked us into coming to the island."

"Cruz, what are you talking about? You said you can't investigate a homicide."

"I know. I can't."

"Then what do you mean?"

"We'll find out when we get back to the hotel. I told them that they had two days to get the police here. So they'll spring whatever they're going to spring on us today when we get back."

"What do you mean? What do you know?"

"Dot, the police should be here."

"Yes, but they told us why. Sounded plausible."

"That's why I don't believe it."

After nearly six hours underwater, we returned to the hotel islet for docking. The nautilus had its own mini-kitchen so robots served our hot lunch. The kids couldn't be happier. They ate their sandwiches standing at the bay windows, not wanting to miss seeing the next fish or sea creature. Cruz Jr. saw his squid monster in the distance one last time before we surfaced.

The door opened and Dot was on the lookout for the hotel staff, but no one was there. Strange, we thought. Not even Runner or Modula greeted us. We also realized that we hadn't seen any of the authors in a while.

The family and I returned to our bungalow. Cruz Jr. had his head resting on my shoulder as I held him. Things had switched. He was sleepy and Kat was wide awake and wanting to play. We were all quiet until we were inside our rooms with the door closed.

Of course, Cruz Jr. needed to take his shower, but I was going to lay him down on his bed. He wouldn't sleep through the night if he fell asleep so early. So he'd take his shower later in the night. I walked back down the stairs to the living room where Kat was playing with her brother's toys.

"Cruz, we have an email," my wife called out.

I came back downstairs without Cruz Jr. Dot sat on one of the living room couches. She had a tablet in her hand.

"The hotel?" I asked.

She extended her hand. I took it and sat down next her.

"I hate it when you're right," she said.

I read it out loud, injecting all the sarcasm I could manage.

"The latest news regarding the stunning murder of legendary author and TV producer, Rod Stellar, on Jules Verne's Island! His body was found dead on the exclusive resort island. But in a surprising development we learned that the island dispatched famed Metropolis private detective, Mr. Cruz of the Liquid Cool Detective Agency, to take charge of the situation in the meantime."

"Island owner, Mr. Lucien Derez, has further told reporters that, while legal jurisdiction is determined, he expects the civilian detective to resolve the case before police arrive. Mr. Derez said in a direct quote, "With only ten people on the island, if he can't solve the case before the police do arrive, he can't be that good of a detective, despite the hype.""

I shook my head in disgust.

"I told you they set us up," I said.

As anyone would tell you, I didn't like to be scammed, not even the attempt. My family and I loved our vacation so far, but still— we'd been lured to the island under false pretenses. I gave them an ultimatum to call their bluff and they responded. What were they ultimately up to?

Dot had been on the vid-phone calling friends back in Metropolis. She was finding out what was going on in the news back home. Once again, my name was on the newsfeed. It was like kindergarten. I was being taunted. I had to solve the case before the police arrived or I wasn't any good. The fact that it was a police matter, as all homicides are, and the fact that I was on vacation with my wife and two kids, didn't matter. But facts never matter to the mob. I could've found Askey and punched him in the nose, but he was just a lackey. The island owner was the one who was worthy of some Cruz violence but he was, conveniently, not on the island.

"But we're on vacation," I declared.

Now I was sitting on the couch holding Kat with her favorite cat doll. Dot stood there, facing me, arms folded.

"Cruz, you have a rep to maintain. What would happen to that rep if the media reported that some big murder happened on the island where you're staying—"

"Dot, we're on vacation with my family. You were the one who scolded me."

"Yes, Cruz. I know. I'm your family, remember."

"My wife told me not to investigate. She told me that we're on vacation. She told me no detective stuff."

Dot tried not to laugh. "Cruz, listen carefully because this will probably be the only time you hear me say this in our entire lives. I was wrong."

"Oh my God, Kat!" Kat jumped, startled, looking at me. "Your mommy admitted she was wrong. Husbands of the world, we have won a decisive battle today in the war!"

"Okay, Cruz. Have your fun. But back to what we're talking about. You can't allow a big murder to happen—"

"It happened before we got here."

"And you didn't solve it or at least help solve it."

"I am not a police detective."

"You're a detective."

"When it comes to a homicide, I might as well be a pizza delivery man."

"You're a detective. You have to detect."

"But we're on vacation."

"Cruz, you can't fool me. I know you're ready. I know you've been investigating. I'm married to you. Where did you go last night?"

"I went for a walk," I answered.

"At one a.m.?"

"Yeah. I couldn't sleep."

"You are such a liar. I don't know what you were doing, but I know it had something to do with the case."

"Who's my client then?"

"Your reputation is your client, Cruz."

"I don't know if my wife will let me work for free without a real human client."

Dot laughed.

A knock at the door. We looked at each other.

"Finally," I said. "Askey and company are here."

"How do you know?"

"Deductive reasoning. I'm a detective. They figured they gave us enough time to read the news article and get all the emotions out of our system. Now, they're ready to tell us what's going on, or a version of the truth."

I was right, of course. We opened the door and there stood the trio—Askey in the middle, Modula and Runner on either side. We let them in and we all sat down in the living room.

Before he sat, Askey handed Dot a slim palm device. "I was able to get the contracts signed," he said.

I looked incredulously at both of them.

"My goodness," I said. "You're bribing my wife right in front of me."

"No one is being bribed, Cruz," she said.

"If you say so. What exclusive arrangement has Jules Verne's Island granted Eye Candy Image Salon?" I asked.

"Cruz, we can talk about that later."

"So, Mr. Askey," I said.

"Yes, Mr. Cruz."

"Have you practiced your lines?"

"Lines, sir?"

"We read the latest news. Your big boss is trying to goad me into investigating the case. I knew when you and your chef promised I wouldn't have to involve myself in this murder case, you weren't being truthful. So, let's hear it. What are you here to say?"

"Mr. Cruz, we do not have the expertise to manage this situation."

"Won't the police be here in less than forty-eight hours?"

"No, sir. The legal issues are more severe than any of us could have imagined. I'm here, on behalf of the police, to...deputize you as a legitimate law enforcement detective. I apologize that I do not know the proper legal terms."

"Mr. Askey, you are not a ranking police officer," I said. "You can't deputize a ham sandwich."

Runner leaned over and showed me another tablet.

As I looked, the smile on my face grew. The signatures of the police chiefs of multiple countries, including America, including Metropolis.

"How did you get Chief Hub to sign off on this madness?"

"Chief Hub," Dot said, taking the tablet from me.

"You know Chief of Police Hub?" Askey said. "Well, you would. You live in Metropolis. I was told he was the first to sign off on the idea of having you take a more direct role in the investigation."

"Cruz, this document says you have full authority to investigate this murder, including arrest, until police officials arrive. Full authority, Cruz." Dot said it with a big smile.

"What happened to our vacation?" I asked. "We didn't see Center of the Earth World, International Earth World, and Mysterious Island World."

"Daddy, I want to ride more animals."

Cruz Jr. was behind me, climbing over the back of the couch with his "I literally just woke up" look.

"Cruz, you have a case to solve," Dot told me. "There're clues to find and evidence to gather."

"Oh really. I thought the potential bad guys were the tourists and staff that left the island before the body was found?"

"But there could be accomplices," Dot said. "We don't want the bad guys to destroy all the evidence and get away scot-free."

"Bad guys?" Cruz Jr. said, perking up and sitting in my lap next to Kat.

I gave my wife a look. "Accomplices?"

"Accomplices," she repeated, nodding.

"There are no accomplices," I said.

"What do you mean?" Dot asked me.

"Mr. Askey, one of the main reasons civilians can't investigate homicides is because of the liability—"

Runner touched the screen of the tablet in my wife's hand.

"The owner will cover you under the island's liability clause to shield you from any adverse lawsuits."

"Lawsuits?" Dot asked. "Why would you get sued? By whom?"

"We're famous, remember," I said. "People are always looking for a payday."

"Mrs. Cruz, your husband will be legally protected in all aspects of his investigation."

"One more thing," Dot said. "Will my husband be compensated for this?"

"We are being compensated," I said. "We've gotten a free vacation."

My wife suddenly covered my mouth to keep me talking further, and my kids, being the followers they were, did the same with their hands.

"Will my husband be compensated for this?" she asked.

Runner touched the tablet screen again.

"Yes, Mrs. Cruz, the owner of the island will definitely compensate your family for the inconvenience of intruding upon your vacation, and resolving this situation in the island's time of great need."

My wife freed my mouth and my kids playfully did the same.

"So I can talk now?" I asked.

"You can talk," she said. "Cruz, you really need to work on your client acquisition skills."

"I thought I was on vacation."

"I just got the family a payday."

"No, Dot. They already were going to pay me. Our friends are prepared for every possible contingency to ensure there is no chance of a negative response from me. Isn't that right, Mr. Askey?"

"Well, Mr. Cruz, that is my job."

"Good, then you can get started," Dot said.

"I can?"

"Mr. Cruz," Ms. Modula began, "your wife did ask you a question before that I don't believe you answered."

I looked at her with squinted eyes. "What question didn't I answer?"

"What question didn't he answer?" Dot asked.

"I'm glad someone is paying attention to this mystery," I said.

"You asked him, 'what do you mean' when he said 'there are no accomplices,'" Runner said.

"Yes, I did ask that." Dot looked at the three staffers. Her smile was gone. She was probably asking herself, how did they catch that? She looked at me again. "Cruz, what did you mean?"

"There are no accomplices."

"But there could be accomplices."

"Dot, there are no accomplices because the person who murdered Mr. Stellar is still on the island. Five writers. Five staffers. Including Askey, Modula, and Runner sitting here in our bungalow."

Dot jumped up from her seat. "One of them could be the murderer? How could you know that?"

"Mr. Askey told me."

"He told you?"

"Yes. You were there. When I asked if the visitors and staff that left the island the night and morning before the body was found were being held, he didn't answer. That meant 'no.' That meant they knew that none of them were the murderer."

"One of them is the murderer." Dot jumped in front of the kids and me. She glared at the staff. "You'd better not try anything. I'm wearing my heels. I've killed people with these heels. And I'm a cyborg too!"

Everyone knew me by my trademark tan fedora and slicker in Metropolis, and beyond. But since I was on vacation, I'd been walking around hat-less. However, I never went anywhere without it. I opened one of my suitcases I'd placed on top of the bed and took out a box.

"What's that, Daddy?" Cruz Jr. asked, standing beside me.

All I had to do was open it and he smiled. I placed it firmly on my head, then I took out a smaller circular box and opened it. Cruz Jr. laughed and clapped. I placed his black fedora on his head.

"Now we're dressed properly," I told him.

They were right all along. I had been investigating. I had started from the time I left the office with Mr. Vec at Metro International. I was no doofus. If something sounds too good to be true, it is. I never thought for a second that my family and I would be able to enjoy a free vacation on a super-expensive, exclusive island in the French Caribbean without getting involved in some kind of madness. Not a chance. The plot began before my family and I happened into the airport; it was a coincidence that we were there. But once they—whoever "they" were—involved us, we were in their mouse trap. However, whenever you trap a mouse in your trap, do make sure it's a mouse and not a lion. Things tend to go wrong if you're that careless.

I wanted to get an early start. So Cruz Jr. and I would grab breakfast. Dot and Kat had left an hour before us. Dot said she had to do some quick shopping. I had no idea what she was up to but didn't spend any time thinking about it.

We hadn't seen any of the writers in a day, but when my son and I walked through the lobby there was AC Vulcana reading on her tablet. She looked like she was coming out of the food hall from breakfast. She looked up, saw us, and smiled.

"What do we have here?" she asked. "Matching fedoras."

"Yes, he's my business associate."

"Mr. Cruz, you can't use your kids as a conversational crutch forever?"

"I know. But I'll play the card as long as I can or until my kids feel they're too cool to talk to their parents anymore, whichever comes first."

"How's the investigation going?" she asked.

"Quite well. I've narrowed down the list of suspects to ten."

Of course, I walked right past her to the food hall with Cruz Jr. following. I glanced back and she was watching me all right.

I returned my gaze ahead and saw Mr. Askey approaching us from the lunch room.

"Mr. Askey. Just the man I needed to see. Will you join my son and me for a quick word?"

"By all means, Mr. Cruz."

"Is he a bad guy, Daddy?" Cruz Jr. asked, pointing to the manager.

"Possibly, but let's keep it to ourselves."

"He can hear us, Daddy."

"He knows we're play talking."

I looked up and smiled at Askey. He nervously smiled back.

Almost forty minutes later, Cruz Jr. and I came out of the main entrance of the hotel building from breakfast. My son was talking a mile a minute, focused on when he was going to be able to ride more animals on the island. Rather than take the path to the bungalows I led us straight ahead where AC and Rich Maxima stood talking. I knew they were watching for when I came out. They saw me and stopped their conversation.

"Hello neighbors," I said as I stopped in front of them with Cruz Jr.

"Daddy, are they the bad guys?" Cruz Jr. asked.

"Possibly," I replied, then I asked the two authors, "What's the latest idea in sci-fi these days? I never did get a chance to ask you about your trade."

"Travel through wormholes. Time travel and alternative histories are always popular," Maxima replied to humor me.

"Personally I prefer the freakish stuff. Gender bending, the risqué, the erotic sci-fi," AC said.

"Hey," I said, pointing to her. "Keep it clean. My son is here and this is a family-friendly island."

She laughed.

"If you all were born maybe a few centuries earlier you'd be making real money," I said.

"Or we'd be broke," she said.

"What you said doesn't sound like new ideas to me," I said.

"Mr. Cruz, there are no new ideas. Only the old dressed up to look like the new," AC said.

"Not a good thing to be more cynical than me."

"Well, we are. Tell me, Mr. Cruz. How's the murderer hunt going?" AC asked.

"There is no hunt. I told you."

"Yes, you told us lies," Maxima said with underlying anger.

"Lies mixed with truth," I said.

"And we have to figure out which is which?" AC asked.

"Yes."

"What happens if I'm the murderer?" she asked.

"Murderess?" I corrected.

She smiled. "If I were the murderess, I'd figure out a way to get off the island before the police arrive."

"Hardly."

"Why is that?"

"You make a pretty good living as a writer. Actually, you make a great living. There's no way you'd jeopardize that by having the government freeze your accounts."

"I have more than enough to live. You see how I dress, live. The bare minimum. No fancy clothes and shoes or fur coats for me. I usually don't even bother much with the makeup."

"Not easy to live on the lam with the police after you."

"I've done it before. Researching for a book."

"Well, it's all academic."

"Academic?" she asked.

"What does that phrase mean?" Maxima asked. "Academic. People say it but if you think about it, it makes no sense."

"Mr. Cruz, let's jump to the punch line. We know you're dying to tell us. What's academic?" AC asked.

"There's no way off the island," I said.

"Why do you say that? There's a fleet of emergency lifeboats encircling the island," Maxima said.

"Oh, you are planning to escape before the police arrived. Yeah, I thought the temptation would be too great."

"I'm not scared of the police," AC said. "I'm scared of the sons of bitches who'll come after them."

"The media," I said.

"We've heard how clever a boy you think you are, Mr. Cruz. Personally, I think you're another of these over-hyped citizen celebrities who lucked out on one case and has been riding it to the bank ever since," Maxima said.

"Lots of criminals thought so too. They're either dead or in jail."

"I still say your smart detective routine is an act. You're just a dummy. I see your kids. They're going to be dummies too," he taunted.

I grinned. "Interesting. Why are you trying to goad me into kicking your teeth to the back of your skull?"

"Go ahead and try," Maxima taunted. "I'm a black belt in three martial art forms."

"I don't know what you're up to now, but I'll figure it out. I always do. Oh, and you can tell all your friends no one is leaving this island before the police arrive. All the emergency lifeboats are on lockdown, command codes courtesy of the island owners."

The two authors stared at me. They appeared to be wondering whether I was bluffing or telling a joke. It dawned on them that I might be telling the truth.

"You can't do that!" Maxima yelled.

"But I did."

"When did you do that?" AC asked. "You've never been out of our sight."

"I managed. Should have left when you had a chance. I wouldn't recommend swimming to the mainland. All kinds of things swimming around in that ocean. And don't bother with your scuba gear in your rooms. I spoke with Mr. Askey and he's having the hotel staff confiscate it all, and those of you with jetpacks too. Dummy!" I pretended to look behind them. "Oh, sorry. I thought I saw that dog of yours."

The authors weren't amused at all. Maxima tried to sucker-kick me like I knew he would, but I was ready for him. I karate kicked him in the face before he could finish the move. He fell to the ground on his back and I saw the glimmer in his hand.

"Supersonic run!" I yelled at Cruz Jr., and I dove for cover as my son bolted away. I heard the first shot. Maxima missed me by a mile.

"Stop!" AC yelled at him. "Are you crazy? The man has his little kid with him."

She stood in front of Maxima. Maxima had a murderous snarl on his face but he stopped his advance. He saw that he wasn't the only one on the island with an illegal gun. I didn't have my prized omega-gun, but the laser gun nestled in my hand would do the deed, and I had it aimed at his head.

"Stop this, this instant, both of you!" AC yelled. "Neither one of you should have guns! Men! We already have one corpse on the island. We don't need another."

AC faced me but moved backwards to push Maxima back too. "I'd say you two little boys need a time-out away from each other. Cruz Jr., is it?" she said to my son. "Take your father back to his room before he gets in trouble."

Cruz Jr. appeared and ran to me. He had a genuine looked of worry on his face and pulled me in the direction of the path to the bungalows.

"You're lucky she's here," Maxima yelled at me.

"She just saved your life, you has-been writer."

"Stop talking, both of you!" AC yelled. She continued to push Maxima back. He tried to get around her, but she kept him moving back to the entrance.

I had a gun. One of the writers had one. Who else had their own toys? And, thanks to me, there was no way to get off the island until the police arrived.

I kept my eyes on them as Cruz Jr. held my hand and led me away from the two authors. As if on cue, the other authors appeared. They all watched from afar. AC and Maxima reached them and I could see them talking. All of them studied me. What devious plots were they concocting against me? Creative types can be very, very sneaky if they put their minds to it. But then I was a creative type too. They wrote stupid books in their basements. I built a world-class hovercar in mine when I was in high school. We'd find out who could be the sneakiest.

"Where have you two been?"

Dot stood in the kitchen as Cruz Jr. and I came in through the door of our bungalow. I stopped.

"Dot, why are you wearing a Sherlock Holmes hat?"

"Just something I picked up."

I noticed on the couch that Kat was wearing a little Sherlock Holmes hat on her head too.

"Dot, I am not Sherlock Holmes."

"I can be your deputy."

Dot had something in her hand as she walked over to Cruz. Jr. and took off his black fedora.

"Deputy?" I asked. "Are we gunfighters at the O.K. Corral? What's that on my son's head, Dot? You got a Sherlock Holmes hat for him too?"

"Cruz, we have work to do."

"*We?*"

"Yes."

"Where did you get these hats, Dot? This is a sci-fi island. Why would they have Sherlock Holmes merchandise?"

"Because Sir Arthur Conan Doyle was also a sci-fi writer."

"He was?"

"Yes, he wrote *Lost World.*"

"He wrote that? The island with dinosaurs."

"No, a secret region of South America with prehistoric animals and creature men."

I smiled. "Dot, how do you know this?"

"Cruz, I do know stuff too."

"They sell this in the store?"

"The island has a full merchandise store of classic and contemporary sci-fi writers and in Sir Doyle's case, a companion section of Sherlock Holmes merchandise."

"So why are you putting strange headgear on the heir to the Liquid Cool Detective empire?"

Dot laughed.

"What about Kat?" she asked.

"Firstborn is always the heir. She can be the VP."

"Or the co-heir?"

"Co-heir? There's no such word...or concept."

"You know...like in marriage. Husband and wife, you know."

"Oh, yes, I see. Yes, it's becoming clear to me now."

"Is it?" Dot said with her arms folded.

"Yes. Co-heir. I remember that word now."

"I'm glad your memory is returning."

"Yes. So I am." I looked at Cruz. Jr. "Cruz Control, you, me, we men will talk privately off-line."

Cruz Jr. giggled, clapping his hands and nodding.

"You two do know I'm still standing here?" Dot said.

I didn't think I'd get away with it. I told my wife that there was no way I'd walk around in public with my family following me wearing Sherlock Holmes' hats. We'd be the laughingstock of the island, and that would adversely affect my ability to be regarded as a professional and solve the case before the police arrived.

My wife looked at me and said, "I can't find fault with the logic of your argument."

Kids wearing a Sherlock Holmes hat was one thing, but not a grown woman. I took my wife by the hand and walked her a bit away from the kids.

"Dot, this isn't a game. There's a real corpse on the island, and someone killed him. Be like me, the opposite of you. Trust no one. I'll focus on the case. You focus on Junior and Kat. We can act lighthearted and it's all fun, but murder mysteries are not fun and games. Someone's dead."

"Cruz, what do you know?"

"Lots. I know stuff and since I'm a detective, I'll go detecting now."

"Go find our bad guy," she said to me and gave me a kiss.

Now that's how you start a murder mystery!

Finally, darkness was falling. I still hadn't gotten used to the Caribbean nights. For Metropolitans like me, we were used to it being dark during daylight hours. Here it was sunny even at night.

I stepped outside of our bungalow. My mind flashed to my posthumous mentor, Wilford G. This was the kind of night he would have stepped outside for a smoke and a bit of life meditation. AC thought I was the archetypal detective, but it was Wilford G. who was the real deal. I'd never be a smoker and I did my best meditating fast asleep under my favorite thick, fluffy blanket in my bed at home. But I had work to do.

Dot was overjoyed at the prospect of "playing detective." I, however, being a real one, knew that "being" a detective was rarely fun and games. Outwardly, I kept my cool, but inside, I expected everything to go wrong—always. That's why I'd live a long life as a detective and solve my cases.

Foremost in my mind was my family. Yes, we were on an idyllic island resort, but there was also a dead body, and someone on the island killed him. As of now, everything was fun and games. But I didn't expect that to last forever. If that changed, I didn't want anyone to think they'd get anywhere near my family. I'd stepped outside because we had a prowler.

Whoever the person was, he or she clearly knew all the blind spots of the island's surveillance cameras around the bungalows. I knew them too after a couple of days of study. I stepped outside and stood on the walkway in front of our bungalow and stared. I couldn't see who it was—they were too far away, and behind bushes and trees—but I was staring in their direction. The person obviously didn't know I was the stakeout king. I could stare at a target, sitting or standing, for days, and had in the past. I had no equal.

The person was quiet, but in their haste to run, I heard some breaking twigs of brush. If the person knew all the blind spots of the surveillance cameras, the person also would know where to run to escape.

I could have given chase, but with my wife and kids inside, that wasn't going to happen. If Dot had been awake, or I'd first gotten them into the bungalow's panic room, maybe. Knowing that someone on the island was interested in me was good information.

Time for bed, I said to myself and went back inside. Early the next morning, I'd sneak back out to survey the area for footprints. Maybe I'd get lucky and identity the murderer that way.

Dot actually didn't want us to go to another theme world on the island. She said I had to solve the case but I ignored her because the family had to have its fun. Now, Cruz Jr. and Kat were asleep; Dot was taking a nap. I, on the other hand, was in the master bedroom working, doing more Net research and waiting for my call.

My mobile rang. I recognized the number. I flipped it on and there was the tiny face of PJ on my vid-screen.

"So the wife called you?"

"Cruz, your wife tells me that your head is not in the game," PJ said.

"My head is in the game."

"A-B-C, Cruz. Always Be Closing cases."

I laughed.

"This is not funny. Solve the case, catch the bad guy."

"I'm on vacation."

"Forget vacation. You Americans take too much vacation."

"Says the woman from a country with six months paid vacation."

"France does not have six months paid vacation. Three months. All work and no play makes people unhealthy. Studies have proven this."

"French studies don't count, and I haven't had a vacation for years."

"That's your fault."

"Oh, what's your new title for this week so I know what to say in public? I thought you were the secretary."

"High-class private investigation establishments do not have secretaries. How many times do I have to tell you this? High-class clients are not dealing with secretaries. That's Free City stuff. High-class clients deal with executives. Like VP of Client Concierge Services."

"What were we talking about again? I just forgot."

"No vacation for you when there are cases to be solved."

"I'm surprised at you, PJ. Who's the paying client here? Who's paying the bill? The hotel hasn't paid me anything yet. The island bribed us with the free vacation and said they'd pay me, but nothing has come in. All they want me to do is babysit until the police arrive. No paying client means no work from me. I thought this was your golden rule as well as mine."

"You have many paying clients. That's what VPs of Client Concierge Services do. I get the paying clients. You solve the case."

"What are you talking about? Who would pay me to solve this case? This is a police matter."

"It is a police matter seventy-two hours from now. It's a Cruz matter until then. And never you mind who the paying client is. What do I always collect before you're allowed to work a case?"

"Retainer. Who paid you a retainer?"

"The money has already been deposited in the Liquid Cool bank account."

"What? What's going on here?"

PJ had my partial attention.

"I sent you bios."

"Bios?"

"On the potential murderer. All the writers."

"All of them?"

"Yes. I listed them in the order of who I think is most likely the perpetrator based on my analysis."

I burst out laughing.

"Stop laughing."

"Analysis? What analysis?"

"Like...who tried to kill who in the past."

I wasn't laughing anymore. Now she had my full attention.

There was a real case all right. If Dot and I were time travelers we should have peeked ahead, because if we had known then what we would later learn, we would have grabbed the children and swum for the mainland no matter what sharks or isopods were in the ocean.

"One more thing, PJ. I want you to call me tomorrow morning. I'll text you with a time."

"To say what?"

"I'll pick a few things from the bios for you and make a script."

"Script? Like movie script? What are you up to, Cruz?"

"Never you mind. Do you want me to Always Be Closing Cases or on vacation?"

"I want you to solve the case so we don't have to refund the retainer."

I came through the main entrance of the main hotel lobby. From everyone's initial expressions, I realized that none of them had seen me wearing my tan fedora before. My tan slicker would remain packed. This was the Caribbean after all, and it was too hot for that. The authors were upset and had the hotel staff surrounded.

"Why did you take our scuba gear from our bungalows?" one asked. It was Jean Code.

"Where's my jetpack? That's an expensive piece of machinery. You have no right to confiscate it," Rich Maxima said.

"Is it true that all of the island's emergency lifeboats are locked down?" Dave Blackhat asked.

Askey raised his hands in the air with a smile. "Ladies and gentlemen, I have all the explanations to your questions. It is not as dark and sinister as you make out."

"Is that even legal," AC Vulcana asked, "to allow a civilian to disable the island's emergency lifeboats?"

"Who cares?" Marlan asked. "We don't need them. There's multiple ways off the island."

"That's not the point, Marlan," she said.

"Ladies and gentlemen, I am just following the orders of my boss with the direction of law enforcement authorities."

"Following orders? That phrase has been used before in history." AC was one of those people who always had something nasty to say to get under your skin.

I knew their inquisition of the hotel staff would go on for some time. I gestured to Ms. Modula. She joined me at the main reception counter away from the crowd.

"Yes, Mr. Cruz?"

I noticed that Runner had joined us too.

"Yes, Mr. Runner?" I asked.

"Mr. Cruz, the guests have informed us that you have an illegal weapon on the island."

"You mean a gun?"

"Yes, Mr. Cruz. A gun. Please give it to me."

"Did Mr. Maxima give you his?"

"He did, sir. We insisted. We're insisting the same of you."

I reached around my waist to the back, then gave him my gun. He, of course, didn't know it was my throwaway gun. My real gun was secretly hidden in the bungalow.

"Thank you, Mr. Cruz." He took the gun and walked away.

Before I could even get out a word to Ms. Modula, AC Vulcana was beside us.

"Mr. Cruz, what on earth is that on your head?"

"I'm a private investigator, AC."

"An expert on murder investigations."

"Not an expert. That's for the police."

"As you've said many times before, but Mr. Askey has said you've been given expanded duties by the police themselves. Duties, which we've already known you possessed from the start. What's the colloquial again for your profession? Private detective is far too formal."

"Do you mean private eye?"

"Yes, private eyes. Slimy little men in trench coats chasing after cheating husbands and wives, skulking around snapping pictures."

"There's nothing little about me, never owned a trench coat, and I wear a tan slicker and a cool hat. And there's a whole range of things private eyes do and can do besides spousal infidelity cases."

"Yes, I'm sure."

"Shouldn't you be off...writing?"

She grinned. "Okay, okay. I'm leaving. I am on vacation too, Mr. Cruz." She shuffled away to join her colleagues, still angry with the hotel staff.

"Yes, Mr. Cruz, how can I help you?" Ms. Modula asked.

"We're not going to get anything accomplished with them. I'll skulk back in my slimy clothes when they're gone."

"Yes, that might be best. They're very upset with us at the moment."

"Spoiled brats. Send them to their rooms with no snacks or toys."

"I wish we could, Mr. Cruz."

"I'll be back."

I ended up not returning that day. Instead, I took the family to the Mysterious Island theme world. They must have used the best augmented reality technology on the planet to create the raging sea storms, then there was the volcanic world itself constantly rumbling as volcanoes erupted with lava. All of that was the backdrop to the family chasing and being chased by man-like orangutan pirates disembarking from their own ancient ships and shooting laser guns at us. Cruz Jr., Kat, and Dot got to play laser tag with these "pirates," though I still wasn't completely comfortable with lifelike androids after my A.I. Confidential Case. Wilford G., my posthumous mentor, rest in peace. The family was happy, so I was happy—on my vacation.

Early morning the next day I arrived in the main lobby. Six a.m. and Ms. Modula was at the front counter on shift.

"Good morning, Mr. Cruz. We were expecting you yesterday."

"Change of plans. I decided to squeeze in one last vacation stop for the family."

"Very good, sir."

"Is the business center open?"

"Oh yes, Mr. Cruz. It's at your disposal."

"I'm going to do a lot of color printing. Also, I'd like to use one of the empty walls. There." I pointed as I walked to the elevated cul-de-sac sitting area on the side of the main hallway to the lunchroom. "Can I use that one to tape my photos too?"

"Tape photos, sir?"

"Yeah. You know, like in police TV shows where they hang up photos of suspects on their white board. We don't have a whiteboard, but the hotel has plenty of white wall surface space. I can use that to hang up photos of our suspects."

"Suspects, sir?"

"Yeah. Our suspects in the case."

I walked about ten paces to the main cul-de-sac sitting area. I liked the location.

"This would do nicely," I said. "I can hang up all the photos of suspects. Like right here, I could even tape your nice photo."

She was not amused. "Wouldn't it be better for you to use one of the private conference rooms, sir? They are available. Our largest is available and would serve your needs."

"I couldn't do that. I like it out here."

"Why wouldn't you want the privacy for your investigation? Our largest, private conference room would do nicely."

"We may have a murderer running around. I set up shop in a private conference room. He or she could sneak in there, bump me off, and leave my wife a widow and my kids orphans. Nah, that would not do nicely. Out here is fine."

"Are you saying we are still in danger, sir?"

"We don't know why Mr. Stellar was killed so we have to assume that we are." I patted a section of the white wall of the sitting area. "I'll use here."

By seven a.m., my make-shift police suspect whiteboard was looking impressive. I used some erasable ink to write on the glossy wall. I had one column called "Hotel Suspects." Ms. Modula was extremely agitated to see her photo on the wall.

"Where did you get our photos?" she had asked me.

"Oh, different places," I replied.

I had a column called "Author Suspects," then a column called "Others," and finally "Not Suspects" which included pictures of Dot, Cruz. Jr. and Kat. My family was quite photogenic, but I'm biased.

At this time, I noticed that Mr. Runner had arrived to join Ms. Modula. They were whispering away to each other from the front counter, straining their eyes to see what I was writing on the wall. Soon Mr. Askey strolled into the main lobby from the elevators and I saw the three of them talking. He disappeared and when he returned, he had a pair of big binoculars. The three of them shared it amongst themselves and then the chef, Mr. Stryper, arrived, and he joined in the binocular sharing. I cringed at the nastiness I was witnessing. That one pair of binoculars...passed around all those hands...pressing against all those eye sockets. I wanted to take another shower, but I had work to do. As long as they kept their binoculars away from me.

Then it began for real. The authors arrived. Marlan Overspeak was first. The crotchety old man had his own binoculars (bonus points for him for exercising proper public hygiene) and started laughing to himself as he scanned my Suspect Wall. When AC Modula arrived, she hung with her fellow author for a while but then proceeded to walk right up to my area. She stood about six feet behind me with her arms folded in front of her. It didn't take long for the "pack" to join her—all the other authors walked in. The hotel staff came out from behind the counter and stood with them.

"Do you really think cops solve cases like this?" Jean Code asked me. "That's only in the movies."

"No, they don't solve cases with the whiteboard, but law enforcement does use it to visualize their suspects and organize their findings. It's a tool, not a gimmick. Haven't you ever written about a police station in your books?"

"I write sci-fi," she answered.

"There are no police stations in sci-fi," Maxima said.

"Not in mine," Dave Blackhat said.

I ignored them and started writing the words "Main Suspects" on the wall. That got everyone's attention.

AC smirked. "So Mr. Cruz, the famous detective. Who goes in that column?"

I glanced back at her. I returned my attention to the wall and moved her photo to that new column. I glanced back with a smirk. She was holding back a grin. I returned her photo back to the Authors column.

"I noticed something, Mr. Cruz," AC said. "Maybe it's a Freudian slip on your part. You have the lovely family under 'Not Suspects,' but you don't have your photo."

"Ms. Vulcana, this exercise is not for me. It's for the police. I wouldn't be excluded immediately because I've killed someone."

"You mean shot and killed a criminal on one of your many grimy private eye escapades."

"Obviously, I don't mean that. Police don't care about that. That's self-defense and there's a record of those being righteous shootings."

"You killed someone?" AC asked

"Yes, which you should keep in mind. Yeah, when I was five."

AC laughed. "You killed someone when you were five."

"Yeah."

"Why would you do that?" Maxima asked.

I walked right up to him. "He tried to take my lollipop away. I didn't like it. I really, really didn't like it. He paid the price for getting on my bad side."

I turned around and went to my work of reviewing notes from my mobile.

"He's lying," Dave said.

"We heard about you, Mr. Cruz. You just lie to throw people off track," Jean said.

"I say you're a liar," Maxima said.

"How much you want to bet?" I asked him

"I'm not betting you anything. But I am saying you're a liar."

My mobile began to ring. I answered it. There was the face of my cyborg secretary, PJ.

"Hey PJ. I have you on speaker and I'm going to put you on the table here so I can take notes."

"Okay. Who are those people behind you?"

"Them? Oh, they're all the murder suspects."

"What do mean? The murder suspects I'm calling you about?"

"Yeah?"

"Are you crazy?"

"No, I'm not crazy, PJ."

"This is a private conversation!"

"Why does it need to be private? I have nothing to hide."

"You want the murderer to know what you're doing."

"PJ, the murderer already knows what I'm doing. It's a small island. Besides, they're not going anywhere. PJ, I'm out here in the public. What are they going to do?"

"They could shoot you?"

"PJ, if they did that, then we'd know who the murderer is."

"Yes, that's true. I see what you're doing. Okay, I'm not going to say it's completely smart yet. If you find the murderer and get back to Metropolis, I'll say you're smart."

"Do you work with him?" AC butted in on our conversation.

"Yes, PJ is my employee," I said.

"I'm Exec VP of Concierge Services for the Liquid Cool Detective Agency."

"She's my secretary," I said.

"Exec VP!"

"Did he kill someone when he was five?" AC asked.

"Yes, Cruz would be a kindergarten felon if they had laws for such things. Not like me, a real felon. It was some big bad guy. He deserved it. Cruz shot him with his grandma's laser gun."

"I don't believe either one of you." AC seemed genuinely disgusted. She took out her mobile, moved to the corner, and started texting someone.

"PJ, ignore these people. What do you have for me?"

"Cruz, what if the murderer is all of them?"

"PJ, that's only in the movies. It can't be everyone. Besides not everyone is here, so they wouldn't take the chance."

"What do you mean by that statement, Mr. Cruz?" Mr. Askey asked. He looked around. "Everyone on the island is here."

"Mr. Stellar isn't."

"Well, Mr...obviously the deceased isn't present, but everyone else is."

"PJ, you're on."

I heard a bit of commotion behind me. AC stood from the floor. "He's telling the truth."

"What?" Jean asked. "He actually killed someone when he was a toddler?"

"Five is not a toddler," I corrected.

"How do you know?" Maxima asked AC.

"One of my sources works in Police Intelligence. I asked if it was true. He said 'yes.'"

"What?" Maxima exclaimed.

Everyone was looking at me.

"Stop looking at me," I said.

"Mr. Cruz, tell us the truth just this once," Marlan asked. "Why did you really do it? It wasn't because he was a lollipop snatcher."

I looked at him. "Marlan, I'll tell you because I like you. My grandma was being robbed in broad daylight by some crazy thug. I got my nana's little laser pistol from the glove box in her hovercar and shot him. Hit him in the throat. He tried to run away, slipped on the pavement, broke his neck and slid into a speeding hovertruck that was illegally too low. Splattered him everywhere."

"Ouch," Marlan said.

"Exactly," I said. "Didn't lose much sleep over it though."

"So death by throat-shot, broken neck, and splattered by hovertruck," AC said.

"How gruesome, Mr. Cruz," Ms. Modula said.

"My act was considered the original act of death, and there was actually a reward for his capture—didn't say he had to be alive, so I got that money. My folks put it in a bank account for me and I used it to buy my first hovercar part at sixteen. Actually, that was the main money I used to build my red Ford Pony."

"You built a red horse?" Dave asked.

"No! A Pony is an advanced hovervehicle originally built by the Ford Motor Company. The Pony was a classic model. Don't you know anything about hovercars? 'You built a red horse.' Even my little son knows enough not to ask such a stupid question. I'm going to tell him you said that so he can laugh at you every time he sees you."

Dave began to say something—

"Silence! I'm working. The only person talking should be PJ. Shhh. PJ, you're on."

I heard gasps of indignation and Marlan's chuckling in the background.

I stood at my "white board" with marker in hand. My mobile—PJ's face on the screen—sat on a hovertray drone, courtesy of hotel staff, beside me.

"Okay, PJ, what do we got on AC Vulcana?"

"She was married to the dead man when they were—"

Rich Maxima looked at her. "You two were married?"

"Yes. It was a long time ago."

"I didn't know you were married to Rod."

"It was a quarter of a century ago. It's so long ago, it's almost like a forgotten memory. Do you know what you were doing a quarter of a century ago?"

"Not married to Rod."

When they first arrived, AC and Maxima were walking shoulder-to-shoulder in each other's orbit. They might as well have been holding hands. Now, Maxima was slowly moving away from her. At this rate they would end up on opposite ends of the lobby.

"People, Mr. Cruz thinks he's some great detective. He's trying to get a rise out of us," AC said.

"Seems like he's succeeding," Jean Code said.

"I'm going to sit next to you," Maxima said and changed his seating.

"PJ, ignore the suspects," I said. "Go on."

"Cruz, I don't know why we're talking in front of the suspects," PJ said.

"We talked about this already. Let's keep going. How old were AC and the dead man then?"

"Dead man?" AC said. "We were practically kids back then and he wasn't dead. What a thing to say."

"He was nineteen and she was eighteen," PJ answered.

"How long did they last?" I asked.

"I'm standing right here," AC said.

"Three months," PJ replied.

"Kids?" I asked.

"Certainly not!" AC yelled.

"No kids," PJ said.

I looked at her. "That we know of."

All the writers looked at her. Maxima gave her a dirty look.

"We didn't have any kids," she said, unconcerned. "He's trying to get a rise out of us."

"Succeeding again," Jean said.

"Silence!" I yelled. "I'm working here. If you all can't be quiet I'm going to have to ban you from my work area."

"Where's the family, Mr. Cruz?" AC asked.

"Safe and far away from you crazy maniacs."

"I bet he has them in the hotel's panic room," Marlan said.

I pointed at the man. "Bingo!"

"Panic room?" The hotel staff looked at each other. "How do you know where the hotel panic room is?" Askey asked.

"Not your panic room," I said. "The other one. So don't...panic. You can still get away when we find out who the murderer or murderers are and they try to eliminate witnesses."

Marlan began laughing. The hotel staff wasn't.

"Your humor is lost on us, Mr. Cruz," Jean said. "In any event, no one should be in any panic room." The woman truly had no sense of humor.

"Where's our panic room?" Dave asked.

"You won't catch me dead in some metal box," Maxima said.

"Panic rooms are not metal boxes," I said. "You think I'd have my wife and kids in a metal box? It's better than the bungalows—much larger, multi-levels, gym, pool (not using that), running track, VR room, business center. Lots for the family to do while I do my work. PJ, let's continue and we'll ignore the suspects."

At that moment Dot came through the lobby entrance. You should have seen their faces. Some of them were actually scared, forgetting that my family was also on the island.

"Well, look at this," AC said in that annoying tone.

I looked. Dot had put her Sherlock Holmes hat back on. I saw a blur and Cruz Jr. was standing next to me with his black fedora. Dot had the hoverstroller with Kat, who was also wearing a Sherlock Holmes hat.

"Why are your wife and daughter wearing deerstalkers?" AC asked. "Are they detectives too?"

"You can play, but keep an eye on your sister," I said to Cruz Jr.

He smiled and was gone. He'd run around, stop and see what his sister was doing before bursting into another fit of play.

"So Mrs. Cruz, if he's Sherlock Holmes, you must be Ms. Watson. That means you're the chronicler. What's this case of his called?"

"I always thought one of his cases should be called the Matrix Murders," she said.

I pointed at them all. "This is my story, so I get to name it."

"What matrix?" Jean asked. "There's no matrix here."

"Exactly."

My wife could see my mobile. "Hi PJ."

"Hello. Is this what you two call a vacation?"

"Tell me about it," Dot said.

"Matrix means," AC said to Jean, "among other things, a place or point from which something originates or develops."

"Good grief, writers," I said. "Why not call it the Supercalifragilisticexpialidocious Murders then?"

"What will you name it then?" AC asked me.

"I was thinking of A Cruz Family Murder Mystery."

"Is that the best you can do? That's stupidly contrite," AC said.

"I'm a detective, not a writer. And it's not stupidly anything. It's classy, has charm. The Cruz family is a classy outfit, I'll have you know."

"Cruz, you got to do better than that name," my wife said.

"If I was a studio exec and you came to me with a script with the name 'A Cruz Family Murder Mystery,' I'd throw you out of my office," Maxima said to me.

"If I had a script I wouldn't be going to the likes of you. Besides, you're just a writer. No one cares what you think," I said.

"The world would come to an end without writers," Jean said.

I started laughing.

"Writers write the publications you read, instructions for the medicine you take, speeches for actors and politicians; we write for the real world and the virtual world. We even write scenarios for robots and computers that run our world. We write far more than books. The world would end without writers. If you had any intelligence you'd know that what I said is both profound and true." Jean gave a good little speech.

"Stop making me laugh," I said. "I can write my fortune cookie messages and I don't need any of you. I have a case to solve. Making me laugh will not get you off my 'Likely Suspects' list."

"Detective? That's the joke," Maxima said. "I knew you were a faker from the first time I saw you on the news. Who wears a hat? Who wears a tan coat? Standard colors are black, brown and gray. Non-conformists are not to be trusted."

Maxima's rant went on for a good ten minutes. It was bizarre. I stood there with my mouth slightly open. It was amusing at first, but then I wondered if he was gripped by some kind of talking fit. I continued to watch him to make sure he didn't fall over in a coma. I wondered if I needed to smack him or kick him to snap him out of it.

Someone did what I was thinking. AC walked over to him and slapped him.

"Oww!" Maxima yelled.

"When he does that, slap him across the face," AC said.

"Why did you do that?" he asked.

"You were losing yourself in the part."

"I don't have a clue as to what you're talking about. Don't hit me again."

"You know you like it."

The two lovebirds were standing next to each other again. Jean was smart enough to step a few paces away from them. I looked at her and nodded in approval.

"What else about AC Vulcana and the deceased?" I asked PJ. "What other connections?"

"Besides being each other's ex-spouses, that's it," PJ said.

"Ex-spouses. That was over a quarter of a century ago!" AC reminded us.

"Let's stay on this theme of who's playing house with who," I said.

"Playing house?" Marlan laughed.

"You even talk like a cartoon detective," AC said.

"He is a cartoon," Maxima said.

I held up my hands. Everyone went quiet and looked at me.

"Okay, I warned you," I said. "You could observe if you remained quiet, but you will not behave yourselves, so I'll have to cordon off the work area."

"I've been quiet," Marlan said.

"Yes, you have. You can stay. The hotel staff can stay, but the rest of you have to back away. Ten feet away."

"I'm not leaving," AC said and sat down on the ground. Everyone suddenly sat down. They were all quiet. I looked them all over. Marlan chuckled from his couch.

"Okay, you'll all get one more chance, but I need to work. I have to put together a full report of my findings, not just for the owners of the island but the police. This is serious."

There wasn't a peep from anyone. Dot was smiling and Kat watched me as if amazed. I'm sure she thought I was about to put on some show for her. Cruz Jr. was behind us all "training" for his preschool half marathon. Not really, but the boy never stopped running.

"Okay." I turned back. "PJ, let's continue." I turned to the screen but no PJ. "Where are you?" Her face appeared and she was laughing, but the mute was on. "You tell me when you're ready to work."

She turned off the mute on her end. "I'm ready," she said, stifling more laughter.

"AC was married to the deceased when they were kids, but that's nothing. Anything more recent?"

"Do you want all the personal connections first, or the rest too?"

"No, let's stick with this theme. Personal connections first. All the personal connections. Anyone else married, divorced, separated?"

"No, but—"

"Yeah, but. Dating. Who's dating who? Who has dated who?"

"You just mean among the suspects."

"Yes, including the deceased."

"Well, that's it on the dating angle," PJ said.

"Business connections?"

"No flags there either. That Mr. Marlan has more company affiliations, ventures, book deals, movie deals than all the others combined."

"Anyone sue or try to sue another? Any complaints with any business commissions or associations, or the like."

"No."

"Financials?"

"That author David Blackhat is richer than all of them. How can you make so much money writing science fiction for kids with only fluffy fur aliens? That doesn't make any sense."

"PJ, I'm going to say to you what I say to Phishy: focus. Any unusual activity?"

"Unusual activity, I'd say."

A sea of hands raised up.

"You all are not supposed to be here. So, no, I will not be calling on you. I'm a detective. Do you think when I investigate I have my suspects sitting behind me at the desk in my office, waiting to truthfully answer any and all of my questions? Of course not. Be quiet and listen."

The hands reluctantly went down.

"Rich Maxima's money is all going to family."

"All my payments are for child support," Maxima blurted out.

"You have too many kids," PJ said. "You need to be fixed."

Everyone laughed.

"I've been trying," AC said.

"Just child support?" I asked PJ.

"And alimony," she replied.

"Lots of ex-wives."

"What else?" I asked PJ.

"The rest of them have large payments going out too. Large payments. No pattern."

"It's our money," Dave said.

"Large payments," PJ repeated.

"What's it for?" I asked.

"My payments have to do with blackmail," AC said out loud.

Everyone looked at her.

"But it's all been handled."

"Okay. Let's save your explanation for last," I said.

"Let's save mine for never."

"Then I'm putting a red mark next to your picture on the big board for further police questioning."

"You do that," AC said to me.

"What do the two of you have your hands raised for?" I asked. "Marlan?"

Marlan lowered his hand. "My payments are my business and not yours."

"Red mark for you too. Mr. Blackhat, you have answers for me?"

"Not out here."

"Okay, private talk."

I glanced back and saw that more than one of the writers was taking notes on their devices, and so were Ms. Modula and Mr. Askey. I shook my head and went back to what I was doing.

"Ms. Jean Code?"

"Stuff it, Detective."

The writers chuckled.

"Big red mark for you then. So all our writers are making big payments, but only Mr. Maxima has a legitimate explanation. PJ, anything more?"

"That's all I have. Good, I'll call later about that other thing. Bye."

"Bye, PJ," Dot called out, and Kat instinctively waved bye.

"Ciao."

PJ's face was gone from my mobile's screen.

"What other thing?" AC asked.

"The secret to solving the case," I replied. I moved to the pictures of the authors and put a red mark next to all of them except Maxima. "This is a good start."

"This is a joke," Maxima said. "You're a joke."

"Remember he's a slimy detective. Most of his cases, despite his supposed fame, are Peeping Tom infidelity cases," AC said.

"Not really, Ms. Cheating Wife," I said.

The writers looked at her, then me.

"Yes, he's right," she said with a smile. "The last and final husband. So if he's looked me up on the Net, it means he's looked all of us up."

"I have."

"The Peeping Tom detective," she said.

"Actually, peeping spousal surveillance cases account for only a quarter of my cases. Quarter are civil investigations like workers comp fraud, asset searches, some missing persons, if there is a trail to follow. Quarter are corporate investigations. Quarter are working for the courts—mostly process serving, fugitive locates, surveillance. My big famous cases get all the attention but are rare."

"The big cases are important," my wife added.

"Today, my plan was to start with the writers and I did. So really all of you—except my family—can go away. I've asked this question before but have never gotten an answer. Shouldn't you be writing something?"

"We, Mr. Cruz, are on vacation," AC said.

"Vacation? That's what I'm supposed to be on right now. When I find out who murdered this guy, I'm going to sue the murderer for ruining my vacation! Get away from me, all of you."

"That's it?" Jean asked. "Red marks besides our pictures?"

"I've already created full profiles on all of you. PJ's call was just to see what the police databases turned up."

"Full profiles? You're a detective, not a profiler," Jean said.

"Actually I am a profiler," I said. "I was certified by the Feds earlier this year. I can't practice, of course, since I'm not a federal agent, but the skills are the skills. And I'm certified."

The faces of the authors told me they weren't entirely comfortable with the information.

"You do a couple of hours of talking to your employee and scribbling on the wall. Is that the end of your detective workday?" Marlan asked.

"No. The island owners gave me full access to all the island's surveillance cameras—both legal and illegal. I'll go through that all tonight."

The writers looked at each other.

"Illegal cameras?" Dave asked.

"Yes, this resort has them."

The writers were staring at the hotel staff, who looked like they wanted to run.

"Don't look at them. They didn't know."

"Illegal means illegal," AC said. "They can't record anyone illegally."

"Yes, AC. The government doing things that are illegal. Yeah, you're right. That's never happened. That never happens."

The authors were nervous.

"Anyway, I'll review them, and the police are reviewing them now remotely. I'm fairly certain the Metropolis Police will get jurisdiction of the case. And you know how our police are. When they know you did it, you can fly to Pluto and they'll track you down. My workday hasn't even begun. Time for me to go."

I looked at the hotel staff. "Tomorrow, I'll put together your profiles."

"Us?" Mr. Askey said.

"We're staff," Runner said angrily.

"I'm not accusing you of anything. But the police are going to ask one question when they arrive: 'Where was everyone that was on site at the time of the murder?" That would be you. Five authors. Five hotel staff. Have you seen these surveillance tapes?"

"Ten little Indians," AC said.

"Oh, that reminds me. Just to play it safe. I'd recommend staying in groups, and when you're in your rooms to keep all windows and doors locked and don't let anyone in."

"What are you suggesting?" Dave asked.

"Nothing. But nothing wrong with playing it safe either."

"None of us in this room murdered Rod," AC snapped.

"I'll go watch those surveillance tapes of the island, including this building before, during, and after the murder. I'll be saying good night to everyone early. Kids, we'll be eating lunch and dinner in our bungalow today. Special dessert too!"

"Yeah!" Cruz Jr. somehow appeared in front of me, cheering. Don't ask how he got there without being seen by the naked eye.

As the family and I left the hotel lobby, we could feel the stares burning holes in our backs.

When we returned to the bungalows, Dot was laughing like a kid.

"That was smooth! Increase the pressure on them. Did you see their faces? One of them is the murderer for sure. When are you going to do the individual questioning?"

"Not sure if I will yet."

"What do you mean?"

"They're too clever. They've been trying to confuse and deceive me from the start, every bit as much as I've been."

"Cruz, tell me. When did you really start investigating this case? Truth. I'm using my 'I'm the wife' card."

"From the moment we were on the plane here."

"I knew it."

"That's why I'm the famous detective in the family," I said.

"Yes, you are."

"I go into their domain to do an investigation, they'll eat me for lunch. When police interrogate people it's at the station, not at the suspect's comfy home or office. I need to have them come into our domain, our universe, or a setting they're not familiar with to take away their advantage."

"Just like the police do."

"Yes."

"So you can trick the murderer and have them reveal themselves?"

"Dot, no one ever confesses, except for the occasional crazy. That's why you need witnesses and evidence."

"How do we get witnesses and evidence? The surveillance tapes?"

"Possibly. I'll see what's on them."

"Cruz, where's the smooth plan? Is this how you solve your cases? Are you winging it?"

"Dot, it seems that we've switched bodies. For the millionth time, we're on vacation, or it seems I am on vacation and my family wants to play detective."

"Cruz, you'd better solve this case. No vacation until this case is solved. Chop, chop. Didn't you tell me the police will be here in seventy-two hours?"

"Yeah."

"Then you have less than seventy-two hours. Your rep is at stake!"

The awful thing about the detective business is that you're only as good as your last case. The wins must never stop. Clients are a mean bunch. They can quickly go from: "Get me Cruz!" to "Who's Cruz?" So in that sense my wife was right. But I had solved enough high-profile cases that I wouldn't be losing my clients anytime soon.

I didn't wake up any of my family. I let them sleep through the night where they were. Dot on the couch. Kat and Cruz Jr. were on the carpeted floor. Kids could sleep anywhere. I covered all of them with blankets, and I returned to the upstairs bedroom to continuing viewing and fast-forwarding through all the surveillance tapes before, during, and after the time of Rod Stellar's murder.

I didn't believe it was a coincidence for a second. I strolled along the path from our bungalow alone, and as I neared the main hotel building there was AC Vulcana and Rich Maxima. She always had that superior smirk on her face. Maxima always looked like a bully and a punk from his near snarl at me. How long were they waiting? I also noticed Maxima's bandaged hand, and the fact they were both holding real-books."

"How's the sleuthing going?" she asked.

"Quite well. Thanks for asking," I said. "What's this?"

"We thought we'd give you some complimentary copies of a novel or two that we wrote—for the family."

"Your child-appropriate ones or the adult-themed ones?" I asked.

"You even know my pen names." She chuckled. "His are general audience. My favorites are always my racier novels. Your wife would enjoy them. From my reverse harem sci-fi."

"I don't know what that means, but knowing you, it's dirty."

AC laughed. I took the book she handed me, which had a black cover with a single eye in the middle. There was no way I was allowing that real-book anywhere near my family.

I turned to Maxima and asked, "Did you find it?"

"What? Find what? What are you talking about?"

"Whatever you were looking for?"

"What are you talking about?"

"I see your right hand is bandaged. You're not a pansy, so you wouldn't bandage your hand if it wasn't serious. And since the bandage isn't stained red anywhere, it must be your second change of dressing, which you did this morning. Whatever you were doing happened last night. So, did you find what you were looking for?"

Maxima glared at me. AC's smile grew a bit larger.

"No response?" I asked.

"You think you're so smart," he said.

"Since I know how to look for things without cutting my hand, yeah, I'm smarter. What do you two want? You were waiting for me. Where are your conspirators? Are they stationed on the other side? Oh, when I get inside, I'm moving you to the Possible Suspects column, Rich, my boy."

"What?"

"You're a criminal. In fact, you're all criminals. I knew there was no way any legitimate writer could afford to rent out an entire luxury resort island for themselves, even pooling your resources."

"We have business ventures besides our book sales!" he yelled at me.

"Ignore him," AC told him. "He's doing it again. Trying to get a rise out of you. He's fishing, I believe that's the mystery detective jargon for this situation."

"Thanks, AC. You're taking an interest in my profession. However, I'm not fishing. Rich Maxima is my number one suspect for the murder of Rod Stellar, your ex-husband and on again-off again lover."

"Why you—"

Maxima swung at me, but I stepped back in time. He didn't connect but I got a good look at the solid muscles of his arms and back. If it had connected, I'd be back on the ground. But I didn't wait for him to swing back around. I reacted and kicked him in the head. Anyone else would have been on the ground or at least dazed. He had been kicked before and shook it off. He was mad! My hands were up and ready. Maxima did the lowly unthinkable. He kicked me in the nuts with enough force to turn me from Cruz to Cruzalina. But the joke was on him.

"You're a dirty fighter. If you did that in a MMA cage, they'd shoot you. The other fighter, the referee, or the audience. You're lucky it's just me. How do you like it?"

Maxima was on the ground, holding his foot, writhing in pain, crying like a baby—literally.

"That's what you get for trying to kick me in the nuts. Didn't I tell you I was a profiler last night? Yes, I'm wearing a groin guard, you dirty fighter. I read your criminal complaints. Now you can bandage up your foot to match your hands."

I'd almost made a fatal mistake. I started walking away, glancing back, and saw Maxima reaching into his jacket for something. He had another gun! It was tiny and black. He shot it at me and I blocked the pellet with AC's book.

"What did you shoot at me?" I yelled. As I walked to him, he tried to back away. "What did you shoot at me? Did you shoot a smart bullet at me, you dirty fighter?"

I grabbed the books on the ground and started smacking AC's book hard against them. The pellet was embedded in her book. I knew I looked like a certifiable maniac smacking that bullet, but I wanted it smashed. I threw it to the ground once, then again. I picked up AC's book and looked at it.

"Here's your book," I said and threw it at him.

"No!"

AC was already running away. Maxima tried to get up. The book landed on him. *Boom!* He was knocked off his feet into some bushes along the path.

He screamed and aimed his little pellet shooter at me again. But I was aiming my real gun at him. AC ran back and jumped between us.

"Come over here so I can kick you in the face again," I said to him.

"Will you two adolescents stop it!" AC yelled at us.

"Keep control of your man," I told her.

141

"Go to your whiteboard," she yelled at me.

"I will. And number-one suspect it is. Red marked and red circled for you!" I yelled at him, backing away down the path to the hotel.

First thing in the morning I'd call the front desk and had them rearrange the lobby a bit. For the cul-de-sac sitting area where my whiteboard was, I had them set up chairs in three rows a comfortable distance back. I knew I'd be the star attraction on the island until the police arrived, so I wanted my suspects happy in their chairs and within sight as much as possible.

I'd been standing at the whiteboard when I heard giggling and turned. I had not just one "deputy," but three of them. My wife had our kids back in the Sherlock Holmes hats. I guess my wife didn't care if the suspects laughed at me.

"Sellout," I said to Cruz Jr. He grinned, obviously not knowing what I meant. "Where's your black fedora?"

His smiling disappeared, replaced by an "Oh no!" expression as he ran off.

I had the hotel create "premiere" seating for my wife—a chair bigger and plusher than the others. Kat had her hoverstroller, and Cruz Jr. would be running around so he didn't need a chair. I returned to my work—on my vacation!

Then they came in—the writers. Runner had been called beforehand, and I saw him leave the hotel with a hoverchair with leg attachments. He was with the writers pushing Rich Maxima in it. His right foot was wrapped in a balloon cast, no doubt also packed tight with ice. Runner set him at the back of the writers' chairs. The others sat down. I glanced at them occasionally, but I was more focused on my work.

"Heard you had some excitement this morning," Jean Code said.

"You mean kicking Rich in the head," I answered without turning around.

"What was that explosion I heard?" Marlan asked with a chuckle.

"You mean me blowing Rich into some bushes with his own bomb." I turned around and there was Runner standing with his hand outstretched.

"Cruz, you're a liar!" Maxima yelled at me.

"How're you feeling from when I kicked you in the face and blasted you into the dirt with your own bomb?" I asked.

"Bomb?" Askey asked, shocked.

"It wasn't a bomb," AC said.

"But I did kick him in the head," I said.

"It was a stun pellet," Maxima said, "not a bomb." He gave me the nastiest look he could manage, like he wanted to spit at me.

"You're asking to get kicked in the head again," I said.

"Come on and do it!" Maxima yelled

"What's wrong with you two?" AC yelled. "Why can't you two behave yourselves?"

Now Dot was giving me the evil eye.

"It's not my fault," I said to Dot. "He attacked me."

Dot wasn't convinced. Runner was standing there with his outstretched hand all that time.

"Please give it to me," he said.

"You should be careful with him," AC said. "He might take that to mean something else."

I reached into my jacket and gave him my second throwaway gun.

"Is this the last one?" he asked.

"It is. And did you get his explosive pellet shooter?"

"I did. Mr. Cruz, I'm going to watch the surveillance tapes to make sure this is the one you aimed at him."

"It is."

"Okay."

He turned to look at me.

"I don't have any more."

He turned to walk away. I glanced at the authors. They sat there watching me stone-faced.

"I told AC and my pal, Rich, already, so I should tell you. Rich Maxima is our prime suspect."

"That is garbage!" he yelled from his hoverchair.

"How can that be, if he was with us all the time?" AC asked.

"Good question," I said to her, "but I'm just gathering the information. Today, we turn to the hotel staff."

"Mr. Cruz, neither my staff nor myself had any involvement in the murder. You know this," Askey said from his place near where my wife and daughter sat. Modula and Runner joined them.

"Where's Mr. Stryper?" I asked.

"He's cooking lunch," Runner replied.

I walked to my whiteboard. "There are three different groups of suspects, not including me."

"Three?" AC asked. "What three? The hotel staff and us writers, excluding you and your family—what is the other group?"

I immediately saw it. I ran to Ms. Modula, startling her.

"What was that face for?" I asked.

"Nothing? I didn't make any face," she said.

"You did or didn't?"

"I didn't."

"Is there someone else on the island besides the other people?"

Her left eyebrow rose. "Other people? There are no other people on the island besides us here."

"Who else is here?" I asked.

"No one else." Modula looked at me with a combination of surprise and anger.

"What other people are you talking about?" AC asked.

"There is no one else on this island," Askey declared.

"There are other people on the island," I said.

"There is not!" Askey said. "There is no one else on the island, Mr. Cruz."

"What are you talking about, Cruz?" Jean asked.

"This island has advanced sensors," Runner added. "There isn't anyone else on the island."

"How many people on the island?" I asked.

"Fourteen," Runner answered.

"Are you sure?"

"Of course, we're sure," Askey answered.

He walked to the main counter. We all followed him like a herd of cattle; even Maxima in his hoverchair glided closely behind the pack. He went behind the counter. I stood right in front of him. The

145

rest of the hotel staff followed the manager behind the counter, and they all watched the screen as he typed.

"Mr. Cruz, there are ...I'll tell you exactly how many people are on the island. See, there are fourteen people on the island." He looked at all of us and then his staff. "All of us. You and your three family members."

"And?" I asked.

"And? There is no 'and,' Mr. Cruz. There isn't anyone else on the island."

I pointed at Ms. Modula. "Yes, there is. Look at her face."

"Why are you picking on her?" Runner asked angrily.

"There's nothing wrong with my face!" Modula yelled.

She saw the look on the writers' faces. She realized that she looked guilty and looked away. Askey and Runner were looking at her, and we could see the doubt creeping into their faces.

"Mr. Askey, your employee could well be concealing the murderer."

She laughed. "That's crazy." Her emotional state had completely flipped. She was the outraged victim one moment, now she was calm and cool.

The manager stared at her. "Is there something I should know, Ms. Modula?"

"Nothing, sir."

"Is there someone else on the island with you?" he asked.

She ignored him at first, but the resolve began to crumble before our eyes.

"Oh my God," AC said and looked at me. "How did you know?"

"Mr. Cruz, can I speak with you privately?" she said.

"No!" It wasn't just my wife who yelled it out; so did all the writers and other staff.

"It's the boyfriend," I said.

She broke down. "He's right, sir."

"Ms. Modula, you know the strict regulations for the island and its staff."

"Yes, sir. I know and apologize."

"There will be a reprimand in your file for this."

"Yes, sir."

"Mr. Cruz, on behalf of the island I apologize for this breach of island regulation by my senior staff."

"It's a beautiful island resort," I said.

"No excuse, sir."

"I hate this," I said. "The suspect list is growing, not shrinking."

"There is no way," Modula said. "I swear."

"Mr. Cruz, is that the other people on the island you were talking about?" AC asked me.

"No."

"What do you mean 'no'?" Dave and Jean asked at the same time.

I ignored them and walked back to my wall. I picked up the marker and began to write: First I wrote "Ms. Modula's boyfriend," then a question mark under "Hotel Suspects." Then I wrote "Night People." Under "Other Suspects."

"What!" Marlan said. The entire pack of authors and staff was behind me. "That was the name of a sci-fi book I wrote. I don't like the sound of that. What night people?" he asked.

"Because they come out at night."

"There are no other people," AC said to everyone. "You stumbled upon her boyfriend. Now you're trying to use it to your advantage."

"We'll see at dinnertime," I said.

"Like a murder mystery dinner," Dot added with a smile.

"Oh, I have a task for you to prepare. Remind me," I told my wife.

AC began to laugh. "You two are too much."

"Before I move on, let's talk about our other three hotel staff suspects," I said.

"What?" Runner said.

"Mr. Runner, could you get Mr. Stryper from the kitchen? It's only fair that he be here if I'm talking about him."

Runner really didn't like me anymore. Askey gave him a nod, and Runner grudgingly walked off to the kitchen.

"Is your husband always like this?" AC asked Dot.

"You mean solving cases?"

"Making everyone around him want to do bodily violence against him."

Dot smiled. "As long as he solves the case."

"I still don't think he can solve anything," Jean said.

"He wants us to think he's clever but all he did here is maybe see the hotel staffer with her boyfriend when they were unaware. He is, after all, a Peeping Tom. Then he comes out here for the great reveal. Nothing sophisticated or magical about that." AC was quite happy with herself.

"No one saw us," Modula said emphatically.

"Then how did he know?" AC asked her.

"I don't know."

"Will you tell us, Great Detective?" AC asked.

"No."

Runner returned with Stryper. He also had a sour face, so the two men had been talking.

"You'd better not accuse me of anything," Stryper said.

"I wouldn't think of it," I said. "You're the chef. I need you to remain on our good side."

"You better believe it."

"I wanted you here to know that I've completely cleared you as a suspect."

He nodded, satisfied.

"How are you clearing him?" Dave asked. "What is that statement based on?"

"He's the only one among all of you with an alibi."

"Alibi? How?" Runner asked.

Stryper gave him a dismissive look. "I couldn't have an alibi?"

"What is it?" Runner asked.

Stryper looked at me. "What alibi do I have?"

"You were in the kitchen and your office on camera before, during, and after the murder."

Stryper smiled wide. "Yes, I was."

"Mr. Stryper, you are excused to cook our wonderful lunch."

"Thank you, Mr. Cruz. You and the family will get a special dessert today."

"Thank you."

Stryper marched off. The other staff weren't pleased.

"As for Mr. Askey and Mr. Runner, PJ sent me your files and you were both clean."

"We could have told you that," Runner said.

"Though—"

"Though what?" Runner asked.

"Nothing."

"You can't say nothing."

"How long have you worked at the island?" I asked Runner.

"Ten years."

"Nine years," I said. "The year after the writers began renting it for their retreat."

Runner said nothing. The writers glared at him.

"What are you suggesting, Cruz?" Jean asked.

"Nothing. And Mr. Askey—"

"I have been an employee of the island for fifteen years and before that worked for the owners for ten. My record is impeccable."

"Any debts?"

"None. I do not believe in debts, drinking, smoking, or criminality of any kind. I'm a lifetime employee of this megacorp."

"Your file said that too. Your record is spotless. Any family?"

"Mr. Cruz, I must insist that you cease this interrogation of me. I am not a suspect. I have no motive whatsoever to ever harm Mr. Stellar. None. I was with Ms. Modula and Mr. Runner during the whole period."

"Yes, you all have alibis too. We'll come back to you two." I looked at Ms. Modula. "You didn't think I'd drop it so easily, did you? Let's go meet him."

"Meet who?"

"Your boyfriend."

"No!" she said with a sneer.

"You don't have to tell me where he's hiding."

"He's not hiding and he isn't the murderer."

I pointed to the clock. "My advice to you would be to get your boyfriend in here with all of us before the night people get here."

"Stop saying that," Marlan said. "It's creepy."

"Mr. Askey?"

"Yes, Mr Cruz."

"Let's go to Ms. Modula's room."

"No!" Modula yelled.

The island manager looked at her briefly, then back at me.

"I forbid it," she said.

"I'm sorry, Ms. Modula. I will grant Mr. Cruz's request, especially given the circumstances."

I heard Marlan chuckling as we all followed Askey to the elevators.

"What floor?" Maxima asked.

"Third," Askey answered.

Maxima wasn't going to wait for the elevator. He was already flying his hoverchair up the stairway. The elevator arrived. Dot pushed Kat in her hoverstroller in first, then we all piled in.

"What about little Cruz, the detective?" AC asked.

"He'll be here," I said.

Just as the elevator was about to close we heard the feet, then the boy jumped in.

"One day you're going to hurt yourself," Dot said to him. He smiled and took her hand.

"Yes, we wouldn't want another cyborg in the family," AC said.

Dot and I gave her a dirty look in unison.

"I could bionic head-butt you, but I'd mess up my makeup," Dot said to her.

The elevator opened and Modula burst out, running!

I was actually running through the hallway after the hotel staffer. I knew what she planned to do but she was fast. All she had to do was touch the door panel and it would open for her biometrics and she could lock us all out. But I couldn't catch her. A blur passed me. It was Dave Blackhat. Modula reached her hotel room and pushed open the door, but Dave threw his body at the door, preventing her from locking it.

Modula tried to pummel him, but she was petite and he was on the brawny side, so he didn't mind.

"Ms. Modula!" Askey yelled when he entered the room.

She stopped her attack.

"I like the design of our bungalows better," AC said.

Everyone was in the room, including Maxima. My wife and Kat arrived last with the hoverstroller. Kat and Cruz Jr. were smiling and laughing. At least they were having fun.

"I say we search the room for the secret boyfriend," AC said.

Modula was beside herself as the writers fanned out in the spacious two story hotel room. I waited with the hotel staff; the three of them stood quietly in the living room. Dave had checked the first-floor bathroom and closets to return and wait with us.

Marlan checked the kitchen and balcony. The two woman and Maxima went upstairs. They soon came down together.

"Mr. Great Detective, there's no one else here," AC said.

"Why did she run then?" Maxima asked.

"For once, he asks a smart question," I said.

"Come over here so I can run you down with my hoverchair," he snapped at me.

"Did you check everywhere?" I asked.

"Of course," Jean answered with annoyance.

Ms. Modula kept her gaze toward the floor and remained quiet.

"Let's go upstairs then," I said.

"We were already upstairs and looked," Jean said.

I ignored them and double-timed up to the second level of the room. Soon all of them joined me in the master bedroom. Modula was sweating.

"Did you check under the bed?" I asked.

"Check under the bed? There's nothing to check," Jean said.

The bed design was not on wheels with space, but rested on the floor. I walked to it and pushed a button on the side and it rose. I leaned down and grabbed something under the new space beneath the bed.

"How do you know the layout of my room?" Modula yelled at me.

"I know the layout of this room, the hotel, the bungalows, the island."

Everyone looked at each other.

"What's this?" I said.

I pulled out a leg, then dragged out the struggling man from underneath the bed.

"This looks like a man," I said. "The boyfriend is here."

He wore a robe and pajamas and kept his face pressed against the carpeted floor. I gave a little tap with my foot.

"Hello."

"Leave me alone! Get out of here!"

"Is that any way to talk to the man you hired?" I asked.

More than one person said, "What?"

"Cruz, what are you saying?" Askey asked.

I turned the man over. "It's Mr. Derez, the island's owner. He hired me to solve the case."

On second thought, I probably shouldn't have sprung it all on them like that. Modula ran out of the bedroom, crying. Askey fell to his knees, about to faint. Runner was like a stuttering fool, and the writers were petrified zombies. Dot just lay down on the carpeted ground.

"Cruz, you're too much," she said.

Kat got out of her stroller and lay next to her, thinking it was nap-time.

Cruz Jr. slowly walked over to the man, who was fully weeping, and pointed at him while looking at me.

"The bad guy, Daddy?"

"Not sure yet. But let's not tell him that."

"I am utterly humiliated!" Derez yelled. "Mr. Cruz, you're fired!"

PART SIX: THE BODY?

I grabbed Cruz Jr., gave Dot the signal, and we were out of there. Derez was still weeping and everyone else was still in shock. Dot and I moved down the hallway to the elevator. We passed a crying Ms. Modula along the way.

"Cruz, where are we going?"

"We'll skip lunch with them and come back for dinner."

"Shouldn't we be here?"

"No. This bunch will be completely useless for the next few hours. We don't have time to hang around and waste that time. So we'll squeeze in another theme world."

"What? But you've been fired."

"He didn't mean it. But let's hurry just in case." I looked at the kids. "We're going to the Center of the Earth World!"

"Yeah!" Cruz Jr. said.

"Yeah!" Kat repeated in her tiny voice.

"Yeah," Dot said in a completely flat, unenthusiastic way.

I had a feeling that this would officially be the end of the "family vacation." Someone had to get murdered for us to get a proper vacation. I didn't like that at all, but it seemed true. We were on this island resort that was beyond our ability to pay for. Maybe one of us, two if we stretched. But a family of four? Families are expensive!

When we left our bungalow with the kids we had to go back multiple times. We forgot Kat's beach slippers and her water wings. We forgot Cruz Jr.'s jacket in case it got unexpectedly cold. Dot forgot to forward the home phone. I forgot to call my folks before I left. We both forgot to call our credit card companies to tell them we were out of the country. The bottom line was that we hadn't been on vacation in such a long time we forgot what to do, and we had two high-maintenance kids in tow.

Dot still didn't think we'd be able to sneak into another theme world.

"Cruz, I don't think we should go to the Center of the Earth World. We can go, but I think we should relax at the beach. You got a chance to relax but not me. The kids can play in the ocean."

"Okay, we'll skip the theme world."

Relaxation at the beach. Dot and I sat in our beach lounge chairs facing the sand and beach. The kids were in complete sight at all times. Cruz Jr., in his trunks, had his own snorkel gear—tube and mask. He'd been in a pool before but not the ocean. He was still walking out into the water, stopped when it got to his waist, and ran back. Kat was in her one-piece swim clothes but wouldn't walk past the water being ankle high. Every so often they looked back at us.

"Come on, Cruz," Dot said.

"The water looks clean, but is it?"

156

"Stop it. Come on."

The kids weren't going to do anything until we came out in the water with them.

"Where's the squid monster, Daddy?" Cruz Jr. asked me when I got to him.

"Is that why you won't use your gear? There is no squid monster. Put on your water mask and see underwater for yourself."

Soon Cruz Jr. was walking fully submerged underwater. Every time he came up and he went back down holding his breath longer.

Kat was getting the hang of her water wings and Dot was showing her how to swim with both arms, then to start using her legs.

The lounge chairs were hover-enabled, so we moved them into the ocean so we could sunbathe and the kids could play in the water around us.

My wife had noticed that I was wearing one black glove, and I was actually wearing a different pair of shades. She knew I was up to something but didn't ask. As we floated in the ocean on our chairs, I could still casually work on the case. I watched the display in my glasses. With the flick of my gloves, I could switch from the normal view to see the family, and with another flick return to what I had been focused on. We were being watched for some time from the bushes by someone.

Even with the best sunscreen, it could be risky lying out in the sun when your body wasn't unaccustomed to it. We were Metropolitans. We lived in a supercity where it rained most of the time, wearing our slickers and wet-wear. Didn't get the chance to wear swimming trunks and bikinis too often there.

The kids had another great day. We'd brought sandwiches for lunch but the kids barely ate. They wanted to stay in the water. Kat was on her way to being an Olympic swimmer. Cruz Jr. was perfecting his sea floor exploration skills. Dot and I were happy to just vegetate in our lounge chairs. We didn't need to do anything else to be happy.

All four of us walked back to the bungalow. Without our wristbands, we wouldn't have even known it was dinnertime. Caribbean days were so misleading for us. The sun said noon to us, but it was after six p.m.

"Dinnertime," Dot said.

The kids applauded. Cruz Jr. ran ahead as always. Kat was chasing after him.

"We have another hotel person suspect, but we're doing battle against these murderous writers," Dot said.

"Dot, don't jump to conclusions. Who said the murderer was one of the writers?"

"What? I thought you did."

"I never said that."

We arrived at our bungalow and entered. Being the paranoid person I was, I checked around each room. Dot followed me.

"Kids, get ready for dinner!"

The kids ran to their rooms.

"Cruz, what are you saying? If it's not one of the writers, then who? The hotel staff?"

"What I did say is that the murderer or murderers could be anyone. Except those in this bungalow at the present time."

"Yes, Cruz. I think it's a safe bet that our kids are not the murderer. More than one person? The writers or the hotel staff?"

"Or others?"

"Yes, you threw that out there before but I forgot. Night people, you said."

"Yep."

"What does that mean? What others, or night people?"

"There are other people on the island."

"What people? Besides the island's owner?"

"Yes."

"How do you know?"

"I saw them walking around."

"When?"

"At night. A few nights in a row."

"How did you know it wasn't the writers or the hotel staff?"

"Because one time I could see the hotel staff in the hotel, and I saw the writers in the dining room. You and the kids were in the bungalow. And these other people were wandering around the grounds watching them. And I was watching them."

"Cruz, this isn't funny anymore. Let's get off the island. I was wrong. You were right. This is for the police."

"Too late. We're stuck on the island like everyone else until the police get here."

"What are we going to do?"

"I'm going to find out who the murderer is—the writers, the hotel staff, or these strange people lurking around. But we have to get dinner."

"Cruz, this is so, so far from fun right now."

The island owner, Mr. Derez, wore a sharp suit, appropriate for the Caribbean. Light fabric, tans. He sat in his chair with tan loafers, with no socks. Unlike before, his black hair was slicked back and groomed. His hands rested on the table, clasped. His demeanor was focused but with a hint of sadness.

We sat in Askey's office, just the two of us at a small office table. Askey had called me at the bungalow. I was expecting the call. Here I sat across from him saying nothing, only waiting.

"Of course, you are not fired, Mr. Cruz. My outburst was uncalled for. You caught me quite off-guard. I am not a man to be exposed in that way. My behavior was out of shock and desperation."

"Why did you hire me? Really? It was never to take charge of the situation or be a presence on the island as the lie began at Metro International. Your intention was to get me involved in this investigation from the beginning."

"I hired you to be a decoy, I'm ashamed to say."

"Mr. Derez, are you involved in the murder of Mr. Stellar?"

"No! Heavens no. I had to avoid the scandal. My family's name is very important to me."

"Aren't you married, Mr. Derez?"

"I'm separated. Divorce pending. Can you imagine what this would do to my family name, my reputation, my company?

Legendary author murdered. His business partner and island owner secretly on the island too, shacked up on the island with his mistress. I couldn't allow anyone to know I was here. And no, I didn't murder Rod. He was a business partner and friend. Besides, I was in the hotel room all the time, nowhere near the scene of the crime."

"Who did it then?"

"One of the writers, of course."

"Not hotel staff?"

"No. Why would they harm Rod? He was a VIP guest, as far as they were concerned."

"You said you and Mr. Stellar were business partners and friends."

"Yes. Rod's a shareholder of the island. He was the one who began their writers' retreat ten years ago, and was only approved by the island's board because of Rod's personal involvement as a share holder."

"What's the purpose of this retreat? Renting an entire island, kicking off all the tourists seems like the height of indulgence for half a dozen people and a loss to the island."

"Not at all. Tourism competition is fierce during the summer, and this is the Caribbean. There's a lot more popular and inexpensive choices for people. Rod convinced the board that the mystique of an annual writers' retreat of the world's top sci-fi writers would help us attract higher-end tourists who would be more receptive to a classic literary, high-brow pitch. The response monetarily has been substantial to the company.

"Also, we use the time for automatic maintenance and any upgrades to the island as needed. Tourists tend to frown on that type of thing when they're present. When tourists are here, our services are around the clock."

"You hired me as a decoy?"

"The writers would focus on you and I'd be left to sneak off the island, then I could personally see to the police investigation. But then you locked down emergency lifeboats. I noticed that the command codes you said were the new ones do not work. The new plan was that Ms. Modula would get me onto one of the hovernautiluses as soon as we'd be certain no one would see me. Granted, Mr. Cruz, my plan was stupid and had little chance of success. However, when you're as terrified of even the hint of scandal as I am, what else would I have done? How did I know Rod would get killed?"

Derez touched his mouth as his voice trailed off in sadness.

"What now, Mr. Cruz?"

"Stay with your staff."

"Could I not remain here out of sight?"

"They all know you're here, so might as well stay with them."

"Very well."

"Who do you think killed Rod?"

"I have no idea."

"Any idea as to why?"

"No."

"But you believe it's one of the writers?"

"Yes. It couldn't be any of the island staff. We all have solid alibis."

"Does Mr. Stellar's death have any other negative impacts to you, the island, or the company?"

"The writers' retreat will be over, my tenure as the island's overseer will be terminated, I'll probably lose my controlling interest, my divorce will invariably become much more complicated, the many business ventures in real estate, publishing, and movies that I had with Rod are probably in jeopardy too. Other than that, nothing."

The family and I had arrived for dinner. This time I was the only one wearing a hat—my trademark tan fedora. Dot didn't need the hoverstroller because Kat only wanted to run and chase after her brother. Looked like all that ocean swimming strengthened my daughter's legs. Soon she'd learn her brother's ninja teleporting skills too.

Runner met us at the main lobby entrance.

"Excuse me, Mr. Cruz," he said.

"Yes, Mr. Runner?"

"Would you, or your family, have by chance seen one of our island drones damaged or saw one crash?"

"Crash?" Dot asked. "Does that happen?"

"No, Mrs. Cruz, but one of our drones is missing."

"Sorry to hear that, Mr. Runner," I said. "We didn't see anything, but we'll keep an eye out."

"Thank you, sir."

"Is everyone in for dinner?" I asked.

"Yes. Everyone is there. Service began only a few minutes ago."

Ordinarily, the kitchen would be open 'round the clock, but with a drastically reduced island tourist population and cooking staff, hours were set. You missed it and it was vending machine food only for you.

We entered the dining area again. Buffet-style again too. My eyes immediately looked for Maxima. He was still in his hoverchair. He saw me and made squeezing gestures with his hands, grinning.

Dot led us to the tables where the authors were sitting, already eating, to greet everyone.

"Join us," Marlan said.

The family and I got our food and sat with them again. We all sat in the exact same spots as we were the first dinner we had with them.

I looked around and I didn't see any of the other hotel staff, except for Runner who waited in the corner.

"The rest of them are hiding in the kitchen," Marlan said to me.

"Mr. Derez too?" I asked.

"Oh, yeah. He's there."

"What can you all tell me about Mr. Derez?" I asked the authors.

"Is he a murder suspect?" Jean asked.

"Depends on what you tell me about him."

"We don't know much about him," AC said. "Personally, I think I've only met him a couple of times. Rod was the only one of us who interacted with him all the time over the years."

"They were business partners," Marlan said. "Over twenty years."

"This situation. It's funny the things men do," AC said.

"It's called love, AC," Jean said.

"That's one word for it," she said. "Mr. Great Detective, what now? When do we start with witness statements?"

"Oh good, you're following the standard detective checklist too," I said. "The police will have to do the formal witness statements. Even if I did them and there were any inconsistencies, it wouldn't matter. When the case begins, the only witness statements that count are the ones done by the police and the DA's office.

"I need to focus on the motives for murder next: means, methods, and opportunity. Motive is third on the list. Including who has alibis."

"Third?" AC asked. "What happened to first?"

"AC, you're not paying attention to the detective checklist. First is the crime. Second is the suspect or suspects. I'm working backwards at this point. I'm on the second point. How many suspects are there?"

"You said something about night people the other day," Dave said. "Why did you say that? Who are you referring to and why do you call them that?"

"Because they come out at night."

"I said it then: There are no other people on the island besides us," AC said.

"Like Mr. Derez wasn't here," I said.

"You stumbled upon her boyfriend and you're trying to use it to your advantage to get a rise out of us," AC said.

"Yes, you did say you would explain it at dinnertime," Marlan said, "which is now."

"I said: Like a real live murder mystery dinner," Dot added.

"And I said, I had a task for you," I said to my wife.

"Do you two always play games like this?" Jean asked.

"This is the first time I've worked with my husband on a case," Dot responded.

"What task did he have you do?" Jean asked her.

"I can't tell you."

"What about these night people?" Dave asked.

"Wasn't that the name of some strange gang in Metropolis?" Dot asked me.

"Yeah," I replied. "Near Mad City. But Wilford G. had Junior clear them out of there for good."

"Junior?" Cruz Jr. asked, looking up from his food.

"Not you, Cruz Control," I said to him.

"What are we talking about?" Dave asked.

"We know what you're doing, Mr. Cruz," AC said. "You invented these other people on the island to try to trick the murderer—you believe it to be one of us—into thinking such people exist to keep them pinned down."

I jumped up from my chair, drew, and fired a laser round at the windows.

Everyone ducked or dove to the ground for cover. I holstered my weapon and stood there with my hands folded. Heads lifted from the floor. Everyone could hear it. Someone was running away outside!

Maxima jumped out of his hoverchair, bolted for the windows, and pulled back the curtains. Dave and Jean joined him.

"What do you see?" Jean asked.

"Look!" Maxima yelled. "Who is that? Look, over there!" He ran away, out of the dining room.

Pandemonium. People ran after Maxima, while others first ran to the window to look out. It was night but far from being dark since we were in the Caribbean.

Soon all of us were in the main lobby moving to the entrances. Maxima walked back in with an exasperated look. He was a bit out of breath from running. We all noticed the hotel staff had joined us—Askey, Runner, Modula, the chef, but not Mr. Derez.

"What is going on?" Askey asked. "Why did you shoot your weapon? Who was it?"

"The other people. The night people," I said.

"It's not night!" Jean said.

Marlan stepped forward to me. "Mr. Cruz, if you don't start talking right now, you're going to be the next one murdered here—by us!"

"I don't know who they are. That's why I'm investigating, or trying to."

"How many other people are on the island?" Maxima asked, standing next to Marlan.

"Why ask me? Ask the hotel manager and the island owner. They're the ones with the fool-proof sensors that can tell us all how many people are on the island, except for island owners."

Marlan clenched his fist as if he was about to punch me in the head.

"There's at least four of them but could be more. I saw them watching us," I said.

"Four!" Jean said.

Everyone was looking at each other, then back at me. It was the first time I'd seen the authors frightened. Even AC had that deer-in-the-headlights look, as if she wanted to be on the next flight off the island.

Askey looked especially distressed. "This is all a bit too much for me. I need to lie down."

"Maybe your boss can give you the day off," Maxima said.

"Ms. Modula, call your boyfriend and tell him to give your boss the day off," I said.

"There we are," AC said. "That's more like the sleazy Metro private eye peeking through door holes, figuratively speaking, that is."

Ms. Modula cried out in rage and attacked me. Well, she started pummeling me with both her fists. Since she was like five feet tall, it was the equivalent of Cruz Jr. Play-fighting, so I ignored it and let her punch herself out. She stopped and ran away to the back offices, crying.

"Mr. Runner, please go get her and keep her in this main area with all of us. She could still be the murderer, and who knows if she has a weapon in there. In fact—"

I grabbed my family and pushed them behind one of the columns, and I peeked out in a defensive position. Some were disgusted by my action, others laughed.

"You're a bastard," Maxima yelled at me.

"Come over here so I can kick you in the head again," I said.

He was about to charge when AC yelled at him. "What's wrong with you? Are you so easily provoked? Ignore him. Mr. Askey, get to your terminal and tell us how many people are on the island."

"Yes, and Chef, please escort Mr. Derez here too. We want everyone to be together," I said.

The chef disappeared.

We all moved to the hotel back offices. We gathered in Askey's nice office as the manager moved to his computer and activated it. Runner returned with Modula and she sat down on the chair. She was still crying but if looks could kill I'd be vaporized to dust. Runner closed the door and joined us.

"Mrs. Cruz," he said to my wife.

"Don't worry. I'll get the gun back for you," Dot said to him.

I was about to say something when we all heard a knock. Everyone looked at each other. Askey gave us all a look.

"Open the door," he said.

"Wait," I said and pulled my gun.

"What's that for?" Modula yelled as she jumped up from her chair.

"Haven't you ever seen a murder mystery movie before?" I said. "Everyone thinks it's one person, then some poor Joe opens the door and gets blown away by the murderer."

AC laughed.

"This is ridiculous," Askey said. "I'll open the door."

"No, you stay here and tell us who else is on the island," Marlan said to the manager, restraining him.

"Okay, Mr. Cruz," AC said. "That means you open the door."

"Sure, but I'm not the only one in this room with a gun," I said.

Everyone looked at each other.

"What does that mean?" Dave asked.

"Come in!" I said.

The door opened. Chef and Mr. Derez casually came in. Sighs of relief.

"Look what the great detective is doing to us," AC said.

"Mr. Derez, join the party," I said. "There are other people running around the island."

"Other people?" Derez moved to Askey at the terminal.

Askey had Marlan on one side and Derez on the other, with Dave and Jean breathing down his neck. The rest of us waited on the other side of Askey's desk.

"There are—That's not possible!" Askey yelled.

"Is that the number?" Marlan asked, pointing to the screen.

"Yes," Derez asked.

"There's a total of twenty-one people on the island?" Marlan asked.

I looked around. "That means, besides the fifteen here, there are—"

"Six additional people on the island," AC said.

For a long moment, everyone stood there quiet. No one said a thing. My kids were looking at everyone, confused as to why no one was talking.

An idea hit me and I didn't like it.

"Follow me," I said to my wife.

I opened the door of the office and led my family out. I led them to my whiteboard in the hotel lobby sitting room. I pulled one of the chairs from the ones arranged for the authors and sat. Out came my mobile and I scrolled down the screen.

"What are you doing, Cruz?" my wife asked.

"Looking at my suspect notes," I said.

"Mr. Cruz, is one of these unauthorized people on the island Rod's murderer?" Derez asked me.

The hotel staff and authors had followed us out into the lobby area.

"One moment, Mr. Derez. Oh, here it is. Profiles of Suspects. Authors. The deceased. Rod Stellar's novels. What kind of author was he? Here it is. One of his popular works was a story where the protagonist pretended to be dead."

"What!" AC yelled.

I saw the looks on everyone's faces.

"That's not possible," Maxima said. "We were here. We saw it."

"I'm a certified medical technician," Jean said. "He's dead."

"He wouldn't," Maxima said. With that, he pulled his gun from his jacket and ran to the kitchen

"What are you going to do?" "Where you going?" "What are you doing?" everyone yelled.

For a man who was supposedly injured enough to still be in a hoverchair, he could run fast. We all were running fast, but Maxima must have been an Olympic sprinter in his spare time when he wasn't writing. I wondered why he didn't help Dave and my son capture Ms. Modula when we were chasing her.

Blast! Blast! Blast!

We all entered the kitchen and one of the walk-in freezers was open. Maxima stood there with a frown.

Runner walked to him. "Please give it to me," he said. Maxima handed him the gun. Then Runner turned to me.

"Not yet. We could still have problems today." I turned my attention to Maxima.

"Rich, that was one of the dumbest things I've ever seen, and I've seen a lot," Jean said to him. "If he wasn't dead before, he is now."

"So if he was alive before, you murdered him now," I said. "Yes, that's real smart. Did you bother to look to see if there was even a body in the body bag before you began shooting?"

"Why would I do that?" Maxima asked. He looked at the bag.

"I take that to be a 'no.'"

Maxima reached down and pulled at the bag, but obviously something was wrong.

"What is this?" Maxima yelled. He opened it and there were only laserized parts of beef. "Where's the body?!"

Askey ran to it and looked at it. He frantically looked it over. "But that is the bag Mr. Stellar's body was in." Again the man looked like he was about to faint.

"Are you all punking me?" I asked.

"Why would you say that, Mr. Cruz?" Askey said.

"Are you all making a reality show and there are hidden cameras somewhere?" I asked.

"There was a real murder here, Mr. Cruz!" Askey yelled.

"Rod was murdered, Mr. Cruz," Derez said. "I can assure you my company isn't into publicity stunts of any kind."

"I knew this was strange from the start. The police allowing you to store a corpse in a freezer," I said.

"They didn't allow us to do anything, sir. It was what was decided by the authorities in this situation. The entire scene was documented and all the actions we took followed their instructions," Askey said. "The body was preserved as good as if it were in cryo; we adjusted the temperatures per the authorities."

"All the surveillance cameras were also set up based on police instructions and the attorneys," Derez added.

"Where's the body then?" I asked.

"I—I—," Derez stuttered.

"It's one of those murder mystery dinner things to mess with us," I said, looking at my wife. She gave me a suspicious look.

"Mr. Cruz, there was a murder!" Askey yelled.

Everyone looked genuinely shocked.

"Mr. Askey, do your walk-in freezer doors close by themselves and lock?" I asked.

"No," he replied.

"Why would you—" our chef began but stopped.

"Then why are we all locked in this freezer?" I asked.

"Is it getting colder?" Dot asked.

"That would be because we're locked in the freezer."

My wife punched me in the shoulder.

"It's a good thing this isn't the scene of the crime," I said. "You all would have seriously contaminated evidence, if there was a real body."

"There is a real body. Mr. Stellar is dead," Askey said again.

"Forget that! We have to get out this freezer," Maxima yelled and snatched back his gun from Runner.

"Don't!" Chef yelled.

Too late. The first round he shot he almost hit himself with the ricochet, and the second one almost took out AC. I guess that was his subconscious way of telling her that they weren't boyfriend and girlfriend anymore. Fortunately, my wife had shielded Kat and I jumped in front of Cruz Jr. Good thing Maxima didn't hit my family, or there would have been some serious violence in that freezer.

Then AC revealed she had her own gun. It was a mini-laser gun from her purse. No ricocheting, but still didn't get us out. Then it was my turn. I blasted that entire walk-in freezer door with one shot from my omega-gun.

"Mr. Cruz, how many guns did you bring to the island? That was a different gun from the other one," Mr. Runner said.

I ignored him and walked out.

"Who locked us in the walk-in freezer?" I yelled.

I saw a humanoid robot approaching and I aimed my weapon.

"No!" The entire hotel staff, except for Derez, tackled me.

"That's Manny," the chef said.

"Manny? You have robots running around this island?"

"We use kitchen robots," Chef said.

"You're a chef but you have the robots doing all the work. What kind of chef are you? And I don't like humanoid robots."

"Humanoid robots steal human jobs!" Dot yelled at them.

"Did you have the robots cooking my family's food?" I asked.

"I cook the food. The robots do prep and assist. That's all," Chef said.

"Did you lock us in the freezer?" I yelled at the robot.

The robot was five feet tall, more like a metallic skeleton, but with a head attachment that looked like an upside-down bucket.

"Why are your robots locking people in freezers?"

174

"Mr. Cruz, the robots operate automatically in case a door is left open, a stove or oven left on, lights still on. One activates and takes care of it," Askey said.

"Aren't they programmed not to close a walk-in freezer without looking first to see if anyone is inside?"

"It's not his fault, Mr. Cruz. It is standard protocol that no one goes in the freezer alone and that one person always stands outside," Askey said.

"How many brothers and sisters does Manny have?" I asked the chef.

"I have three kitchen robots," Stryper responded.

"How come we didn't see them before?" Dot asked.

"I have lunch and dinner prepared before guests arrive," Chef said.

"Let's see them," I said.

"Could they be the night people the great detective is trying to scare us about?" AC asked.

"The island sensors don't show robots only flesh and blood humans," Askey answered.

Stryper showed us where the robots were kept when not working. It was like a wide closet where all three stood, shoulder to shoulder. Manny walked in to stand in his spot like we weren't even there. We had to step out of his way.

"Nothing unusual here," Chef said.

"Well, Manny, we'll talk later," I said mockingly. "However, nothing is changed. Since there's no body, there's no murder. I'm going back to my vacation with my family."

"Mr. Cruz, there was a murder!" Askey insisted.

"We saw it," Jean said.

"We all did," Marlan said.

"Do you really have the medical training to determine if someone is truly dead rather than just taking a nap?"

"Mr. Cruz, that's insulting, but the answer is yes," Jean said.

"Taking a nap? You don't need medical training to know whether someone is dead or asleep," Runner said.

"My hotel staff is also medically trained," Askey said. "They verified Ms. Code's determination."

"He's dead," AC said.

"Where's the body then?" I asked.

"We don't know," Jean said.

"You all thought he might be alive. Dirty hands, karate man shot him multiple times to make sure, which if he really is dead means you are now suspect number one—again."

"I wasn't thinking! I didn't kill anyone!" Maxima yelled.

"Rich, ignore him. Rod wouldn't be alive and hanging out in a body bag in a freezer in the dark. Think!"

"Yeah, you're right."

"Mr. Derez, no body, no murder, no investigation. I'm going back to my vacation," I said.

"But what about the other people?" Askey asked.

"What about them? If no one's murdered, then everything is fine as wine."

"There was a murder!" AC yelled.

"Where's the body?"

No one said anything.

"Unless you see the body yourself, you will not continue your investigation?" Derez asked.

"Doesn't a murder mystery need a murder?" I asked.

Derez touched his forehead with his eyes closed. He composed himself. "Please, Mr. Cruz. You must continue."

"Don't look at me. The first thing the police are going to ask you and everyone present at the time is: where's that body? You think I'm a hard case. What do you think the police are going to do when they travel out of their jurisdiction almost two hours to your island for a homicide and there is no body and no murder scene? They'll put all of you in the system just to mess with your lives. Your new vacation will be a jail cell."

"Did you even visit the crime scene before?" Jean asked.

"I did. The day I arrived. Mr. Askey showed me when he showed me the grounds. I walked around the scene. Visual inspection only. Not a full forensic examination, but the police will do that."

"Mr. Cruz, then we'll find the body," AC said.

"You do that."

"I have to say, Mr. Cruz," AC said. "Well played."

"Meaning?"

"I bet you're the one who moved the body."

"When? You and your friends have been watching me and my family, sneaking around our bungalow, following and watching us in all the theme worlds we visited. When?"

She gave me a smirk. "Well played. We'll find that body."

"When you do, tell me and I'll find your murderer."

I tipped my hat. "Good night, everyone. My family and I are back to our vacation. If Mr. Rod Stellar was murdered, this is a lucky break for the murderer. Without a body there will be no investigation, assuming it's never found. However, if the body was moved by someone other than the murderer, then he or she has the added burden of not knowing why. Then there's always the possibility, despite the claims, that Mr. Stellar is in fact alive and hiding out like Mr. Derez was. Then we have the fact that the police will be here soon."

"Yes, they will be here," Derez said.

"No, I'm not talking in a general sense," I said. "Soon. As in specifically on the way. Very soon. I spoke with the police chief yesterday. Metropolis was given official jurisdiction. They'll be here with a full homicide unit and forensics team. Alive or dead, if Mr. Stellar is on the island, they'll find him. If he's alive, he's going to jail. If not, his murderer or murderers will be. Good night!"

We left them there.

PART SEVEN: BY THE NUMBERS

Dot was quiet the whole way as we returned to our bungalow. I could see her glance at me occasionally from the corner of my eye.

"Cruz, you're not good as a detective; you're dangerous. I see why you catch all the bad guys now. You're relentless. If I were the murderer, I'd want to turn myself in now. The body's gone. The police on the way. You're obviously doing all kinds of stuff in the background. What about these night people? Should you have told them?"

"Maximum pressure, Dot."

"You're devious too. Who are they? Are they real? They have to be. You shot at them. We chased them. Who are they, Cruz?"

"I can guess who they are."

"Who?"

"Stowaways I bet. This writers' retreat has been going on for ten years. It's just the kind of thing super fans might do."

"Stowaways?"

"Yes. Kids. Nerds."

"Kids and nerds. These are your night people."

"Yeah."

"Cruz, I appreciate your efforts to put a positive spin on the situation, but if there is a murder and there are unknown people on the island, I think it's best to stay indoors until the police arrive."

"What about our vacation?"

"Forget vacation, Cruz. After that performance, the murderer will be so wound up they he or she may want to kill a whole bunch of people. We should stay in the panic room until we know what's what."

"Panic room?" I asked. "You mean the Panic Palace! Isn't that right, Cruzie and Kat." I threw up my hands and a giggling Cruz Jr. did the same, then Kat. Both kids had been standing there all the time watching us talk.

Cruz Jr. raised his hand.

"What?" I asked.

"He wants to carry Kat," Dot said.

"He can carry her?"

"Our son is strong, Cruz. But only for a little while."

I tried not to wince as Dot lowered a smiling Kat into her brother's arms. He actually looked like he knew how to properly hold a baby, until he almost slipped. Dot caught her. I had to turn my eyes away.

"Dot, don't drop the baby on the ground."

"Cruz, I'm not dropping anything here. He's your son."

"A toddler cannot take responsibility for a baby drop. The adults will be the ones going to jail."

"Yeah, you would know about that. There, you did it again!"

"What?" I asked.

"You smoothly maneuvered the conversation away from what we were talking about."

"What?"

"No what, Cruz. We're talking about strange people on the island, and you've wound up the murderer so tight that they'll go amok. In fact, are the police really on their way? Truth, Cruz!"

"They are."

"So if there is no murder, they will need someone to take to jail."

"Yes, they'll want to handcuff someone and take them away."

"Then you'd better hope there was a murder."

"Maybe the murderer is not murdered and the police can take him away. That would be a happy ending, wouldn't it?"

"That would be a happy ending in somebody's world. But, Cruz, we don't live in that world."

I pointed at Dot. "Don't drop our daughter on the ground."

"Don't point at me. He's your son."

I glanced back and there was Cruz Jr. looking like a little adult, holding Kat. He saw me looking. A smiling Cruz Jr. and Kat. Now that's a Hallmark moment during a real quality family vacation...well...until later that same night.

"Where's the body?" "Is Mr. Stellar really dead?" "Who murdered him if he's dead?" "Where is he if he's not dead?"

Dot had been interrogating me, but she got no answers from me.

"Dot, this is an ongoing investigation so I can't disclose anything."

"Cruz, that's what the police say. You're not the police."

Since I didn't sleep in hotel beds, I had my CDC sleeping bag all set up on top of our master bed. To the outside world, that meant that no unauthorized personnel would be allowed. My wife always smelled nice, so she was always authorized. The kids were in their beds, so any nastiness they had in their diapers/pants was far away from me. Actually, I liked the concept of the diaper. It became unsanitary you ripped it off and threw it away forever. None of this washing and reusing clothes thing. In the CDC, patients wore paper clothes that could be discarded and burned daily. I liked that. Yes, I realized that something had triggered my germophobia, though I didn't know what. I'd sleep on it and maybe figure it out in my dreams.

Well, the Cruz family was asleep. We were all in the master bedroom. We opted not to stay in the "panic palace" because it terrified Kat. Not sure why because she wasn't scared of the walk-in freezer. We were all supposedly away from all the crazy maniacs on the island. Just after three a.m., both Dot and I sat up in the bed.

"What was that? Was that an earthquake?" Dot asked me.

We both looked at the kids—both were fast asleep, then we looked at each other.

"What was that noise?" I asked.

I rolled out of bed and pulled out a briefcase. I opened it and it was a bank of monitors.

"Where did you get that?" Dot asked me.

We could literally see all over the island. I flipped switches and the views of the monitors changed.

"Did we really hear an explosion?" Dot asked.

"I don't know."

All the bungalows were there, the hotel, nothing seemed off. Both our eyes opened wide when we got to the docks.

"Oh my God!" Dot yelled.

There was no way to adjust the monitors remotely. But at the docks, we saw what looked like a body in the water. I bolted out the bedroom door then stopped, realizing I'd better put on some proper clothes.

When I reached the docks near the main hotel building, there was already a crowd waiting.

"What happened?" I asked.

The authors and all the hotel staff were on the docks, except Maxima, Dave, and Runner.

"I saw bodies in the water," I said.

"Some kind of hovercraft exploded," Jean said. "We don't know if it was landing or leaving."

I saw the missing men. They were in the water, swimming and diving.

"Be careful!" Askey yelled.

I was glad I didn't have to dive in myself. I was more than happy to let those guys do the noble work while I watched with everyone else.

"Are you going to help?" AC yelled at me.

"Why aren't you helping?" I asked. "I thought women were better than men."

"We are, but men obviously have more upper body strength than women. I can't grab any bodies."

"Anyway, I can't swim," I said. "I sit on the beach but don't go in the water."

"We saw you in the water," Jean said.

"Spying on me and my family, huh? If you remember I was in the water for the sake of the kids. They were swimming. I was standing in the water to my waist or lying on the hover-lounge chair. That's all."

She scoffed at me.

Dave appeared near the docks. This part I could do. I pulled him out of the water. Maxima popped up from the water and jumped out as if he was half-man, half-fish.

"What happened? What exploded?" I asked.

"It crashed," Maxima said.

"What did?" I looked at Askey and Derez. "One of the hovernautiluses."

Askey nodded. "Yes."

"Who was piloting it?" I asked.

"We don't know," he said.

"Your night people, I imagine," Marlan said.

Runner appeared in the water and we all helped him onto the dock.

"No one," he said. "We're too late. Whoever was in the craft is probably at the bottom of the ocean."

"We can look for bodies tomorrow," Maxima said.

Runner shook his head. "The currents are too strong. We're not likely to find anything in daylight either."

"How many hovernautiluses are left?" I asked.

"Only the one," Askey replied.

"You should lock it down too," I said.

"Who was in the craft?" AC yelled. "What about the surveillance cameras?"

"There's a problem there," Askey said.

"What?" more than one author asked.

"Was it Mr. Stellar?" I said.

"No," Askey replied. "Why would you say that?"

"Just a guess."

"We told you, Mr. Cruz. Mr. Stellar is dead. What I was about to say is there is no surveillance tape."

"Why is that?" I asked.

"Someone covered up the cameras."

I looked at everyone and they looked back at me. They were nervous.

"We need the police here now," Dave said.

"Who are these night people on the island, Cruz?" Marlan had genuine anger in his voice.

"Who has guns beside me?" I asked. "AC. Maxima. Who else?"

"I do," Marlan said.

"I have your two weapons," Runner said.

"Lock yourselves in your rooms," I said. "Tomorrow morning I'm going to track down these night people, even if I have to hunt them all day."

"Hunt?" AC said.

"Yes, hunt. I want to know exactly who they are and keep them in my sights at all times. If as you claim, Mr. Stellar is dead, then either one of you killed him, or one of them. I'd like to know, or at the very least keep you all together until the police arrive.

"Did any of you directly see the hovernautilus crash?" I then asked.

"It must have," Maxima said. "I got out here and heard its engines going."

"You didn't directly see it?"

"No. Not directly."

"What are you getting at?" Jean asked.

"Maybe someone wasn't taking off and it crashed. Maybe someone blew it up to crash it. The body we saw was them abandoning the craft and swimming away."

"This can't be happening," Dave said. "What are you saying? Someone intentionally destroyed the hovernautilus? Why? What would they gain by that? Especially if they were the ones who killed Rod."

"That means we only have the one left?" I asked Askey.

"Yes, that's correct," the manager replied.

"I don't know," I said to Dave to answer his question. "I don't know what's going on, but I feel like the situation is escalating."

"Escalating to what?" Maxima asked.

"Ladies and gentlemen, I think it best from this moment on not to be alone at any time. I believe our lives are in danger and its likely one or more us may be murdered before the police arrive."

Utter silence. Didn't even hear any crickets in the night. They were all speechless and scared.

"No, Cruz!"

My "deputy" was annoyed as we faced off in our bungalow's kitchen. Cruz Jr. and Kat looked up at us standing nearby, trying to figure out what we were fighting about.

"Dot, this is dangerous."

"You're investigating without backup."

"Dot, I can't run around investigating with my wife and kids with me!"

"Cruz, aren't you only searching rooms?"

"Dot, it's still dangerous."

"Cruz, you know who the murderer is."

"I don't."

"Are there really night people on the island?"

"I'm not going to answer that question."

"There! I knew it! You're weaving such a web of confusion the murderer is a hot mess right now."

"Dot, I have to go! I have five rooms to search before they wake up."

"Cruz, I'll watch the kids. You do your thing. You won't even know we're there."

The night before I suggested that the hotel staff stay together in one room and the authors in their own room. Everyone could protect their own group. Everyone was eager to do so with the scary picture I painted.

I couldn't believe I was actually about to engage in illicit searching of the authors' individual bungalows with my wife, two-year-old daughter, and four-year-old son. It was certifiably insane.

"Are you going to break in?" Dot asked

We had reached Maxima's bungalow. I reached into my pocket.

"Much more advanced than that. I got the master key card."

"How?"

"Derez authorized it, before I discovered he was on the island."

"I wouldn't rule him out as a murderer despite his claim of an alibi."

"The only ones ruled out are you and the kids."

"Well thank you, Cruz. Good to know."

All the bungalows on the island were the same layout. Individual two-story vacation homes. We entered the first one.

I went in first, quickly looked around to make sure no one was present, then gave my family the signal. In crept my family like a bunch of criminals. My family the cat burglars. Twinkle from my Biopunk Blues Case would be proud. This was exactly the kind of experience that kids remembered. "Oh, Judge, I turned to a life of crime because I remember when I was an infant I went sneaking into other people's homes with my parents and it was fun."

"Where do you want me to search?" Dot asked.

"Everything on the first floor—kitchen, closets, cupboards, desks, under the furniture. I'll search upstairs."

I'd expected Maxima's place to be a pigsty with clothes on the floor and old food everywhere, but it was orderly and neat. The master bedroom was the same. I quickly searched all the closets and drawers, looked under the bed, the bathroom, empty luggage. Maxima also had additional guns, which I made note of. The medicine cabinet was filled with male enhancement pills. There was a laptop and it was password protected. I had to try. The only thing out of place was a pair of muddy boots—freshly muddied. Maxima had been hiking somewhere, but there was no other gear.

Dot hadn't come across anything on the ground level, so we hurried out for the next bungalow which was Jean Code's. Finally, a writer who looked like she was actually writing! She had multiple laptops (all password protected too), pads, tablets, white boards with plot points everywhere. She was a packrat. But it was exactly the profile of a true working writer. While Maxima's place showed he spent most of his time upstairs not writing, Jean looked like she spent all her time writing in the living room and kitchen on the ground level. The upstairs bedroom was Spartan, and the only thing in her medicine cabinet was a single bottle of aspirin.

However, this time Dot and the kids did find something. My wife had turned it into a kind of a game for the kids.

"Kat found it," Dot said. "I told you we could find clues too."

The surgical gloves I had given AC as a joke.

"It was hidden under the cushion in the living room couch. Why would she do that?"

"I gave it to AC, so why does she have it?"

"Why did you give it to AC?"

"To confuse them. Jean will have some 'plaining to do."

Next was AC Vulcana. Her bungalow exactly matched what I expected. No clutter of any kind. A single laptop and one tablet with stylus on the dining room table. There were another laptop in a bag on a dining-room chair. Based on a quick peek of the balcony through the curtains, I imagined she spent all her writing time between the dining room and the outside balcony area. Upstairs was virtually empty, but I didn't see any female things at Maxima's, and I didn't see any of his things in her bungalow. That made me wonder. Her medicine cabinet was a bit more interesting: anxiety and migraines were her ailments that needed attending. Nothing else was to be found.

"What are we looking for, Cruz?"

"Nothing specifically. We're doing our due diligence. Checking out the places of our suspects to see what's there to see."

"As long as you're not expecting to see a dead body."

"No chance of that."

"There is a dead body, isn't there?"

"There is."

"And you know where it is?"

"I do."

"Just as I thought," Dot said.

We reached Marlan's bungalow and we had entered the Alpha Male pigsty. There was clothes, cigars, cigarettes, plates, beer bottles, wine bottles, ash, laptops, writing tablets, styluses of different colors, garbage everywhere. There was also a gun in the bathroom on the toilet. He had quite a few bathing trunks all over the bed. His medicine cabinet had lots of drugs but nothing illicit. All what I would term "old people's medicine."

Dot found another gun in the refrigerator along with some data sticks.

"You're checking the refrigerators too?" I asked Dot.

"Of course, Cruz. Criminals hide stuff in refrigerators."

"One more," I said.

Dave Blackhat was the last bungalow to search of the group. Dave was the least talkative of the authors, at least since we encountered him. They said he was the wealthiest of the group with his science fiction for children. When we entered it was like we entered the room of a king. Expensive slippers, silky bathing trunks and robes, tons of men's jewelry, even though we never saw him wearing any of it, were all over the living room, kitchen and dining area. His laptop and writing stuff were on the carpeted floor. I walked upstairs to leave my family to finish their searching; they all seemed to have their own routine at this point. The door to the master bedroom was closed but the bathroom had its own open entrance. It was filled with lotions, body sprays, facial cleansers, skin scrubs, fruit extracts, nothing in the medicine cabinet. I opened the second door to the master bedroom.

"Ahh!" I think that's what I screamed.

I was in the master bedroom, saw what I saw, and was outside the bungalow running like a madman toward the beach. I had no idea how long I was running, but I think I ran around the entire island at least once. I couldn't be sure of my memory when I had an OCD-germophobic "episode." Then Dot appeared beside me, running.

"Cruz, what are you doing?"

"Running?"

"Running where?"

"Just running."

"For how long?"

"Not sure. When I get tired."

"That could be a long time, Cruz. I think you need to stop running."

"No, I have to keep running."

"What's the cause of this fit of yours?"

"A monster of unspeakable nastiness."

I saw Dot turn her head to the side. I think she was laughing.

"If you're going to laugh at me, you can go find your own path to run."

"Cruz, listen to yourself."

"I am."

"We talked about this."

"No, we didn't and I don't want to talk now. I want to be left alone to run."

"Then how will you see my magic trick?"

"What magic trick? Since when can you do magic tricks?"

"Cruz, do you want to see the magic trick or what?"

"What's the trick?"

"I don't tell you. You experience it."

"Go away." I ran faster but Dot wasn't letting me get away.

"Here goes," she said.

"What are you going to do?"

"It's a pet!"

"Pet? What are you talking about?"

"The monster. It's a pet."

I stopped in my tracks and stared at her. My face was going through a whole series of contortions—shocked, disgusted, pensive.

"Who keeps a giant isopod as a pet? That's nasty. That's a giant isopod, Dot, in the hotel's bungalow."

"I know," she said.

"How do you know?"

"Because he has pictures of it."

"He writes of books with giant creatures on alien planets. He's the alien if he keeps giant creatures in his hotel room. Giant creatures have giant germs. Giant isopods. Dot, do you have any ideas the violent germs that must infest a giant isopod? Isopods are an infestation, so we're talking about an infestation upon infestations. And those germs must have their own germs. It's a biological apocalypse on the very island we're supposed to be vacationing on with our kids!"

Dot had stood quietly all this time watching me rant and rave, smiling. I calmed myself then smiled too. I nodded.

"Impressive," I said. "Quickly analyzed the patient. Introduced a new focus to distract them from their unhealthy fixation. You're good, Dot. You could be a certified germophobe psych counselor for the CDC."

"I thought I already was. The title is: wife."

I laughed and gave her a hug.

"Where are the kids?" I yelled.

We raced back to Dave's bungalow where Cruz Jr. and Kat were waiting quietly. Big brother holding his little sister's hands.

"J.R. is a big boy."

"I am," he said.

"Did you see any bad guys?" Dot asked him.

"Not yet."

"Not yet," Kat repeated.

"Oh, I see one now," Cruz Jr. said.

We followed Cruz Jr.'s finger, pointing to something behind us. We turned. Dave Blackhat stood there wearing a red silk robe and flip-flops.

"What are you doing here?"

"Nothing," I answered.

"Were you in my bungalow?"

"No."

"You were in my bungalow."

"No."

"Yes, you were."

"My ma always said to beware of the quiet ones."

"Meaning what?"

"I'm going to find Mr. Askey and see if he has a flame thrower."

"Flame-thrower?"

"We can't let a giant isopod loose crawling around the island spreading disease and pestilence!"

"What? No! What are you talking about?"

"I'm going to burn it!"

"Burn what?"

"That giant isopod you have!"

"Herbie? No!"

"You named the monster Herbie? You're one sick puppy! Burn it!"

"No! Herbie's my pet!"

Dave jumped me and tried to strangle me. My entire family had to help beat him back and restrain him. I had him pinned to the ground.

"Are you really naked under that robe?"

"I took a shower and came back here for my clothes!"

I jumped off of him and backed off.

"Why were you in my room?" he yelled.

"Go put on your clothes! Maybe Herbie can help you before I burn him."

"You harm my pet and I'll kill you."

"Hey!" Dot yelled at him.

"He's threatening to kill my pet!"

"My husband is right. A giant isopod?" Dot yelled.

"What's wrong with an isopod for a pet? It's no different than any of the other wildlife people adopt, anthropomorphize, and give free reign of their inner sanctum."

"Humanity left the jungle eons ago, so I am not interested in having its wildlife in my home and defecating in the corner," I said.

"You must have been a fun child." It was Marlan's voice.

"Marlan, I was never a child. I was born fully adult and sentient," I said.

"That we can believe." Marlan wasn't alone. All the other writers were with him.

"They were in my room," Dave said and entered his bungalow by eye-scan.

"Did you find what you were looking for?" Maxima asked.

195

"They met Herbie," AC said. "I'm sensing a bit more stress in our great detective."

"I hate germs and isopods, especially giant, genetically engineered ones that carry bigger germs."

"Listen to the great detective. Scared of germs. You should carry protection."

"Cruz travels with his own bio-suit," Dot revealed.

"You travel with your own bio-suit?" Maxima said in disbelief.

"I do. Why do you ask? And no, you can't borrow it."

The writers laughed.

"Where's Dummy?" I asked AC. "I haven't seen your better half lately." Maxima gave me a dirty look.

"He has free reign of the island. He'll show up when he wants. Have you searched all our rooms?"

"We did."

AC held Maxima back from charging us.

"Someone needs to stop you," Maxima said.

"Entering our rooms is illegal unless you have a warrant," Jean said, "especially when you don't even believe a crime has taken place. Did you search the hotel staff's room?"

"I did," I told her. My wife gave me a look of surprise. "All I want to know is where's the body of Mr. Stellar."

"You tell us, Great Detective."

"My family and I will return to the hotel for me to update my white board. I'll also let Mr. Askey and Mr. Derez know that we didn't find any murder weapon."

"Murder weapon?" Marlan asked. "Rod was stabbed in the back."

"No he wasn't," I said.

"How would you know?" Jean asked.

"I examined the body when I first arrived on the island. Before the murderer made the body disappear. I need to find these night people not because I think they killed him. I think they are eye witnesses to how he was killed and by whom. See you all at lunch."

I seemed to have perfected the ability to leave the authors speechless, but this time so was Dot.

"Come on, family," I said.

Cruz Jr. and Kat pulled their mother along to follow me to the main hotel building.

"Did you really search the hotel staff's room?" my wife asked me as we entered the hotel main lobby.

"No point. The day we found Mr. Derez in Ms. Modula's room ruined any chance of finding anything incriminating in their rooms. I'm sure all of them 'tidied up' their rooms in case I decided to drop in. We'll have to leave it to the police to do a real thorough search."

"They might be careless and leave something out."

"Maybe, but I have something more important to do. I'm leaving you and the kids here in the main hotel. I'll sneak out the back."

Mr. Stryper manned the main counter alone. He watched us as Dot got closer. We waved.

"Good morning, Chef!"

He smiled and gave a wave too.

I lowered my voice. "You and the kids stay here."

"Where are you going?" Dot asked in a whisper.

"I should be back by lunch. I have some island recon to do. The hotel staff and the writers will want to know where I am too. Keep them preoccupied."

"How?"

"Dot, you know how to keep people preoccupied better than I ever could. You work in a high-end salon every day."

"That's true."

"Make the sitting room near the whiteboard your base. There's plenty for the kids to do."

"Is what you're doing dangerous, Cruz?"

"No."

"Are you going to find these night people?"

"Among other things."

"That sounds dangerous, Cruz."

"It's not. I'll be back before you know it."

I gave her a kiss. Lifted Kat up and gave her one on the cheek, making her laugh. Cruz Jr. tried to run, but I lifted him up and gave him one too on the cheek.

I left them and walked as if I were going to the whiteboard and sitting room area, passed it as if going to the dining area, passed it, then dashed down the hallway to the rear entrance. That rear entrance could be seen from the dining area, so I turned and made a right turn. I'd get out of the hotel unseen from one of the business center rooms. I still had the master key card.

I'd been infected with a bio-toxin in one case, been to the Moon and back fighting another cabal of criminals in another, and all I wanted was a simple vacation with my family. I didn't think that was too much to ask, but here I was running through the forested areas of the island making my way to the highest point of the island—a forested mountain at the far end. As a city boy in Metropolis, naturally I did a lot of driving—flying my hovervehicle to all ends of the supercity. But I did a lot of walking too, so marching to the other end of the island wasn't a problem for me. It would take me over an hour to get to my destination. My hope was that my wife would occupy all our suspects for the entire time I was gone. Unless one or more of them realized what I was doing. I had to move quickly.

Knock. Knock.

I tapped on the side of the mountain. The door blended in perfectly. Unless you knew it was there, it was invisible, but I knew it was there. I knocked again.

"I know you're in there, so let me in. Contact the Metropolis Police Department. They can verify my identity. I'm Mr. Cruz of the Liquid Cool Detective Agency. I'm directly contracted with the owners of the island. This is a homicide investigation. I'll wait."

I didn't have to wait long. There was a click and the mountain-face door opened. As I stepped inside, into the darkness, I made sure to also grab my omega-gun from inside my jacket.

There were two of them. One sat behind the counter watching a vast array of monitors. The second man stood in front of the counter with his arms crossed. Both wore white short-sleeved uniforms. Both men never took their eyes off me. West Indian men who could spot a non-Islander tourist like me a hundred miles away.

"Did we see you grab for your gun when you came in?" the standing man asked. "Why did you do that?"

"It's habit. I didn't know who was in here," I said.

"If you knew we were here, then you knew who'd be in here."

"I knew security would be in here, but that's all. I like to be careful."

"Keep your hands where we can see you," the man behind the counter said.

"What kind of island security guards are you? Where's your guns?"

"Are you Americans all the same?" the seated man asked. "Why do we need guns? We're island security. We sit and watch. We're not police. Neither are you."

"Why are you here, Mr. Cruz, of the Liquid Cool Detective Agency? We've been watching you good for a while. We've never seen a tourist behave in the manner you have. We've been calling the police every day to tell them what you've been doing. Blowing up things. Sneaking into resident bungalows not your own."

"Was that a body you moved to the Center of the Earth World?" one asked.

"Yes," I said. "Do you know who killed him?"

"How do we know? We're not the police."

"You've seen everything else on the island, but not that?"

"How do you know what we've seen?"

"Because genius, I'm in touch with the police every day too. Who killed Rod Stellar?"

"Why are you asking us these questions?" the standing guard said.

"Why didn't you visit us the first day you were here?" the other asked.

"I wasn't asked to investigate then and I wasn't asked to solve the murder until a day ago, though I knew I'd have to from the first day."

"Why are you here then, Mr. Cruz?" the seated man asked.

"If you didn't see who killed Mr. Stellar, then that means you two did it."

The seated man stood up.

"Why are you saying lies? We killed nobody. We're island security. We never leave this facility."

"I have six people who say you have."

"No one else is on the island. We saw what you did."

"Why did you kill him?"

"I told you to stop saying lies," the standing guard said again. "We should never have opened the door and let him in."

"I'm sorry to tell you this, but I have to make sure you two stay in here until the police arrive."

"You're sorry?" one asked. "You should be."

I had my gun pointed at them. "I need you two to come out from there. I know this facility has holding cells. Maybe you're guilty, maybe you're innocent, but I need to confine you until we can find out which."

"Listen to him. He walks in here and tells us he's going to arrest us. Arrest us in our own facility. Who are you to do this? You're a tourist to our island. This is our island."

"Please don't do anything rash," I said. "I'm investigating, but I'm still on vacation. Let's walk over to the holding cells."

201

"How do you know about our facility?" The guard's eyes were tearing up he was so outraged. I was sure he felt beyond disrespected.

"I told you. I've been in contact with the police too. We need to have you both confined."

The man behind the counter sat down, then he jumped up from his chair again. That's when the shooting began. He fired at me. I fired back.

"Daddy!"

I strolled through the lobby main entrance. Cruz Jr. ran to me, then Kat. Cruz Jr. was getting a bit chunky, but I lifted him up in one arm. Kat wanted "up" too, so up she went in my other arm.

At the whiteboard Dot was holding court. All the authors were there in their section of chairs, and the hotel staff had created their own section on the other side. What got my attention was that Dot wasn't at the whiteboard alone; AC was standing next to her. Both of them had markers in their hands.

"Dot, why is one of the suspects writing on the whiteboard?"

I set my kids down when I reached the group.

"Cruz, she's not writing on the white board. She's assisting me."

"Did you accomplish your task?" AC asked me.

"I did."

Since she wasn't using it, I grabbed AC's chair pulled to one side of the whiteboard and sat down.

Everyone seemed surprised that I had to sit down. My kids walked over to me, worried.

"What's wrong, Daddy?" Cruz Jr. asked me.

"What's wrong, Da-Dad?" Kat asked.

"I'm fine."

"Cruz?" Dot said. "What happened? Did you find them?"

"Who?"

"Who? Your night people," AC said.

"Oh, them. No. I had to visit some other people."

"Other people? Besides the night people?" Dot asked. "How many other kinds of people are on the island?"

"All in good time, my deputy detective. It's time to use the detective checklist and review what we have."

I stood and Dot eagerly handed me the marker and took my chair. Runner jumped up from his chair to give it to AC.

"Don't bother yourself," AC said to him. "I can stand and when I get tired I'm completely content with sitting on the floor. I'm not a germophobe like a certain person. You wouldn't have survived too well back in the Pleistocene Age when we all lived in caves and swung from trees. We weren't too much into washing and daily hygiene either back then."

"They didn't have hovercars back then either, so I wouldn't have stayed. Let's see what my wife has added to the whiteboard."

Dot had actually added all kinds of biographic information on our suspects. Age, place of birth, current and past residences, hobbies, pets—I saw the word "Herbie" in Dave's section and cringed, along with other tidbits. All nice but irrelevant. We had a homicide. We weren't preparing for a quiz show. However, Dot had fulfilled her mission. She kept everyone focused on her and in the lobby, not worrying about or looking for me.

"I'll add to the list. Who has guns? Rich, AC, Marlan, Runner, and Stryper."

"You too," Runner called out.

"I think we can say with certainty that neither Dot, Cruz Jr., Kat, nor I are the murderer, since you all called us here after the incident in question. What's wrong with you, Runner?"

"Men," AC said. "I told you."

"Stryper has a gun too?" Askey asked, surprised, but none of the other staff were. Derez didn't care. He sat in his chair and sighed.

"Rich Maxima's bloody hand."

"What? What about my hand?"

"How did you cut it?" I asked.

"Cut myself shaving."

"Says the man with the electric razor in his bathroom. Try again."

"It's nothing. I can't remember."

I began writing on the whiteboard. "Maxima severely cut his hand trying to break into the freezer with Mr. Stellar's body."

"You!" Dave yelled as he jumped up from his chair.

Everyone was looking at Maxima. "You moved the body?" Jean yelled at him.

"I didn't. I couldn't get into the freezer. It was locked. I tried to pry it open with the fireman's ax and—"

"Please stop talking now, Rich," AC said. "I saw the wound without the bandage. We get the picture."

"I swear I couldn't get in. I didn't move the body," Maxima said.

"Why were you trying to get into the freezer? That's the only question I have," AC said.

"I wanted to make sure it was there."

"No. You wanted to get at it because you wanted to move the body," I said.

I started writing on the board again.

"Why?" AC asked him sternly. Everyone was watching for his answer.

"I—I wanted to mess with the detective. I figured he'd get around to the body and I wanted to mess up his case."

"Interfering with a murdered victim's body and contaminating evidence in a homicide investigation," I said out loud as I wrote on the whiteboard. I turned around to face the group. "Dave with the nasty pet."

"You leave my pet out of this!"

"Why would you keep a giant isopod?"

"Why not?"

"You write about fluffy animals."

"So?"

"When did you get Herbie?"

"Years ago."

"You travel with a giant dung-eating arthropod?"

"Herbie eats fishes."

"In my last case, the one on the Lunar Colony, I came across a new genetically created species of isopods that could eat you and Herbie. Because of that case I learned a lot more about isopods. More than I would ever want to know. I learned that here on Earth some genetically modified species were being used by deep sea treasure hunters."

Dave had one of those complexions that telegraphed his true emotions to the world. He turned bright red. Marlan laughed.

"Dave is a treasure hunter?" Marlan said.

"An illegal treasure hunter I'd imagine, because anything a legitimate one found in these waters would have to be shared with all kinds of other countries," I said. "Don't think he'd like that. Dave has very expensive tastes that he has to satisfy."

"Very," Dot said. "Very high-end, expensive things. The ladies must love you."

I turned around and wrote on the whiteboard. "Dave, despite his quiet demeanor, I'm sure is quite the lady killer."

"Are you going to do this with all of us?" AC asked.

"I was planning to. Do you want to go next?"

"Yes, because there's nothing to write. I'm boring."

"You said you were married to Rod."

"Because I was."

"Was?"

She gave me a look. "Mr. Cruz, I am divorced from Rod, a long time ago. I was there."

"Were the papers properly filed?"

"You have to be kidding me! Are you suggesting I'm secretly still married to Rod?"

"Are you?"

"No, I'm not!" She saw Maxima staring at her. "He's making it up. He's trying to get a rise out of us."

"Succeeding," Jean said.

"Maybe you should sit down on the floor now," Marlan told her.

"He's lying. I know I'm legally divorced."

"If not, that could throw a legal monkey wrench in your other divorces. Those stupid men you married might get smart and claim you tricked them, sue you, demand alimony."

"Oh my God." AC was so overwhelmed she didn't sit down on the floor, she lay down. "You're lying."

"Moving on," I said.

"What are you suggesting?" Jean asked. "Okay, Dave had a secret to protect. AC might have a real motive. All you got for Rich is he tried to get at Rod's body. Do you believe there's a body now?"

"I do."

"You didn't seem to ask any follow-up questions about Rich wanting to get at the body," Marlan said.

"Why would I? I'm the one who moved the body."

"You prick. AC is right. You've been playing us from the very start," Jean said.

"Moving on. Ms. Jean Code can you remove your gloves?"

No one had noticed that she had been wearing gloves until then. Her self-confidence had vanished. AC sat up from the floor. Everyone looked at her.

"No, I won't."

I wrote on the whiteboard. "Jean's purple hands."

Jean writhed in her seat and held her hand down. "All right! I'll tell you. Because I didn't murder Rod. I'm only doing research for my books. I go into the theme worlds at night to look around, at the controls."

Askey stood up. "You're breaking into the theme worlds. Corporate espionage?"

"No! It's for my books. I need them to be authentic, realistic. I was doing research. That's all. I use gloves so I don't leave any fingerprints. I lost my box of gloves and got a pair from AC."

Jean's eyes narrowed and she glared at me in disgust. AC turned to look at me too.

"How did you know?" Jean asked. "Did you steal my box of gloves?"

"You searched our rooms before, didn't you?" AC asked me.

"How long have you been doing this?" Askey asked her.

"I do research all the time!" Jean yelled.

"Moving on to Marlan or Askey. Who wants to go next?"

"Me?" Askey said. "There's nothing about me. We've been through this before."

"Yes, you are spotless. What about family?"

"What about—"

"Your daughter?"

"What about her?"

"Has anyone here seen her before?"

"What do you mean?"

"Do they know what she looks like?"

"No. She's never been here."

"Your daughter had a serious accident, didn't she?"

"I don't know..."

"Corporate party. Lots of drinking. You'd think people wouldn't drink and drive these days with all the cheap hovertaxis around. But you still have these old-school, old-timers who still insist on doing things themselves, even when they shouldn't. Wasn't there a guy?"

Marlan stared at Askey with his mouth open.

"That was you?" Askey yelled at him.

"That was Marlan," I said.

Askey stood up, glaring at him. Derez and Modula stood from their chairs too and grabbed him.

Marlan sat down slowly in his chair. Derez and Modula made Askey sit down.

"Marlan almost killed Askey's daughter. Used high-priced lawyers to beat the rap. But it's okay. That's the old Marlan. The new Marlan was the one who got Askey the job on the island. Moving on. Runner."

Runner jumped up from his chair and almost fell.

"No! Leave me alone."

"Falsified credentials to get the island job."

The hotel staff stared at him.

"Runner is what's called a sci-fi super fan. He falsified his CV to get the job for the chance to meet and serve his favorite authors in the universe."

"Yes."

"Mr. Derez and Ms. Modula. We know their story already. Mr. Stryper, our chef, does have a record, but Mr. Derez and Mr. Askey already knew and hired him anyway."

"What record?" Modula asked.

"AWOL from the military, but the case was closed and desertion was changed to dishonorable discharge."

"It was thirty years ago," the chef said from the main hotel counter.

"That too," I said. "There it is, everyone. All the tiny threads the police will comb through with the best investigative and forensic teams in the world. Unlike me, they'll be able to scan every inch of this island for evidence. They have the surveillance tapes, and then there's the real surveillance tapes."

"What are you referring to, Mr. Cruz?" Derez asked.

"You know, Mr. Derez."

"You know about the private island security guards?"

"What private island security?" Askey asked.

"The island is a huge investment that needs to be protected. A handful of guards and drones aren't sufficient. Islands such as these employ secret security and hidden surveillance, unknown to visitors and staff, including island management."

"Yes. The police will review it all."

"Is that where you were, Mr. Cruz," Derez asked, "talking to the secret guard personnel?"

"Not talking, Mr. Derez. Arresting."

"Arresting?"

It was if everyone asked me the same question, including my wife.

"We're wrapping up the case, ladies and gentlemen. The police will be here tomorrow morning early. They will sort it all out and arrest our murderer. My family and I will remain in our bungalow until they arrive. And ladies and gentlemen, I am very much armed so not to be rude or anything, but stay the hell away from my bungalow until the police get here. Night people, you, anything comes near us and I'll just shoot you."

PART EIGHT: GET ME OFF THIS ISLAND!

"Hon, I don't want you to take this the wrong way," Dot said, "but I don't ever want to work with you on another one of your cases ever again."

In the bungalow kitchen, we warmed up food for dinner. The kids were playing in the background.

"Detective life in the big leagues," I said.

"Cruz, I'm completely exhausted and the case isn't done yet."

"You wanted me to solve the case rather than enjoy our vacation."

"I need a vacation from the vacation. Is this how all your cases are?"

"You worked on the NeuroDancer Case with me."

"No, I saved your butt on the NeuroDancer Case because you were being mind-controlled by the late NeuroDancer. That's different. This is working with you as your deputy. And this deputy wants to go home. I actually felt sorry for everyone there in the lobby. You utterly destroyed them. They don't want to be anywhere near you anytime soon. They want the police to get here to arrest them even if they're innocent just to get away from you. Do you do this in all your cases?"

"Most of the time."

"The bad guys don't stand a chance. What is this about you arresting people already? How many other people are on the island? Cruz, who's the murderer?!"

"Cruz, who's the murderer?!" Cruz Jr. had teleported into the kitchen and was standing next to his mother looking at me.

"Cruz, who murderer?!" Kat said after she ran to her brother and stood in front of her mother, looking at me.

"Do you smell that good food? Yum-yum. Let's eat dinner," I said.

"Cruz!" Dot yelled.

"I don't know yet."

"I thought you said you knew."

"Dot, it's possible that the murderer is someone we haven't met yet."

"Not the writers? Or the hotel staff? Or that Mr. Derez?"

"Might not be any one of them. But I did all that to see if one of them might be an accomplice. Namely, Dave Blackhat."

"Yes. He's the illegal treasure hunter. But why only him?"

"Not just him. Maybe Mr. Derez."

"He hired you."

"But he didn't think I'd uncover that he was actually on the island. Askey, I've already ruled out completely. Quiet Dave is my target."

"We need to know who the murderer is."

212

"I have a theory, but I think it's best to stay indoors until the police arrive."

"You're not going to finish the investigation?"

"Dot! I have my wife and two kids here. If the murderer, or murderers, are not the writers or the hotel staff, then this whole thing is a lot more dangerous than we thought. We need the police. I can't investigate with my family on the island."

"Cruz, that is a lame excuse. Finish your investigation. You can't stop now."

"Yes, I can. My priority is my wife and the kids. I'm happy to let this one go."

Dot really wanted me to investigate, but she appreciated that it was "family first" with me.

"Okay, Great Detective."

"So we're talking like AC now. I haven't forgotten you had her at the white board with you."

"Is she the murderer?"

"No."

"Then it's okay. She was my deputy. She has degrees in psychology and psychiatry."

"Explains her medicine cabinet."

Dinner was served. Family fed. Kids to bed. Dot and I loaded up the dishwasher. My brain was always amazed at how many dishes a family of four could use in one sitting. We only had two kids. How did people with four, six and eight do it? I'd run myself over with the Pony.

"Cruz, you didn't hear a word I said." Dot's voice snapped me out of my musings.

"What? What did you say?"

"I asked if your statement about the police being here tomorrow morning was another lie."

"Lie? Dot, it's called misdirection and confusion in the course of my investigation."

"Cruz, will I see police on this island tomorrow?"

"Maybe."

"Maybe?"

"They might be delayed."

"Why?"

"Layla."

"Layla? Who's that?"

"Hurricane Layla."

My wife had the bungalow's TV on to watch the news while she was on the phone calling friends in Metropolis. Hurricane Layla wasn't going to come anywhere close to the island, but it was causing havoc to the mainland. Only the force of nature could stop the advance of the Metropolis Police. Just our luck because we needed the cavalry to show up. That left me to properly secure the bungalow again for the night to my satisfaction. I wanted to ensure no one could break in while we were asleep. Dot already had the kids set up and sleeping in our upstairs master bedroom. I set up my own do-it-yourself traps and alarms on all windows and doors.

I heard a noise and looked up at the ceiling. I ran downstairs to the living room just as Dot was waking up.

"What's that noise?" she asked.

"The last hovernautilus! Stay inside with the kids!"

I'd been wearing my belt and gun holster at all times, so I was out the front door and slammed it shut. I heard Dot yelling at me. Something about the unfairness of leaving my deputy behind—whatever.

The hovernautilus was in the sky, hovering between the docks and the hotel. Was it coming or going? I didn't know what it was doing or who was in it. I was running as fast as I could to reach it. A high-beam light flashed directly on me, blinding me. The craft flew straight up. With my omega-gun in hand, I let loose a volley to get its damn spotlight out of my eyes. I shot out the light then kept firing until I heard the sound I wanted. There was popping, then an explosion. I'd shot out its engine. The hovernautilus began to come down—fast. The craft hit the water with a sickening crash, breaking up into all kinds of pieces.

I'd reached the docks and stood there, waiting. I'd been running and shooting at the same time. But I had company. All the authors and all the island staff were standing beside me, including Derez. They looked at me with apprehension. No more snappy jibes from AC either.

We heard voices and cries for help. Maxima was about to dive in, but I stopped him.

"Don't."

"Why?" he asked me.

"Who's in the hovernautilus?" Askey asked.

We heard voices of men. They were speaking French or some related dialect.

"I thought it was one of you escaping," I said. "I thought it might be you, Dave."

"Why me?" Dave said.

"We can talk about that later."

"You're flashing," AC said to me.

An indicator on my belt was flashing red.

"I don't hear their voices anymore," Maxima said.

"Where are the people who were in the water?" Runner asked.

"They either have a boat or a submersible that we can't see. Ladies and gentlemen, get back in the hotel. Rich, Marlan, and AC—you too Runner, if you can shoot—those men are with the gang who I believe killed Mr. Stellar."

"Gang?" Derez said. "What is happening here?"

"I have to go, but I'll meet you all later."

"Go where? Where are you going?" Derez asked.

"They're trying to get the body. I have to go. Get back to the hotel! Lock it down and watch for them to return. I expect them to be armed."

We all saw it. Tiny flashes of light above the waterline in the distance.

"What are those?" Modula asked.

"Get back to the hotel! I'll cover you."

"Cover us?" Derez said.

"Get back to the hotel, or get shot," I said.

All of us were standing in the open and I didn't like it. I ran behind a tree, keeping my gaze fixed on the flashes. Everyone else ran away. If the flashes were what I thought they were, and they had a sniper scope...I flicked the switch on my omega-gun and fired. I heard muffled screams as the round exploded, I heard things splashing into the water, and saw the tiny flashing of their laser rifle indicator lights disappear into the water.

Time was running out. I was back at the bungalow and had to leave immediately.

"Was that the last remaining hovernautilus?" Dot asked me.

"Yes."

"So there's no other way off the island for us?"

"No, but it's fine."

"Fine?"

"Dot, a change in strategy."

"What's that?"

"You were right all along. I'm a consultant detective working on behalf of the Metropolis Police Department."

"Not really in the mood for Sherlock Holmes references, Cruz. That was a lot of gunfire I heard at the docks."

"Remember, Dot, you're armed too and you're my deputy."

"What about the kids?"

"Oh yeah."

"You forgot the kids, Cruz?"

"No. Of course not. This is why you don't do detective work when you're on vacation with the family. I need you in protective custody. Into the panic room. You and the kids."

"Not you?"

"No. I have to go to the Center of the Earth."

I wanted to kick myself. Anytime one went on vacation you invariably forgot to pack something. I had Phishy send me my omega-gun, but forget to have him send my enhanced glasses. I'd hit what I aimed for at the docks, but I didn't see who it was or how many of them there were because I had no night-vision. I guessed it was about three to five men on a stealth jet-boat—the kind used by maritime smugglers of, likely, drugs and guns.

The paths on the island were adequately lit, but I was heading to another one of the theme worlds that would likely have no lights at all. I snapped my fingers as I jogged. Running all day was Cruz Jr.'s pastime, not mine. All this running for a man who was on vacation. I should have known that it was going to be far more than casually investigating a murder. All the particulars of my island murder mystery were taking form in my mind, and I didn't like what I was seeing. I needed the police here now but Hurricane Layla had other ideas, which was probably why our bad guys were making their move. They knew the police were coming too.

Forty minutes later I had reached the darkened theme world and made my descent down its initial spiral staircase. Kids loved the theme world. Climb from the surface of the Earth to its core, encountering giant plants, insects, crystalline hills, underground rivers, and finally the molten lava plumes and rivers at the core. The attraction was that the kids could actually jump into the lava and splash around, since it was all fake but loads of fun. Even though many feet below me, I could see the lava flowing from where I was.

The design mimicked what it would look like if a giant asteroid smashed to the Earth, punctured the surface, and cut its way straight down to the center of the Earth. There were some half-dozen levels within the different attractions. The spiral staircase was about fifteen feet across and didn't run straight down the center of the hole to the core, but winded down the sides of the gaping hole. One could get off on each level, explore, and return to the stairs.

I wondered if the family and me would be able to return, since our vacation in real terms was over. We got to see three of the five theme worlds—Moon World, Underwater World, and we squeezed in Mysterious Island, so that had to count for something. And we got to enjoy our balloon ride as a family, so we could skip International World if we had to.

Hopefully, I could sneak through Center of the Earth World without incident. The only lights were the glow from the crystal structures on one level, giant plants on another, and the lava rivers at the bottom of the theme world. Then I saw the many flashlights in the hands of the group of people who were two levels below me.

Actually, I'd moved Rod Stellar's body and hid it in the bottom of the Center of the Earth World on our first night on the island. There was a network of giant cooling machines to regulate the temperature of the massive turbines that ran the lava and underground rivers. I grabbed a hovergurney from the hotel's first aid medical room and stacked Stellar's body bag on it. My plan was to use it as a pressure tactic to flush out the murderer or murderers. Together with other tactics, it worked brilliantly. The only problem was that I determined our original list of suspects had nothing to do with the murder, and those who did have something to do with it saw me move the body.

I crouched down on the spiral staircase. Not having my night vision was like being naked in a mosquito swarm. However, I was able to count about ten men by their flashlights. They were talking a mile a minute in French or a French dialect. If I got into a firefight with them, I'd potentially be there all night. I also didn't know how many others might be around who could sneak up behind me if I did open fire on them.

If I got shot, how likely was it that anyone would find my body? They knew I was nearby. The fact that they were here meant they saw me. The two guards in the island's secret security post told me that. They'd also know about the hurricane and were taking full advantage of it, aware that the arriving police would be delayed.

Instinctively, something caught my attention from above. The moon was out but the clouds were blocking a full view. What did I see? People often forgot that humans were animals too, with a sixth sense for survival. Since I didn't have my glasses, I couldn't take chances. I fired a flare up and dashed down the stairs. The flare exploded and I saw them. Two men. They only got off one shot at where I had been, and I fired from where I was. Two down, but now all the smugglers knew for certain I was there.

As I ran down the stairs, I wanted to yell out, "Can you please speak English?" but I knew what they were saying. Cursing had the same intonations in all languages. The only place to go was to the bottom level of the theme world—I had no other choice. It was the only place that was defensible. I'd also have the benefit of better light.

If I wasn't being chased by gunmen, I'd be having fun. Cruz Jr. would be smiling from ear to ear running on the black rock surface of the bottom with raging rivers of lava beside him. What made it even better was that you could jump into the lava and swim around. Fun. I heard the laser shots behind me and dove behind a giant stalactite touching the ground. Laser fire, not fun.

Lots of yelling in French as they ran to me, though they couldn't see me. I peeked out and fired. Hit one. They ran for cover. I shot two more. Some hadn't found cover. I shot a few more. While I waited I noticed that the edge of the lava river was actually close enough. I stretched my foot out and touched it.

"Not hot at all," I said.

A person really could jump in and swim around. Since I had no one around to take a photo, it made no sense for me to do it. I'd have to bring the family back.

"Cruz!"

One of the gunmen called me out by name!

I peeked around the corner and pulled my head back just as the remaining gunmen blasted the stalactite. I had to crawl away as the firing was so intense they blew the rock formation to bits.

Then there was no sound from anyone. I was lying prone against the black rock out of their direct sight. My eyes and gun arm focused. I still didn't hear a peep from any of them. I estimated they only had four or five men left. Assuming no one else showed up.

But I had to assume more gunmen would show up. I rolled over, got up and ran deeper into the world. Good thing I did. My resting place was overrun by gunmen, chasing after me and firing their weapons. There were more than enough stalactites and stalagmites for me to use for cover. It was a seemingly endless underground cavern.

Unfortunately for them, I knew the plans for the theme world and they didn't. The island's secret security post had a hidden entrance, and so did the theme worlds—a network of control and maintenance tunnels. The entrance was hidden in one of the larger stalactite columns. I opened it, passed through, and closed it without a sound. Once inside, I had the benefit of the security monitors. I stood there and watched as the gunman ran right by.

Did they know about the hidden control and maintenance corridors? They didn't. I could return to the surface. However, since I was there, I made my way to one of the cooling machines. Right where I'd put him was the late Rod Stellar, inside the body bag and secured to a hovergurney. The only future engagement for him was with the coroners' division of the Metropolis Police Department.

I'd read stories of detectives and even police detectives getting shot and killed because they forgot to turn their mobile phones to vibrate or off. Even though I was past my OCD days, I OCD'd about it all the time, which was why I had my phone modified so I could simply touch the top of it to know whether the ringer was on or not—a raised ridge closest to me meant on, center meant vibrate, farthest away meant ring. I believe it was a tactile language known as Braille. I'd read about its use before the planet eliminated all hearing impairment. Versions of it were still used by intelligence services. During the entire time my mobile had been vibrating. Dot had been calling me—multiple times. Something was wrong.

I got back to our bungalow and pounded on the door as I kept an eye out behind me. I opened the door but it was chained.

"Dot!"

"Cruz!" She appeared at the door and opened it.

I rushed in, slammed the door closed, and chained it back. Kat was in her arms in a hysterical crying fit. Cruz Jr. followed behind his mother, visibly scared.

"What happened?"

"She won't stay in the panic room!"

"Why?"

"Cruz, Kat doesn't like enclosed spaces."

"It's like a palace."

"It's a giant metal box, Cruz. She can't go in there."

"Does everyone in this family have a phobia? My isopods. You and bridges. Kat is claustrophobic. What's yours, Cruzie? What are you afraid of?"

"I'm, I'm afraid of big, hairy, scary squid monsters, Daddy."

"Good boy. A phobia you'll never meet. That's exactly the kind of phobia to have."

"What do we do, Cruz?"

"We have to get to the hotel now."

"The hotel? Why can't we stay here? You said this was our base until the police got here."

"*Until* I ran into an army of gunmen with laser rifles."

"Gunmen?"

"If we can't stay in the panic room because of Ms. Kat, then it's the hotel."

"Gunmen, Cruz? What kind of crazy vacation is this? You take your family to an island with gunmen and murderers."

"It's not my fault, and you wanted to come here too."

"I could handle the one murderer. I wanted to see you catch them. But now you're telling me there are gunmen. More than one gunman?"

"Hotel! Now!"

"You're sure they're not the murderer."

"We can talk about that later."

"You said there could be an accomplice to the murderer."

"Yes."

"What kind of plan is this?"

"Dot, we can't stay here! All the gunmen have to do is encircle the bungalow and open fire. The laser blasts will cut through every wall like paper and reduce this place to a pile of debris and bodies."

"Oh my God."

"Yes. Oh my God is telling us to get to the hotel."

"Cruz, I'm so angry with you right now."

Dot ran upstairs carrying Kat in her arms. Cruz Jr. followed after her.

"Dot, what are you doing? We don't have to pack anything. Get their coats and that's it."

While she was gone, I ran into the kitchen. I opened the cupboard under the sink and retrieved my silver briefcase and a full knapsack from a secret compartment I created from my own personal—and unauthorized—remodeling. I returned to where I was standing near the bottom of the steps.

"Good grief," I said to myself.

My family came down with their jackets on and all of them wearing hats. Dot and Kat with their Sherlock Holmes hats; Cruz Jr. with his black fedora. I stood there shaking my head.

"What?" Dot said, annoyed. "I had to get Kat's doll. She's in distress."

Kat had her favorite stuffed cat doll in her hand.

"I'm in distress," Dot continued, "because I have a husband bringing me to islands with murderers and gunmen."

"It's not my fault," I said.

This was where things could have gotten interesting in a bad way. We had to get to the hotel. Not far, but with gunmen running around not so easy. I was the only one proficient with a gun; besides, Dot had to hold the kids' hands. Then I realized that I had so struck fear into the hearts of our island writers and staff that they might shoot at anything moving to or outside the hotel.

"You watch out for the gunmen and I'll get us inside the hotel," Dot told me.

"That's a plan. What are you doing?"

We stood outside in the middle of the walking path to the hotel. Dot had her mobile to her ear.

"AC. Yes. We're on our way there. Let us in at the main lobby. Cruz is back and has news. We'll make our stand in the hotel. Yes. Bye."

What on earth did I just witness?

"When did you become best buddies with AC? 'Make our stand'?"

"She's my deputy, Cruz. Let's go. Don't let us get shot by any gunmen!"

I walked ahead a couple of paces, and we stayed along the edge of the path. The trees would be our shields. We could see the hotel, but we'd have to run across in the open to get to it. The entire distance was well lit and if the ground lighting were off, we had the full moonlight from above.

"Okay, this is what we'll do. I'm the shield and you all run with me."

"You're the shield?" Dot said.

"Ready. One-two-three."

We ran. Cruz Jr. ran like a rocket, so Dot had to hold his hand. Along the path and into the main entrance. The outside lights of the hotel were off, including the lobby entrance. The doors automatically opened with Maxima and Marlan, both armed, standing on either side.

"What's going on out there?" Derez asked.

"We heard gunfire," Askey said.

"Gunmen," Dot answered.

"What do you mean gunmen?" Derez asked.

"Gunmen," I replied. "Men with guns."

"I know what the word 'gunmen' means. What gunmen? Who?"

"Smugglers, I'd say."

"Did they kill Rod?" AC asked. She came out of the shadows. All the lights inside the hotel were off too. The only light was the natural moonlight through the ceiling skylight. I hadn't noticed it before.

"I'd say yes."

"Then what we said from the beginning was true," AC reminded me. "None of us were the murderer."

"I noticed that in all this time, none of you suspected each other. You writers didn't suspect your group. The hotel staff didn't suspect their group. Not out of loyalty or friendship or familiarity. You all were certain of it."

"Because we were all together at the times Mr. Stellar could have been killed," Askey said.

"Ladies and gentlemen, this isn't personal. I wasn't here when Mr. Stellar was murdered. I didn't see it. You were the ones here. In investigations, you're a suspect until the facts say otherwise. That's how it works. Murderers lie all the time."

"Detectives lie more," Jean said.

"Yes, Jean. We lie. The police lie. Everyone lies. I lied to find out who killed Mr. Stellar. That's what I was hired to do. I wasn't hired to 'manage the situation.' I was hired to solve the case before the police got here."

"Is it solved, Mr. Cruz?" Derez asked.

"I'm going to be blunt. I took out maybe eight gunmen, not including the ones I shot at the docks. That's the good news," I said.

"The bad news?" Marlan asked.

"There's at least a dozen more, emphasize the words 'at least.' But actually, there is more good news."

"Which is?" Jean asked.

"They can't seem to hit the side of a building. Worst gunmen I've come across, but they don't need to be marksmen with the weapons they have."

"There's one more thing," AC said. "My dog is missing."

"Your dog?" I asked.

"Yes, my dog. He's very precious to me."

"Yet, you called him Dummy."

"It's my dog." AC swallowed hard. She was genuinely upset. "I think they killed my dog. I know it. Rod, him. Us."

"Let them try," Maxima told her. "I'm not going out alone."

"No one is dying in this hotel," I said. "We need to keep our wits, be calm, and be cool."

"You can be calm in all this?" Jean asked.

"Yes, he can," Dot said to them.

"I wish we had your husband's fortitude and experience, Mrs. Cruz," Derez said. "But we don't."

"Ordinarily, I wouldn't mind this, but today, I have my wife and kids with me and that makes me very unhappy. Because if they get shot, I'll get angry. No one wants to see Cruz angry. This is what we're going to do. The hotel is too big for this size of a group to properly secure. We need to stay where we have the best defensive positions. Make them come out in the open."

"We can use the kitchen," Chef said.

"If we had enough ammo, the kitchen would be perfect with its metal walls," I said, "but we don't. We can't be in enclosed spaces and upstairs has too many points of entry like the dining area. We only have four shooters."

"I can shoot," Jean said.

228

"I can too," Modula said.

"I'm rusty, but I can," Mr. Derez said.

"Mr. Runner, how many guns do you have now?"

"Two."

"Marlan?"

"Just my one."

"I have two, also," Maxima added.

"Then we have five shooters. Jean, where did you shoot?"

"Personal use, on the range."

"Modula?"

"Video games."

"Modula gets the gun," I said.

"Playing fake video games makes a better marksmanship than a real shooting range?" Jean asked in a huff.

"Yes," I said. "What do you think the military does? Rich, give Ms. Modula one of yours. Runner, give Mr. Derez your second one. I know where he learned to shoot."

"Where?" Jean asked.

"Mr. Derez works for a foreign megacorp. He has to qualify on the range annually."

"Mr. Cruz is correct."

"See, a real firing range, not a video game," Jean pointed out.

"My wife has the other gun. Her job is to defend the kids. This lobby is our base. Lots of windows. Lots of defensive positions. They want us, they have to come and get us. Even if they try to strafe the building they won't get us so easily."

"Jean, take my gun," AC said. "I'm not really any good with it. It's yours for the night."

"And Chef has a gun. Eight shooters and me," I said.

"Murder mysteries are not supposed to have strafing and shootouts," AC said.

"When the gunmen arrive, I'll be sure to make that announcement. People, take your best positions. We have to defend the front entrance, make sure no one comes through that hallway from the kitchen dining area, or rear of the building. And no one comes down the steps."

"When are you going to tell us what's going on here on this island? What this is all about?" Marlan asked angrily.

"When are the police arriving?" Askey asked.

"Let's get to our positions first, people. We have an entire night to pass the time. I'll feel much more chatty when we're not all standing together in the center of the lobby like a bunch of idiots signaling to the gunmen, 'Hey, shoot us now. We're all standing together in the middle of the lobby like a bunch of idiots arranged for your firing convenience.'"

"Officially, this is the worst vacation I've ever had in my life," Jean announced.

Jean sat with her back against the wall of my whiteboard in the sitting area.

"Are you doing okay over there, Jean?" I asked. "Do you need an intervention? You are armed."

"And don't forget it. Sitting in the dark on the floor waiting for gunmen."

"Think of it as research for your next book," I said.

I sat behind a section of the reception counter on the other side. It was the perfect spot for me to be able to view all three pathways to the main lobby. My silver briefcase was open and I closely watched the monitors—six screens of different parts of the island. I had the top three screens locked on the surveillance cameras of the hotel exterior—main entrance, views of the rear and right side of the hotel, and a view of the hotel's rooftop camera covering the paths to the main entrance, bungalows, and docks. The others three screens I had on a ten-second rotation of the entire island.

"Are you seeing anything over there, Askey?" I asked.

"Nothing at all, Mr. Cruz."

He had his own monitor briefcase. Between the two of us we had view of the entire external area of the island, including docks, bungalows, and the hotel grounds. Dave, Modula, Derez, and Askey were at the furthest end of the reception desk, closest to the main entrance. Dot and the kids were behind the counter in the center, which was the sturdiest and had an extra section of counter— double the protection. Runner was in front of them, with AC.

"What's in the knapsack you brought, Mr. Cruz?" AC asked.

"Oh, it has the drone camera I borrowed," I said.

"Borrowed, Mr. Cruz?" Runner said. "You've been quite busy, Mr. Cruz, for someone on vacation. Doesn't that belong to the island?"

"You guys brought me here," I said. "I'm doing what you hired me to do, or bribed me to do. Don't complain now."

"I hope these gunmen of yours are real and not more subterfuge," Marlan said to me.

Marlan and Maxima were on either side of the main entrance, their backs against the wall that wasn't glass. They'd be in a world of hurt if the gunmen shot out the glass of the entrance, but that's where they wanted to be.

"Do you see them, Mr. Cruz?" Askey yelled out.

"Where?"

"The mountain."

"Security mountain. Switching now. Well, look at that. The island's two secret security guards have been let out of their cell. And look at the new laser rifles they're carrying."

"How many?" Maxima asked.

"They're coming," I said. "Looks like at least twenty gunmen."

"Do we have enough ammo for this gunfight?" Jean asked.

"About twenty? That's not so many," Maxima said.

"Do you see them, Askey?" I called out.

"Yes," he answered.

"See what?" Maxima asked.

"There are a lot more of them following," Askey answered. "Mr. Cruz, we should all get to the panic room!"

The line of heavily armed men in fatigues, khakis, and casual wear looked like the United Nations of thugs. While their dress wasn't impressive, their weapons were state-of-the art. They were smugglers, the pirates of the international seas, that you read about in the news. They would run away with their tails between their legs at the hint of trouble from any government. But if you were unlucky enough to encounter them, you'd be no match for them because of their numbers. They always attacked with overwhelming forces. I didn't say it aloud, but the last thing we wanted would be to get into a firefight with them. Even if we won, they could bring down the entire building in rubble on top of us.

"No."

"Why not, Mr. Cruz?" Mr. Derez asked.

"Because the two island security guards have the access codes to all the island's panic rooms. They're expecting us to hide in there. We're going to surprise them. Marlan and Maxima, which one of you is the better shot?"

"I am," Marlan said.

"But you take forever to shoot one shot," Maxima said.

"It's called aiming."

"Gentlemen," I said. "The goal of the day is to make sure those two island security guards join Mr. Stellar. Do you hear what I'm saying?"

"Yeah," Maxima answered.

"If we all do have to retreat to the panic room, we need those two men not to be alive."

"We hear you."

"They're here!" Modula screamed, startling everyone.

I switched the views of the monitors. Five figures were running at breakneck speed to the main lobby entrance. Marlan and Maxima were on their feet and ready to fire.

"No! Wait! Let them in!" I said.

"Let them in?" Marlan said. "Why?"

"Those are the night people," I said and came out from behind my counter spot.

"Night people?" Marlan said. "Are you back to that?"

"You made them up that night," AC said. "It was a trick."

"He couldn't have. We saw them too. People outside running away that night," Marlan said.

"They're young people," Marlan said.

We unlocked the entrance and the door auto-opened as the five twenty-something-looking kids ran in. Three guys and two gals—all dressed in island wear—tank tops, shorts, loose-fitting short-sleeve shirts.

"Over here," I said, directing them away from the door.

Our new group, however, stopped to look at the authors at the main entrance.

"Richard Maxima! Marlan Overspeak!" the tallest one of the group said. He was giddy and looked around the rest of the lobby. "Is that Jean Code? Yes! AC Vulcana! Where's—Dave Blackhat!"

"Please don't tell me it's true," AC said.

"We have to get your autographs," one of the young women said. "I can't believe we're here with you, on the same island, in the same hotel, right next to you."

"Cruz, what did you do?" Jean asked.

"Me? I didn't do anything." I turned to the kids. "Over here behind the counter."

"Who are they?" Marlan asked.

"These are the night people," I said.

"These are not night people," Marlan snapped. "They're kids."

"No, Marlan. They're your fans."

"Super fans," the tall kid said, smiling. "Read every book you ever wrote, Mr. Marlan, sir. Is it okay to call you Mr. Marlan, or do you prefer Mr. Overspeak?"

"Read all his books. That's a lot of books," AC said.

"Three hundred and forty-one, sir."

"How did you get here?" Askey asked.

"Why are you here?" AC asked.

"AC Vulcana! Love your books. Read all of them too. Even the ones under your pen names. We're here to meet our favorite sci-fi writers on the planet and get your autographs and lots of photos."

"Gunmen and groupies," Jean said. "Shoot me now and put me out of my misery."

"Ms. Code, you're so authentic," one of the female fans said. "You're radiating with the humor you infuse into your characters, especially your strong female protagonists."

"Yep, shoot me now," Jean said.

"Please, everyone get back to your positions," I shouted.

"How did you get here?" Askey repeated.

"We have a boat, sir. Hidden on the other side of the island."

"Boat?" Askey asked.

"Where's this boat?" Runner asked.

"Hidden near the Moon Theme World, sir."

"That's near the bungalows," AC said.

"Yes," the tall kid said. "There's a small piece of beach between two quite gnarly sets of reef. But once landed, no one can see us."

"That's where you've been?" AC asked.

"Yes, ma'am. We beat the hurricane to get here. We did have some rough times at sea though," he said.

"We had to find the right moment to show ourselves," another said.

"Since you're trespassers, when did you think that might be?" Askey asked.

"Oh, sir, we were waiting for when the authors had their outdoor barbecues that we've read about. They have them on the beach. They hang out and write and talk about new ideas and projects and new series and characters."

"Yes, we get the picture," AC interrupted the other female fan.

"Were you all spying on us at night?" Maxima asked.

"Sorry, sir. We wanted to see you all and peeked in when you were at dinner or walking to and from your bungalows. We were just trying to get some photos. Sorry we scared you and made you shoot at us. I can't imagine the stress we caused. We're truly sorry."

"I can't believe this," Maxima said, looking at me. "Night people."

"Night people, indeed," Marlan said.

"How big is the boat?" Runner asked.

"It's my father's tri-phibious schooner, sir. Hover on land, float on water, dive to the bottom. Perfect for the five of us to live on, but if we had to cram everyone here onto it, we could. We'd be happy to take you where you want. Or you can take a spin. The key is in it."

"Why would you leave the key in your craft?" I asked.

"Why not?" he asked me.

"So it doesn't get stolen."

"Ah, sir, this is Jules Verne's Island with the greatest sci-fi authors on the planet. We don't need to do that. This isn't Metropolis."

"They'd steal the shoes off your feet while you're walking in them there," a female fan said.

"We can escape the island," Runner said triumphantly to everyone.

"Can we be extras?" one the female fans asked.

"Extras?" Jean asked.

"For the movie."

"What movie?" Jean asked her.

"The pirate movie you're making. We see the armed Caribbean modern-day pirates everywhere. The stealth boats. The guns."

"How many stealth boats did you see?" I asked.

"Three of them."

"How many of them do you think there are?"

"Couple a hundred easy, sir," another answered.

"This is no movie, sonny," Marlan said.

"Not a movie, sir? Looks like a movie production out there."

"It's not. Those are real gunmen and they're coming for us," Askey said.

"Why?" one of the fans asked.

"Yes, why?" AC asked. "That is an excellent question. Maybe our great detective can answer that one for us. Why are a couple hundred gunmen coming to visit us?"

"Because they figure getting rid of all of us is better than leaving us alive to tell the police about them," I said.

"I'm sorry, sir. 'Get rid of us?'" a female fan asked.

"Our great detective talks in euphemisms," AC said. "He means be 'transcended to the next life' without our consent via bullet or laser blast."

"But we thought this was a movie."

"Sorry, dear," AC said. "You picked the wrong night to visit your favorite sci-fi authors on the planet."

I put the five sci-fi groupies with my wife and kids. Modula kept her eye on Askey's surveillance briefcase while Dot watched the screens from mine, with the kids.

"We have to get to their boat!" Maxima yelled.

"But can we make it?" Marlan said.

"Modula, Dot. How's it looking?" I yelled out.

"They're gathering at the ridge line border of the forested area and the recreation grounds," Modula answered.

"How long does it take for an army of gunmen to get here? Are they lost?" Jean asked.

"Cruz, I think they're waiting for something," Dot said.

"Waiting for what?" AC asked.

"Very good question," I said. "Since we have some time, let's put it to good use. Super fans, you stay with my family. Dot will watch the surveillance feeds. Chef, get to your kitchen. The hotel has many bottles of alcohol. Ever heard of a Molotov cocktail? Bring back what you can."

The chef smiled.

"Maxima, Marlan, Runner, Jean, AC! Upstairs. Get chairs and whatever furniture you can drag down here. We want to block up the main entrance with as much junk as possible. Mr. Derez, Askey, Modula, Dave! Through the back to the dining room area and patios. Same thing. We need furniture to block up the hallway.

"Go!"

The authors and hotel staff ran off. I walked to Dot and the kids.

"What are you up to now, Cruz?" my wife asked.

"Switch all the monitors to views of the hotel."

"Why?" she asked.

"Whoever doesn't come back or runs for the boat is your murderer."

My wife's mouth hung open. The kids copied her expression.

"Watch out!"

Maxima being his typical uncouth self threw a stack of chairs down the steps.

"Why are you doing that?" Marlan appeared with a single chair.

"One chair, Marlan! How many people do you think will be stopped by one chair?"

"We're slowing them down for us to shoot at, not stopping them."

"Or for kindling," Jean said as she appeared with her two chairs behind Marlan. "Give us something to burn. That'll slow them down."

The three of them came downstairs. Maxima quickly created a wall with all the chairs they dragged, carried, or threw down to the ground floor.

The hallway past the sitting area with my whiteboard was being plugged up with chairs by Derez, Askey, and Modula.

"Coming down." We heard AC as she and Runner carried each end of a long couch.

"How are you two going to get that down the steps?" Maxima yelled.

"Easy, like so," AC said. They had set the couch at the top of the steps. She kicked it. The furniture slid down the steps with a thud.

"Help with this," Maxima said as he and Marlan moved it to the main entrance.

I stood at the section of the reception area with my wife and kids. The super fans stood behind us, quietly.

"Well, look at them," AC said when she and Runner got downstairs, looking at us.

"What's wrong, Mr. Cruz?" Mr. Derez asked.

The group formed up in front of us.

"Which one?" Dot asked me.

"You're my deputy. You know my methods. Deduce. Your notes are on the white board."

Dot came out from behind the counter. Cruz Jr. ran after her.

"Where's Mommy going?" Kat asked.

"What are you two talking about?" AC asked. "Where's Dave?"

Everyone looked around.

"Where's Chef?" Askey asked.

"The murderer!" AC realized. She ran to the whiteboard to join my wife.

My wife had her flashlight shining on the notes for Stryper and Dave Blackhat.

"Keep an eye on the surveillance feed," I said to the super fans.

The five of them stepped forward and took charge of the open silver briefcase.

"Cruz, why does your band of sci-fi groupies not look like super fans anymore?" Marlan asked.

Dot and AC walked back to us.

"Who are your night people really?" Marlan asked.

"A trick!" AC said. "They wanted to lure Rod's murderer out to steal the boat."

"Sir," one of the super fans called out to me.

I joined them at the monitor. "There goes our murderer," I said. "I'd say the gunmen will be visiting us shortly."

Everyone tried to come behind the counter to see but I kept them back, including my wife.

"All of you can't fit behind here," I said.

"Who is it, Cruz?" Dot asked.

"Dave!" Jean said.

"It has to be the chef," Maxima said.

"But Cruz said he wasn't the murderer," Jean said.

"Why isn't he here then?" Maxima asked.

"It's both of them," Dot said.

"Guessing or certain?" I asked.

"Dave could be a thief but not a murderer," Marlan said. "He writes fluffy sci-fi for kids. He's not capable of stabbing a man like that. It's the chef."

"Our chef?" Askey said.

"Who, Great Detective?" AC yelled.

"Not Dave," I said. "Marlan is right."

"Mr. Stryper was the one running away, ma'am," one of the super fans said.

"You kids are definitely not groupies. You're in this with Cruz," Marlan said.

I looked at the super fans. "Find Mr. Dave Blackhat."

The five super fans moved around the counter and ran through the chairs down the hallway. We didn't have long to wait. The fans returned; two of the men helped a groggy Dave back to us. Blood was dripping into his right eye from his hair. They set him down on a chair.

"Move over, let me look," Jean said, looking at his head wound.

"I'll grab the first-aid kit," Modula said and ran to behind the counter.

"What happened, Dave?" AC asked.

"He hit me," Dave said, eyes closed.

"Of course, he hit you," I said. "You were the only one who knew he was the murderer."

"What? Dave, you knew?" Maxima asked.

"I didn't know, Mr. Cruz. I suspected," Dave said. "But I stopped suspecting when you said it wasn't him."

"Listen to that, Great Detective. One of our own knew who it was from the beginning but doubted himself because of you," AC said.

"I did that to keep you all alive," I said. "I didn't want him threatened until I was sure and knew what was going on, and the police arrived."

"But the police aren't here," Jean said.

"Yes, they are," I said.

Everyone looked at the kids.

"Ladies and gentlemen, meet the agents of CGI," I said.

"CGI?" Maxima asked. "Computer generated image?"

"No! Do they look like holograms to you? Coast Guard Intelligence," I said.

"You're the police?" Maxima asked.

"Agents, sir," one of them said.

"You're the police we've been waiting for?" Dot said. "You're here."

"Well, ma'am, not exactly. The police are still on their way. They sent us ahead because we were already nearby," another agent said.

"You look high school students," Marlan said.

"What exactly does CGI do?" Modula asked.

"They're the arch-nemesis of gun-runners, drug-runners, human traffickers, and modern pirates," I said.

"How do you know these CGI?" Jean asked.

"Cruz, what's going on? I consider myself an intelligent person, but I've given up trying to follow along with you. I'd base a future character in a future book on you, but my fans would find him too annoying," AC said.

"When did you all arrive?" Marlan asked them.

"We've been on the island for four days, sir."

"You've been communicating with our great detective all that time?" AC asked.

"Mr. Cruz is the reason we're here."

"China, I'd say you married a real-life detective," AC said. "He's already to the final chapter while the rest of us are only finishing chapter one."

"China?" I asked. "How does she know your super hero name? Did you already sign her up as an Eye Candy client? Is that how you got her to be your 'deputy'?"

Dot laughed. "Superhero name. I'm not tellin'"

"Mr. Cruz, you didn't tell us how you knew our chef was the murderer," Derez said.

"Your chef speaks French," I said.

They looked at me. "He became a suspect because he speaks French?" AC said.

"Cruz, you wrote that on the whiteboard but that's ridiculous," Dot said.

"Mr. Askey was the one who told me."

"I told you?" Askey asked.

"The smugglers, our approaching gunmen, couldn't be doing what they were doing without an inside person," I said.

"Chef is the acting manager of the island when I'm not here," Askey said. "I'm here summer and fall months only. Chef is here the whole year round."

"That's what you told me. He's been on the island longer than anyone else. Knows all the security, all the security guards. Even hires staff."

"He hires the island's secret security," Derez realized.

"Yes. He even looked the other way when Dave there wanted to do his extracurricular treasure hunting in the area using the island as a base."

"That's why you thought it might be me," Dave said.

"That's why I thought you might be involved."

"Why did he kill Mr. Stellar?" Derez asked.

"Answer is simple, Mr. Derez. Mr. Stellar stumbled onto what they were doing. They killed him, or Chef did. I'm sure that a lot of money is involved. The authors have been using the island for their island retreat and the smugglers have been using the fact that the island is empty of tourists and personnel, except for your small group, for their smuggling. The CGI know the scheme better than me."

I turned it over to the young agents to explain.

"Based on Mr. Cruz's intel, we believe these smugglers have been using the island for their illegal operations. They transport, hide, and store their latest illegal contraband on the island. When the island reopens to tourists from around the world, their army of mules arrives and scatters around the globe with their illegal goods. Mr. Cruz has brought us the break we've been looking for all these years."

"But he'll escape in the boat," Runner said.

"We lied before, sir. The boat isn't where we said it is. And it definitely doesn't have the key in it," another agent said.

"Lying liars everywhere," AC said.

"What are we going to do now?" Jean asked.

"Wait," I said.

"Chef killed Rod," AC said.

"Chef killed Rod," Marlan and Jean said.

"Chef killed Rod," Maxima said. "Rich kills Chef."

"The murderer cooked the food I fed my children," Dot said.

"Mur-rer," Kat said.

"They're coming!" Modula yelled out, looking at the suitcase monitors.

We ran to where she was. I saw what I needed and moved aside for everyone else to get a good look. Others ran to my briefcase monitors to get a view. The gunmen were marching to the hotel in force.

"Too bad this isn't a movie production," AC said.

"Agents, what kind of weapons are you packing?" I asked.

None of the "kids" seemed to be wearing enough clothes to hide anything, but they reached under their clothes and pulled out weapons. They unfolded and cocked their collapsible laser rifles.

"They've reached the bungalows," Modula yelled out.

"Everyone get back to your spots," I yelled. "Did you get a fix on when the cavalry will be here?" I asked the agents.

"There's a break in the hurricane. Police hovercruisers should be en-route," one of them answered.

"I want my family protected. There's a four-year old and one year old," I said.

"We'll handle it, sir," one of the female agents said, looking at my wife. Kat was in her arms and Cruz Jr. climbed up on the counter to see.

"Pirates and smugglers," Askey said with disbelief.

"Using the island for criminal activity," Mr. Derez said.

"Drug and guns are the standard fare in the smuggling trade, but we believe this gang is involved in much more," one agent replied.

"We now know the island's secret security is in league with the smugglers. The same detail works every year during the time of the writers' retreats," another agent said to the group.

"A lot of things are making sense now," Dave said.

"We can talk more later. I need three agents to come with me," I said.

"Go with you?" Mr. Derez asked.

"I'm not going to wait for the gunmen to get here to turn the hotel into Swiss cheese. We need to take out as many as we can and scatter them. We have the element of surprise. They don't know about our officers here."

"Cruz, are you saying you're going back outside?" Dot asked.

"The cavalry is on its way. We're buying time."

"Ma'am, these smugglers are not stupid. The second their radars pick up any approaching craft, they'll abandon the island as quickly as they arrived to escape. That's how they've been in business for so long. Overwhelm the weak and run from everyone else."

"Marlan, Maxima, Runner, Jean, and Modula, who's probably the best shot out of all of you because she's video-game trained like me, keep this hotel smuggler-free. Marlan and Maxima, same plan. If you catch sight of those two secret island officers, body bag 'em."

"Do detectives really talk the way you do?" Jean asked.

"We do," I said.

"What about the chef?" Derez asked.

"He doesn't know about our five new friends either, and that they're armed to the max."

Everyone nodded. We were ready for the fight.

"Agents, keep my family safe," I said to the male and female agent standing with Dot and the kids.

"Bye-bye, Daddy," Cruz Jr. said, waving.

"Da-da," Kat said, waving her little hand.

I waved at them and winked at my wife. "Oh, can't forget my case." I ran to my spot behind the reception desk, closed my silver briefcase, and took it. I rejoined the remaining three agents. "Let's go and create some chaos."

"What do you think you're doing?" I said.

Chef hadn't seen me in the shadows of one of the palm trees. He jumped when I stepped out and asked my question.

"You."

"Yes, me. I asked, what do you think you're doing?"

"I'm going back in."

"Why? No, you're not going back in. Go get on your boat. You coward."

"I'm sorry. I lost my head."

"You're not going back into that hotel with my family. You left and you're not being let back in. Go get on your boat. Send us postcards when you get to wherever you're going."

"I'm sorry. Why are you out here?"

"I needed some air."

"Strange time to be getting some air."

"Why do you say that, Chef?"

"Under the circumstances."

"I could say the same about you. See any gunmen on the way back?"

"Not a one. Mr. Cruz, we need to get back inside."

"No. We're staying out here."

"I don't think that's too smart."

"Chef, what about the boat?"

"I was on my way but changed my mind. I said sorry and I'll say it again. We need to get inside."

"Chef, I need to ask you a personal question. But keep calm."

"Why can't we talk inside the hotel?"

Stryper started moving to the main entrance again.

"Chef, if you move to that entrance, you're going to get shot."

He stopped.

"Why would I get shot? Who's going to shoot me?"

"Chef, they know you killed Mr. Stellar."

"What are you talking about?"

"Maxima and Marlan will shoot you right in the belly. Then they'll pass guns around for the other authors to shoot you."

"Why would I kill anyone?"

"Was it an accident? He stumbled upon your island co-venture with your gunmen buddies. You're making way too much money to let a stuck-up author get in the way. Sure you don't want to run down to the kids' boat?"

"I'm sure. Since it's not there."

"We're making progress. You're starting to be truthful. Does this mean you're about to do something stupid?"

I quickly reached into my jacket with my right hand.

"I wouldn't do that if I were you," he said, with a slight grin.

"Chef, get down on the ground, face down, arms out. I'm going to handcuff you and if you're good we'll keep you in a closet. If not, we'll put you in the freezer. You like freezers. We'll make sure it's closed and locked so Manny doesn't have to."

Chef smiled.

"Don't smile at me. It means you're about to do something stupid."

"I have a surprise for you."

249

"I have one for you too. But you go first. Chef, if you make any sudden movement, I'll shoot you right in the forehead. I'm not playing. I don't play in life-or-death situations anyway, but this time my family is here. That makes me more dangerous than usual."

"I'll make this deal with you. I walk away. Everyone walks away, including your family. I get shot. Everyone dies."

I shot Chef in his thigh. As he fell, I rushed him. Slammed him down.

"Handcuff him!"

The CGI agents came out of the shadows too. One handcuffed him as Chef cried out. The other two agents took a knee, aiming their weapons in the distance.

I dragged Chef back to the front of the hotel entrance. I couldn't see inside but I gestured. The door auto-opened. Both Maxima and Marlan came out with guns pointed at Chef.

"Look what we found," I said.

Maxima just kicked the man in the neck. Chef screamed.

"Gentlemen, put him on ice, if you know what I mean."

"Our pleasure," Marlan said, grabbing him by the legs to drag.

"Search every inch of him first," I said. "Our chef wanted to come back inside, and I don't think it was to make us dinner. I think our chef has a communication device, and he was going to tell his friends outside our exact locations inside. Isn't that right, Chef? Which is why they stopped again. Waiting for instructions."

"Instructions? He's the ringleader!" Maxima said and kicked Chef again.

"They pay me. That's it. I'm not in charge of anything."

"Gentlemen, he's all yours. After the strip search, feel free to interrogate him using any and all methods before you toss him in the freezer. Use the same one where he put Mr. Stellar."

"You got it," Maxima said.

"Askey," I yelled.

The island manager tiptoed outside. He was so nerve-wracked he was trembling.

"Tell me about the autonomous puppets," I said.

My teleporting ninja son appeared and pointed at Chef on the ground. "Bad guy!"

"Cruz Jr., get back inside!" I yelled.

"J.R.!" I heard my wife yell.

All I saw was a blur of moving legs and arms as he ran back into the hotel.

One of the CGI agents with me watched the surveillance monitors at all times. The signal was to whistle the second the hundreds of gunmen began their advance again. But I never heard the whistle, and despite his words, Chef wasn't especially concerned about standing out in the open, under the moonlight, a clear shot for our pirate smugglers. He acted like he was in no danger. Maybe Maxima was right—Chef was the chief bad guy.

It was certainly plausible, but I had to act as if he was just a paid accomplice to the smugglers. Though he was the murderer, there was someone else among the gunmen who was their leader. We had to find that person, or create enough chaos and destruction to make them all flee. We simply had to stall for time and keep them away from the hotel.

"I want to check something," I said to my three agent colleagues.

"Alone, sir?" one asked.

"Yes."

We crouched down behind trees watching the briefcase monitors. The docks were ahead and the hotel behind us. The gunmen were obviously aware of the location of all the surveillance cameras on the island. They remained in the trees outside the tourist zone of the hotel, bungalows, golf courses, and beach. The forested area went all the way to the island's mountain. Outside the tourist zone, at night, all we could see was silhouettes. They'd smartened up and covered up the indicator lights of their laser rifles.

"I say we engage them now, sir," another agent said.

"If we do that, then they'll scatter. No way to control the situation then."

"Then what? We don't even know what they're waiting for."

"We do," I said. "A call from Chef. We don't have a lot of time, but we do have some. I need to check something out. I can move quicker alone. If they move, then engage them. Remember, they don't know about you yet. That's our element of surprise."

"But alone, sir?"

"They want the group. That's what they're focused on. I'll keep an ear open and if the shooting starts, I'll get back here."

"Okay, sir."

"You're checking the International Theme World?"

"Yes. It's the only theme world I haven't been to, and I remembered it was Chef who told the family and me to skip it and do the balloon ride instead. He was right about the balloon ride, but I don't think his suggestion was for my family's vacation enjoyment."

"Their illegal contraband."

"Whatever that may be. I'll take a peek and get back here."

"Twenty minutes there and twenty minutes back, sir. Not to mention the time to take a look around."

"I have some ideas of where to look first," I said.

Once again, I had to do a mini-marathon to the far end of the island. The island was for walking and if you needed transport there was the hovernautilus, but unfortunately the smugglers destroyed them all.

As I ran I tried to use the shadows and trees for cover too. Maybe all the gunmen were together. Or maybe they had lookouts posted in the shadows and behind trees. I had to assume the latter. Fortunately, my new agent friends had augmented vision glasses and lent me a pair. I had my night and infrared vision. My eyes quickly adjusted to the left eye in night vision and the right in infrared.

There was a volley of gunfire in the distance behind me. I stopped. I waited a bit to see if I heard anything else. Not a sound. I could speculate all day about what it was, but my agent buddies had the briefcase surveillance, not me.

As I continued running, I abruptly stopped again. My right eye picked them up right away. Two figures ahead. I switched to telescopic night vision. Two armed figures ahead, looking right in my direction.

They were unable to see me from where I was hiding but knew I was ahead of them. One of them put a pair of binoculars to his eyes. I was standing behind a cluster of palm trees and viewed the two men from the space between them. The men were only twenty feet away or less, on the ground in a downward-sloped patch. He stared at where I was but clearly wasn't positive as to what was me and what were the trees.

The second the man lowered his binoculars, I jumped out and fired. Both men down.

I reached the forested area of the island and quickened my running pace. The entrance to the International World dome was locked during the day, but I had all the security access codes. The theme world was a replica of the global world of the early 1900s. In a time when humans didn't yet live on the Moon and Mars, I guess it was appealing. If it was built here, then there must have been some marketing studies and focus groups that said it would attract tourists. Personally, I had no interest in a time without hovervehicles. The notion of driving on the ground seemed bizarre to me. That time didn't even have mass airplane travel yet. A bit too primitive for me.

Dot and I had looked at the pictures of International World. It was very beautiful. There was minimal illumination as I entered the maintenance access tunnels and climbed down two levels of stairs to the elevators. The stairs continued down to the bottom level, narrowly spiraling down to a single metal column. I doubted that it was ever used, more for emergency purposes.

The elevators were gigantic, made for transporting large crews and machines. The elevators' power came on as soon as I punched in the codes. When I arrived on the bottom floor of the domed theme world, the doors opened to complete blackness. I was so glad I had my night vision. I stepped into International World, though viewing it in the darkness diminished its majesty.

The elevator closed behind me. I spun around and took off my glasses for a moment. High above me I could see multiple flashlights coming down those narrow spiraling steps. The elevator was on its way up, and there was no way to stop it. I was about to have company. But then I was startled out of my skin— the entire theme world came alive. Lights, music, people— autonomous puppets—all came on. I hate puppets!

Then the lights and music went off. I was back in darkness; even the dim safety lights were off. I really, really wished it hadn't happened. Now, I had after-images of all the "people" in their early twentieth-century attire. Big dresses and tall hats. Autonomous puppets. I hated that phrase more than "moving mannequins." Androids! That's what they were. For obvious past reasons, I didn't want to have anything to do with androids. If they were real "autonomous puppets," meaning knee-high puppets without strings that could move, that would be creepy enough, but I could deal with it. Life-size ones I wouldn't deal with. I had wanted to let them loose on the island to confuse the gunmen, but Mr. Askey told me that the androids couldn't move past the barrier of the International World. My glasses were back on.

French speaking echoed everywhere. Yes, the language annoyed me. Yes, my cyborg secretary, or VP of Client Services, was French. But the real issue was that I was annoyed by languages spoken around me other than English. My wife spoke at least three. Cruz Jr. would probably be a tri-lingual before he was seven, then Kat. My parents spoke Spanish, so they were bilingual, and I believe my father spoke something else too. My wife's parents were bilingual. It annoyed me. I like English.

Well, the French-speaking gunmen came down the spiral staircase and spilled out of the cargo elevator, waving around their rifles and babbling nonstop. They were looking for me all right. I didn't need to understand French to know all the things they planned to do to me when they found me. However, I was glad they showed up. They were about to save me tons of time. Rather than aimlessly looking for their illegal contraband, the dummies were going to lead me right to it, since they feared I was after it.

I'd ducked into the Italian section of the massive International World. My perch was the roof of one of the buildings. I watched the gunmen go by the Leaning Tower of Pisa building replica. When they passed, I rushed back down and followed the flashlights.

These smugglers were not intelligent at all. They had no tactical planning or strategic abilities. They moved as a pack with a single goal: find the detective, shoot him, return. Unable to multi-task at all, like leave a couple of guys at the elevator and base of the stairs, in case I double-backed. They were also loud as hell. They clearly needed ninja training lessons from my son.

We passed the Old London section, the Egyptian section with its pyramids (I was starting to get annoyed by the sight of pyramids because they kept popping up in my cases), the India section with the Bombay and Calcutta sub-sections. They disappeared into the Old Hong Kong section. Ahead of me, I glimpsed Old Japan, and I believe San Francisco was after that. The glow of the gunmen's collective flashlights guided me.

Again, I really wondered about the brain-power of these smugglers. One had strayed away from the pack with his flashlight bobbing around. I ducked around a corner; he passed right by me. I looked out and he was still shining his light all around. He was joined by another flashlight. They talked and the same gunman retraced his steps, while the other flashlight flicked off. That got my attention.

I'd hopped back around the wall of the building replica. The first gunman went by to return to the group. I dashed down the alleyway and across the street. The second gunmen who flicked off his flashlight must have been higher up in the smuggler hierarchy, because he showed a glimmer of intelligence. He either knew I was nearby or suspected it. If he had night-sight I could hide among the many "autonomous puppets," and he'd never find me. If he had infrared, he'd be able to walk right up to me, or shoot me from afar.

The only thing for me to do was avoid him. If he saw me, he wouldn't shoot at me. He'd tell all his buddies and they would. The goal had to be to remain undetected. I had to wait until I saw the second gunman, follow him, and do so until he returned to the group.

"Jean!" a voice called out, pronounced the French way.

I carefully moved along another alleyway. A flashlight flicked on and I saw the second gunman go by in the distance. I recognized his overall shape—tall, brawny, bald, bulbous nose. I made sure it wasn't a trick and watched him closely from behind. He rejoined the group. He didn't do a particularly competent patrol job.

Always wear proper footwear. I climbed up one building to get a better look. Thank goodness twentieth century Hong Kong didn't have the two-hundred story megatowers of today. Five stories and I looked down on the gathered gunmen. They encircled a giant trapdoor in the ground in the alley of two buildings. I looked through my mini-binoculars. Stacks and stacks of plastic bags the size of my suitcases. Drugs? I wouldn't be able to get close enough, but I knew where their stash was and soon the CGI would too.

My devilish side wished I had a Molotov cocktail to toss in, but that wasn't my mission. I'd found what I wanted. It was time to go.

I emerged from the underground theme world expecting to hear something. Not a sound anywhere. Not a gunman to be seen. My sixth sense wasn't tingling. What I did see was a bright glow on the other side of the island.

The smugglers had signal jammers inside the International World. My phone had been in nonstop vibrate mode.

"Cruz," one of the agents answered as soon as I dialed the same number back that had called me a million times.

"What's wrong?"

"Where are you, sir?"

"I found where they're hiding their contraband."

I heard the agent informing his colleagues in the background.

"Sir, that is great work. We think the gunmen are preparing to leave. All three of their craft are docked along the island coast near Underwater World."

"I can see it from where I am."

"We're there, sir."

"The bright lights."

"Yes, sir. That's them. All the gunmen are getting aboard."

"They're waiting for their comrades to join them. They're in International World. Those gunshots I heard earlier, that was to warn me about the two gunmen ahead of me?"

"Yes, sir. We knew you'd realize it was a signal. We saw the two gunmen running to you from island surveillance cameras. Didn't seem to be a problem for you."

"Any news from the hotel?"

"Nothing to report, sir. Gunmen never made it to the hotel, only back to their craft."

"I'm on my way to you."

"We're waiting, sir."

The three CGI agents were hidden in the forest line just outside of the beach's edge. One of them monitored the briefcase surveillance monitors. The other two were watching the same thing that caught my eye as I reached them—the three giant, black seacraft anchored just outside the reefs. Smaller hoverplatforms transported a dozen men at a time from the beach to the larger ships.

"Did you see two men in uniforms?" I asked.

"Yes, they're aboard already."

"They're the two secret island security guards."

We heard a barking from one of the seacraft.

"Is that a dog?" I asked.

"We've heard it barking off and on for most of the time we've been here."

"Damn smugglers are stealing AC's dog," I said.

"Here comes the rest?" an agent said, and we all instinctively crouched lower to the ground.

From our left view over sixty men, rough guess, burst out of the forest onto the beach, running to the water to await the return of one of two of their hoverplatforms.

"Are they really going to escape without any of their contraband?" I asked myself.

"The police must be almost here. They can see on their radar."

We heard a boom, then a giant aircraft rose from one of the three seacraft.

"The smugglers have an airship too," an agent said.

"They are going to try to take the cargo with them," I said. "They weren't checking to make sure it was safe; they're moving it. What do you want to do?"

"We could wait, but we don't know when the police will be here."

"You said it yourself though. These smugglers are slippery. They know how to time these things. They'll be loaded and gone before the police arrive. Metropolis Police ain't no joke, but you can't obliterate the bad guys if they're long gone."

"You're saying we should stop them, sir?" an agent said.

"Why not? Their seacraft are probably also subs."

"High-speed subs."

"But the airships have guns," another agent said.

"I agree with Mr. Cruz. Take out the airship when it's loaded. We'll take heavy fire, but we'll make them choose. Contraband or escape. They'll choose escape and we'll prevent their contraband, likely drugs, from ever reaching the streets."

"Works for me," I said.

I'd been watching the airship glide over the water to the International World area. A volley of lasers shot out from its heavy guns in our direction; I barely had time to push the agents out of the way and onto the ground. No need to hide anymore.

The trees and brush all around us were cut to pieces. We also heard voices and could see the bulk of the remaining gunmen running to us on the beach.

"You take the gunmen. I'll take the airship!" I yelled.

"You can't take out aircraft with a handgun!"

I didn't ever get up. I spun around as I grabbed my omega-gun and returned my own laser volley, adjusting the range as I kept firing.

"I'm not close enough!" I yelled and was on my feet running to the airship.

I heard laserfire behind me and saw from the corner of my eye gunmen being hit and falling to the ground. Some shot at me so I shot back, hitting more. They knew about me, but not the agents with their high-powered laser rifles. For the gunmen, the battle was already lost.

The airship seemed to only be able to shoot from its side, but not at anything ahead of it as it flew forward. I stayed in that blind spot as I ran to it. The airship flew in a downward trajectory as if the pilots intended to literally run me down. Not sure why they thought that was a smart strategy, because they faced me with my omega-gun and three other agents with their high-powered laser rifles. All the gunmen on the beach were dead, critically wounded, or running for their lives to the ocean.

The pilots were counting on their aircraft's armor protecting them. Unfortunately for them, they got close enough for me to use my explosive rounds. I blew their canopy window off with one shot, and the CGI agents turned them and the interior of the cockpit to Swiss cheese.

They lost control of the airship; the craft suddenly dove at me. I couldn't stop or run to either side. I had to channel every ounce of strength to bolt forward. There was a reason foot races are *not* held on the beach with sand. That airship literally brushed the top of my fedora so fast that the backwind blew my hat off and me off my feet.

All I heard was the sickening crash into the beach sand. I felt myself being lifted into the air. I saw the three agents. They didn't have to say one word to me. It was now four of us channeling Cruz Jr. Super-sonic-speed running away. We dove behind a sand bank. The explosion was...I'd been in explosions before, but this was of a magnitude beyond comprehension. If we hadn't been behind the sand dune, we'd all four have been dead—vaporized. The blast, the shrapnel of metal and plastic, all of the above would have killed us.

I sat up. We all did and surveyed the area. What had been the airship was now a ball of smoldering fire and metal. There was no beach. In fact, all the sand around us, the bodies of the gunmen, wounded and dead, were all in the ocean. On the other side, all the palm trees and path lamps were gone, blown out of sight further into the island.

"That wasn't a normal explosion," I said.

"The aircraft must have been loaded with explosives."

"An already explosive airship, loaded with more explosives," I said. "I'd call that a dumb thing to do."

"Look!" one of the agents yelled out.

The three seacraft were almost submerged.

"They're getting away," an agent said.

"Don't think so," I said.

They saw them too. Flashing red and blue lights everywhere in the sky. We saw lighted plumes streaking down and landing in the water. Then saw the underwater explosions, one after another. The three seacraft rose from the water as swarms of police and military hovercruisers hung in the sky above them.

"This is the police! Come out on your decks with your hands in the air or you will be fired upon and killed!"

PART NINE: AROUND THE WORLD

Police and Coast Guard marched off landed aircraft in force to secure the island. I watched from outside the front of the hotel entrance with Dot. Cruz Jr. amused himself by running around in front watching the officers and agents, but he really wanted to jump on their hovercruisers. Kat alternated between running after him, or trying to, and being fascinated by all the Metro police officers in their black and silver body armor, wearing their black helmets, and the translucent navy uniforms of the Coast Guard.

"Why didn't you tell me, Cruz?" Dot asked. "You figured this out all along."

"You have an honest face, Dot. If I told you, they'd read it in your face. But instead, as my deputy, you helped me catch the murderer."

"I did?"

"Yes. I needed the time to figure out if it was one murderer, or more, and if there were any co-conspirators. I had to always leave open the possibility that it could have been all of them. An entire island to themselves. Who knows what they could have been up to?"

"Oh, we need to go back inside."

"Why?"

"We interrogated the chef."

"Interrogated?"

"Yes. He was a treasure trove of info. Marlan and Rich were the 'bad cops' and AC and I were the 'good cops.' Then Jean jumped. Mr. Derez, Modula and Runner too."

"What? All of you?"

"What about Dave?"

"We had to confine him."

"Confine him?"

"He tried to kill Chef, but we couldn't allow him to do that until we interrogated Chef, so first we handcuffed him, but he still tried to assault Chef. We had to put him in the freezer."

"Freezer?" I laughed.

"We gave him extra jackets to keep warm and we turned the settings to room temperature."

"What did you learn?"

"Got the whole story from Chef."

"Whose idea was it to even have the writers retreat to begin with ten years ago?"

"How did you know to ask that?"

"That person might be a suspect too."

"We thought the same thing. He said it was always Mr. Stellar's idea."

"Whose idea was it to use the island as a smugglers' cove then?"

"They came up with the idea all on their own. Chef said they made an offer to him he couldn't refuse."

"Or he made the offer to them."

"You think he always knew them?"

"Dave wasn't the only amateur treasure hunter. So was Chef."

"You knew that too?"

"Yeah. I had PJ do backgrounds on everyone. Chef was an amateur treasure hunter going back to when he was a boy. Traveling in those circles you meet people. Like when I was on the hovercar racing scene. You meet all types. You know who are the aficionados, the real racers, the groupies, the collectors, and the gangsters."

"Chef would know smugglers."

"He would. He may have been involved with smuggling, but on a far smaller scale, even before the writers' retreats."

"Dot! Is Dave still in the freezer?"

"J.R.! Kat! Follow Mommy inside."

Dot ran back inside the hotel with our kids following her.

As I strolled into the hotel I saw Chef, handcuffed behind his back, escorted by two armored police soldiers. He smiled as they approached me at the entrance.

"Greed," I said.

"What's that?" he asked. The officers stopped for a moment.

"Nothing."

"You lied to my face from the very beginning. You said I wasn't a suspect. My alibi was solid."

"Everyone's alibi was solid, which meant none of them were. That's how I proceeded."

"I should have shot you when I had the chance."

"Yeah, but I saw you sneaking around our bungalow that night."

"You didn't know it was me."

"Didn't I? You shouldn't have been there to begin with. A dumb move."

Chef was about to respond but stopped himself.

"Was it your idea to turn the island into a smugglers' paradise?"

"If not here, there are plenty of other islands."

"Killed Mr. Stellar because you wanted to be a greedy swine."

"Stellar got himself killed because he was nosy and wouldn't get with the program. It could have worked out for everyone."

"Were you going to kill Dave too eventually?"

"If they hadn't brought you here, everything would have been smoothed out."

"Is that what we're calling murder these days? Good luck, Chef, in prison. At least you have a skill that can come in handy. Gourmet chef and murderer."

"Cooking was never more than a hobby."

"Smuggler from childhood then."

"Pirate."

"But without the eye patch. You have a good trip, Pirate Chef."

"People like me don't stay in jail for too long. I know too much. A valuable government witness."

"An informant against your pirate buddies. Yep, that's a genius plan. You'll live a very long time with that strategy. You have a good trip, Chef. My case is done, and so are you." I nodded to the officers. "Officers, you can take your man away. Which country's luxury prison facilities will he be vacationing at for the rest of his life?"

"French authorities will get the honor."

"How does my cyborg secretary say it? That's TRAY BON. Very good."

They took Chef away out the main entrance. Other officers joined them, and they marched him to a waiting prison hovervan. I wouldn't be seeing the criminal Chef ever again.

"Mr. Cruz." Mr. Derez approached from the hotel's back offices, accompanied by a CGI agent. "You might want to follow us," he said.

"Where're we going?" I asked.

"To see what these smugglers were stockpiling on my island."

Jules Verne's Island was supposed to be an exclusive vacation resort; however, this morning it looked like the landing at the Battle of D-Day (I saw the movie). Hovercruisers hovering tens of feet in the sky, some flying out, others flying in. Metropolis police made up the bulk of the forces, but Coast Guard Intel were in charge and had plenty of personnel themselves.

With the daylight, I could see the entrance to the International World dome was a replica of a nineteenth century railway station of London of that time. Visitors were supposed to file through a tunnel opening, which was the walkway down to the elevators via moving walkways.

Our agent escort led us to the elevators to join other law enforcement, all going about their tasks. Officers and agents were stationed everywhere as guards. We took the cargo elevators to the same bottom level where I'd been the night before, only all was active. I breathed a sigh of relief because all the "autonomous puppets" were deactivated and stacked to the side in a pile.

Ancient Hong Kong was ground zero of CGI activity. We were met by other agents.

"Are you Mr. Derez?" one asked.

"Yes, sir," Derez said, shaking hands. "This is Mr. Cruz."

"Mr. Cruz, our man on the ground," the agent said.

"That's me."

"Good work, Mr. Cruz. We'll show you what we have."

The agents led us into the hiding underground warehouse that I was only able to see from afar the night before. I'd seen the briefcase size plastic-wrapped packets.

"How much drugs are here?" Derez asked.

"Sir, this is the largest stash we've ever seized in my thirty-year career in the service. Even so, this wasn't their prize."

The agents led us to an open spot in the warehouse. One of the agents activated the controls and a section of the floor, ten by ten feet, began to descend. Another secret underground warehouse. All around were giant crates. A few were open and being inspected by an army of agents. Weapons. Machine guns, machine gun rifles, mini-cannons. They looked new and very dangerous. Agents had activated a few to examine them. Flashing lights on the muzzle, sights, side, and body for no practical reason other than for a bearer to show off.

"Your agents on the phone said you were after this group for years," I said.

"Decades, Mr. Cruz," an agent said. "We've been after them for decades. But we never made a dent in their operations. Today, we know why. We thought their base was at sea, one of their seacraft or a stealth super-submarine. They've been using the island all along. If you hadn't notified us, I don't think we'd ever have found this."

"Too bad for them Mr. Cruz came to the island," Derez said.

"Too bad they killed Mr. Stellar," I said.

"Yes, of course."

"Is this the murdered man?" the agent asked.

"Yes," Derez replied.

"We found the body where Mr. Cruz told us."

"Poor Rod," Derez said.

"He tangled with the wrong people," an agent said.

"Did they get any of the weapons out of here?" I asked.

"Weren't you the one who blew up their airship?"

"It was a joint Cruz-CGI operation," I said with a smile.

"My people tell me they loaded up the craft with all their explosives first."

"Oh," I said. "It did feel unlike any explosion I ever experienced."

"Because it was. You're very lucky, Mr. Cruz. That explosion could have blown you all the way back to Metropolis. You wouldn't have needed an air flight back. Unfortunately there would have been very little left of your actual body."

"Mr. Derez," I said. "Sounds to me like I need a vacation."

When I returned to the hotel, the interior still had officers stationed throughout. Authorities had designated the entire first floor a crime scene. The sitting area had the rows of chairs but my whiteboard on the wall was gone.

I strolled into the dining area where I was told my family, the authors, and hotel staff were.

Cruz Jr. and Kat ran to me.

"Daddy," Cruz Jr. said.

I rubbed his head to mess up his hair and he laughed. I picked up Kat. She was in her "I am the queen so please carry me" mood.

Everyone was sitting at the dining room in the same spots as the previous times we'd had dinner. I noticed a man standing at the dining tables with his back to me, wearing a hooded parka. He turned. It was Dave Blackhat. He smiled.

"Join us," Marlan said.

Marlan sat at the head again. I sat down next to him, holding Kat. Cruz Jr. climbed up to sit next to me and Dot. There was AC with Jean, Dave, and Maxima at the other end of the table. Modula, Runner, and Askey joined us from the other table.

"Dave, they let you out of the freezer," I said. "You can take off the parka."

"I prefer it. I don't get to wear one at all. I think I'll have my next novel take place on a frozen planet."

"Will it have fluffy fur animals?" I asked.

"Of course."

I looked around at everyone. Smiles all around.

"The case is solved, Mr. Askey," I said.

"Yes, it is, sir," he said.

"Though there are a few minor points to clear up," AC said.

"What did you all find out from your interrogation of Chef?" I asked.

"That's another thing," Jean said. "Your wife came back in and told us what you said. You even knew the things we got out of him."

"Yes, I passed Chef on the way out. The police were walking him out to a prison van. A bit too cocky in light of where he's going. He seems to think he'll be able to cut a deal with the authorities to get out of jail."

"Inform on his smuggler friends?" Marlan asked.

"That's what he thinks."

"The authorities may call you in to investigate a new murder at the prison. His," Marlan said.

"I can assure you, Mr. Cruz, he will not be cutting any deals with authorities for leniency," Askey said. "The island's company will see to it. We have considerable influence."

"I have no doubt, but even without it, he's not going anywhere. I saw the contraband."

"What was it?" Runner asked.

"Weapons," I said. "Lots. Seems that laser rifles with tiny lights, your choice of flashing yellow, white, blue, or red, are all the rage with the criminal underworld lately."

"Not drugs?" Askey asked.

"They had plenty of drugs too, but they left it behind in their hiding place. It was the weapons they were taking out of there. Weapons enough to equip several armies. And explosives. Either way, who knows how many people on the streets they were indirectly killing every year."

"We found out their whole plot," Dot said. "With the island being mostly emptied of all tourists, except for the writers, and a dramatically reduced staff, including security, they loaded up the island with their illegal goods for those two weeks. Like you said, when the island opened, they had their army of mules take a piece at a time to points all around the globe, and even Up-Top. The island security is tremendous for arriving visitors, but not for departures. The distribution took the entire year to complete."

"Then there would be another writers' retreat to start it all over again," I said.

"Exactly," Dot said.

"And I was right. Chef was their overlord," Maxima said. "They were never going to attack us as long as he was with us."

"Overlord?" I asked. "You mean their boss. The chief bad guy."

"The bad guy?" Cruz Jr. asked.

"They were using us," Marlan said. "Did you figure out who gave Rod the idea for the retreat?"

"Yes, and that brings me to Mr. Askey again," I said.

"Me, sir?"

"Mr. Askey, once this is all over your presence will be required at corporate headquarters. The persons who gave Rod the idea were also the persons who could approve the idea."

"The board?"

"Yes. I don't think they ever knew or suspected what Chef and his smuggler friends were up to, but you'll likely become the new chairman."

Askey, at first, was flabbergasted, then he couldn't stop smiling.

"Which means that more promotions will be coming," I said

Modula and Runner looked at each other, then laughed.

"Mr. Cruz, there are a few outstanding points," AC said.

"Like why I searched your rooms?"

"Yes, that's one."

"I was looking for shoes. The murderer was sneaking around our bungalow one night. Left footprints in the soil. I wanted to see who matched them. Chef, Maxima, and Derez were the winners of the shoe size award. I was able to narrow it down from there."

"I've always had big feet," Maxima said. He grinned at AC and she turned up his nose at him.

"So it wasn't that nonsense you said with him speaking French?" AC asked.

"It was the background checks first. I was sure it was him, but I had to verify and make sure it was only him. I also had to find out if Dave was involved or not. If he was, fine. If not, then he might become a second murder victim. I saw Dave's face when I told Chef he wasn't a suspect."

"I knew exactly what you were doing that night when you sent us all to do our little assignments," Dave said. "I wanted to catch him trying to escape. He caught me off guard."

"I hear you tried to make up for it."

Dave smiled. "I can fight when I need to."

"I heard it was much more than that."

"Dave was going to rip Chef apart if we didn't restrain him," Jean said.

"Dave, aren't you an author of children's fluffy fun sci-fi?" I asked.

"So."

274

"Speaking of violence," I said. "Marlan, are you and Mr. Askey okay? I don't want to read about you two in the news in the future."

"It's resolved," Askey said.

"That was a very low trick you played on us," Marlan said. "It was so long ago. That mean drunk I was doesn't even exist anymore. But it was two separate events. All these years I thought it was the same. How did you find out? How did you find out about any of it?"

"I just read the full police reports. It was all there."

"You read the police report? I was there and I never did. I never did it."

"You weren't the one driving. But your friends in the vehicle decided to pin it on you."

"Yeah, I wasn't all that nice a person back then, but new me and new friends."

"Somehow there was still a cryptic note in Mr. Askey's personnel file about why you recommended him for the job."

"Look at what you were able to make us think with all those independent, tiny bits of info.," Marlan said.

"True, but who cares? Askey is going on to bigger and better things in the company. You have endless material for your next novels. As long as you two knew the truth before you murdered each other."

Marlan chuckled. "That's true."

"We all do," Jean said. "Endless material."

"Tell me, Mr. Great Detective," AC began, but this time she said it with grudging respect rather than the previous sarcasm, "are you really memorizing the mugshots of all the criminals in Metropolis?"

"The brain remembers everything," I said. "We just can't recall all of it. But it's there. It helps my instincts."

"That's your edge then."

"No. My edge is that I study the crimes of our fine supercity—the tactics, the grand schemes, how they got away, how they got caught, players and victims, associates and unsuspecting dupes. Channel all my OCD tendencies into something constructive. I just have to teach Cruz Jr. now."

My son grinned at me, though I was sure he really didn't know what I meant. Or maybe he did. With my parents and the Hellspawn, the urchin probably already could speak multiple languages—unlike me.

"Criminals don't stand a chance with you," Marlan said.

"Another mystery solved," AC said.

"Which brings me to another matter," I said. "Where's my whiteboard?"

I looked around the table. I looked at the staff. Everyone was looking away.

"Another mystery," AC said.

"Dot, who has my whiteboard?"

"Well…"

"Well, what?"

"Opportunities appear, and you have to take advantage of them."

"Dot, you're supposed to be my deputy."

"I took charge of the whiteboard…"

"And?"

"A suggestion was made."

"And?"

"And it was auctioned off to the highest bidder."

"You sold my white board!"

"Cruz, it's the least you can do for what you put us through," AC said.

"Me? You all tricked me into coming here," I said.

"Mr. Cruz," Runner began, "we also expect you to return the island's drone."

"I was using it for personal surveillance of the island."

"Yes, but see to it that it's returned."

I leaned back in my chair. "Dot, I think I need a vacation."

They laughed at me.

We finally walked out of the main hotel. I carried Kat in my arms, her head resting on my chest; she wanted to get inside our bungalow away from the island-wide landing of authorities. Dot managed Cruz Jr., who still looked like he was going to bolt away from us to run onto one of the hovercruisers.

Mr. Derez was speaking with a group of agents and saw us. He said a few final words and walked to us.

"Mr. Derez," Dot said. "The case is over."

"Thanks to your husband," he said. "Mr. Cruz, may I have a final word?"

"We're going back to our bungalow. You can tell me on the way. And I can give you back that drone I borrowed for Mr. Runner."

"Yes, he'd appreciate that. I didn't know it was that easy to hack into one of our drones."

"Cruz is good with tech," Dot added. "Did you know he built his own working classic hovervehicle when he was only in high school?"

"I had read that but thought it was standard puffery of one's resume. Now I know better."

The authorities had finished their own searches of all the bungalows, but officers remained on guard. They were all cleared for use. Derez walked along the path with us.

"Mr. Cruz, it will take time for us to restore the island to normal operations."

"How long do you think it'll take?" I asked.

"Corporate headquarters is determined to restore all normal operations in thirty days."

"That's fast," Dot said.

"But doable. I've spoken with the authorities, and our full maintenance and construction crews will arrive tomorrow."

"Will the scene be cleared that fast?"

"By week's end. There's also Rod's funeral we have to organize. We want it dignified. To take place when the authorities have left and our crews are finished with island repairs and reconstruction. However, there's the matter of the press."

Dot and I looked at each other with smiles.

"Mr. Derez, we don't have to remind you how the media found out I was even on the island."

"No need at all. The saying goes: actions have consequences. Though if I had to do it again, I would. The resolution was better than I could have hoped, considering."

"Yes," I said.

"If you and your wife, could do a last favor for the island. Stay clear of the media. If they should contact you, or corner you on the street, be evasive and refer them to corporate headquarters. These situations need to be properly managed, with as much as possible kept confidential. This is an island resort and ultimately it's all about tourism. The lifeblood of the Caribbean."

I chuckled. "Situations managed. Yes."

"You can even finish your vacation as we spoke about."

"Finish our vacation?" Dot asked.

"Yes, hon. Mr. Derez and I had a conversation."

"Conversation? When?"

"We should end our vacation as we began. A great grand balloon ride, but this time through the International World of Jules Verne's Island," I said.

"Daddy, do I get to ride animals too?" Cruz Jr. asked.

"I think we can manage that. In fact, before we do the balloon ride, we need to visit the Center of the Earth World."

"Cruz, it's dark down there. We should just skip that for the balloon ride."

"But we can swim in the lava."

"Swim in the lava?" Cruz Jr. asked with happy shock.

Even Kat jerked her head up to look at me. "Lava?"

I don't know how Derez managed it, but the CGI and police wrapped up and were gone before night fell. We heard the last hovercruisers depart around nine p.m. The authorities had said we had to remain indoors for the duration of their investigation, which we were happy to do. Even hyper-energetic Cruz Jr. was napping, along with the rest of the family.

At five a.m., Dot got all of us out of bed. At 5:05, I returned to bed and tried to hide under the blankets. At 5:10, she dragged me out of bed and told me she'd get Herbie if I didn't get up. Kat and I ended up being the last to get dressed. Dot and Cruz Jr. had already gotten breakfast by the time we arrived in the kitchen.

The plan was to spend some time in the Center of the Earth World, but most of the day at International World. Runner picked us up in one of the island's new hovernautiluses at 6:30 a.m. in front of the hotel.

"Swim in lava?" Cruz Jr. asked me again.

I had returned, but this time with the family. The kids were beyond fascinated with the effect of the asteroid blasting through the ground to create a giant angular hole to the "center of the Earth."

"I can climb down," a grinning Cruz Jr. said as he started down the hole using the rope ladder and the handholds.

"Not you, Kat," I said. "I'll take you down."

On the first level down were the giant plants, which Cruz Jr. immediately tried to climb.

"Watch out or you'll fall, J.R.," Dot yelled at him.

His attention was easily drawn away by the sight of the giant insects; the realism of robots these days. He ran after them, trying to catch them. Kat, on the other hand, tried to run away from them frightened.

The next level was filled with the crystalline hills.

"Where's the giant animals, Daddy? This land is dumb."

"Don't you see the underground rivers, J.R.?" Dot asked.

He frowned. Not interested.

The last level contained the lava geysers and rivers, with giant stalactites and stalagmites in the underground cavernous level.

"You can swim in the lava," I said.

I found myself walking to the lava river by myself. My wife and kids watched me from afar, unconvinced.

"It's safe," I said.

"It's lava, Daddy! You'll burn up," Cruz Jr. yelled.

My son didn't seem to get that he had on his jacket because the cavern was a bit chilly.

"I'll jump," I said.

"No!" they yelled at me.

Soon enough, I wasn't the only one jumping around in the shallow lava river.

"It tastes like candy."

Dot and I turned around quickly to see the little urchin eating another handful.

"Don't eat the lava, J.R.!" Dot yelled.

Our heads quickly turned in the opposite direction.

"Don't eat the lava, Kat!" Dot yelled.

Splashing around in the synthetic orange lava was one thing; eating it was quite another. We were out of there.

"I want a lava bath!" Cruz Jr. had to be dragged out of the lava river kicking.

In daylight, we were treated to the full effect of International World. I wondered how a balloon ride would work in an underground theme world. We got our answer. The entire theme world rose up from the ground. Our hot air balloon flew itself as before. The kids had their bodies pressed against the glass floor of the basket to get the best look at Old America, Old London, Old Egypt with its pyramids, Old India, then Old Hong Kong and Old Japan.

From high above, the "puppets" did look like real people going about their day. I didn't tell the kids, so they thought they were real in their ancient dress. All of us had our own mini-binoculars, but it was the kids who didn't take them away from their eyes. They wanted to see every last detail there was to be seen.

The family vacation wrapped up in that balloon. We stayed for the rest of the day, only returning to the surface of the theme world twice for lunch and bathroom breaks. Dot and I were actually proud of the kids because kids normally need a lot more bathroom breaks than two. But they wanted to enjoy their first international vacation as much as we did.

It was a great end to our island vacation. Didn't turn out that bad. We returned to the bungalow at night and all everyone wanted to do was sleep.

I stood in front of the hotel building staring at our mountain of luggage.

"How did we get all this luggage on the plane with us? Did it multiply? I don't remember all this."

"Cruz, it's the same luggage we had when we arrived," Dot told me.

"Dot, how many pieces of clothing did you buy?"

"Cruz, this isn't about me and clothes I bought."

"You did buy more clothes."

"Cruz, the kids have new toys. I have *some* new clothes."

"Ha! How many new pieces of luggage did you buy to carry all these new clothes, shoes, and toys?"

"Cruz, it's the same number of luggage. We always bring extra so that we have room to carry back our purchases. Cruz, do you really think people travel to other places and don't buy stuff to bring back?"

"Dot, this is a lot of luggage."

"It's the same luggage we had before. Runner, help me out over here."

Runner's face went white. He and Modula were standing nearby listening to us.

"Leave him alone, Dot. I'm sure they can't wait to have us off their island. Wasn't he one of your deputies? Helping you interrogate the bad guy."

"Yes, that's true."

"So leave him alone and thank him and Ms. Modula for their service."

She gave both Runner and Modula a hug.

We couldn't leave the island without saying bye to our favorite crazy authors. We'd said our goodbyes to Derez and Askey yesterday. Both men were recalled to corporate headquarters by the board of directors. Both Modula and Runner would be running the island and managing a new island staff.

We were back to fun and games in our conversation with Marlan, Maxima, AC, reunited with her pesky dog—now renamed Luv-Dum, Dave, without his parka, and Jean.

"You'll have to be our guest, Great Detective, at a future writer's retreat," AC said to me.

"The writers' retreats will continue?" Dot asked me.

"Are you kidding?" AC said. "Every novelist, filmmaker, screenwriter on the globe and off-world will be beating a path to us."

"We're already sold out," Jean said.

"Sold out?" I asked.

"We decided to expand the retreat to the public going forward," Jean said. "No more shutting the island down for only a handful of people."

"Actually, it was the board's idea," Marlan said. "Besides, writers don't make enough to rent an entire island for themselves."

"Even if we did, we wouldn't," AC said.

"This was fun," Dot said. "We need to do it all again next year."

They were smiling. I wasn't.

Despite Dot's testimony, I still felt that we had twice the luggage going home as when we arrived. Apparently, we were in the same hoverplane that brought us to the island. The same hoverplane I thought was too tiny, and now we had double the amount of luggage.

I noticed that Kat was playing with a new fluffy dolphin.

"When did you get that?"

She was too busy playing to hear me. Cruz Jr. had a new large and long hovernautilus and was holding it in the air, running through the plane.

This time, other than the flight staff and crew, only the Cruz family was aboard. I'm sure more than a few scary sci-fi movies were made about nearly empty planes. I made sure to sit in the middle column of chairs and keep my eyes away from the windows. I didn't want to even think I saw anything, like a hairy gremlin, on the wings.

Also, I found out I was still flagged on the air registry as a "risk" because I was contaminated with a bio-toxin, and had been to the Moon. I'd been cleared by the CDC but I was still on the registry. I felt like some kind of germ terrorist. I told them it wasn't my fault. Fine by me, because I wasn't going to be leaving Metropolis for a while after this "vacation." At least we didn't have any flight attendants spraying us with anything as we came aboard.

The flight attendants on our special flight were the friendliest. They even joined us to watch in-flight movies. The adults watched the movies. The kids played with their toys. Everyone was happy.

"Oh, Dot, I forgot to tell you."

"What?"

"A surprise."

"Cruz, after all this, no more surprises."

"I thought you'd say that. Run-Time is picking us up at the airport to take us home."

"That's the kind of surprise I like."

We'd heard about the hurricane, which was all hype and did no real damage at all. We flew above billowy clouds, headed back to our home supercity of Metropolis. We couldn't wait to touch down on the tarmac at Metropolis International.

I knew I was right! We needed two, not one, hovercarts for all our luggage. We came through Customs and were waved through because we had a special entry pass from the island. No inspection for us.

When Run-Time told me he'd send a Let It Ride driver to pick us up, I didn't know he would be there too. My best friend was waiting for us at the arrival gates with one of his drivers. He waved and we waved back.

Dot gave him a hug and Run-Time and I exchanged bear hugs. Run-Time introduced his driver, everyone shaking hands. Run-Time bent down.

"Hello, Cruz Jr."

"Hello," my son greeted.

"Hello," Kat said.

"Hello, Ms. Kat," Run-Time said.

He stood up and took charge of one of the hovercarts of luggage, and the driver pushed the other one. I gave Dot a look.

"Cruz, not a word!"

"I wasn't going to say anything," I said.

"The real reason I came down is because I truly couldn't wait to hear about this vacation of yours," Run-Time said.

"Cruz!" Dot yelled.

I looked at my wife and saw her looking past me with shock. I quickly turned around.

"It's not possible. It couldn't happen a second time," I said.

He seemed to be coming to us from a VIP waiting area. We noticed the All-Vacationers Travel Hub—the domain of airport travel agents. We saw the glass-walled offices with changing holo-screens of travel destinations. We heard the live music. We saw the man named Vec quickly approaching!

"Mr. Cruz! Mrs. Cruz!" he called out. "You're back. I'm so glad I caught you. My new bosses called, and do I have a vacation offer for you and the family."

"Run!" I yelled.

Cruz Jr. was at first confused.

"The bad guy!" I said.

That's was all he needed to hear. Dot grabbed Kat, and the Cruz family ran through the airport for the departure exit as fast as we could, with Cruz Jr. leading the way.

Now, my Liquid Cool Cozy Murder Mystery with the family was over.

THANK YOU FOR READING!

Dear Reader,

I hope you enjoyed my *Liquid Cool* cyberpunk detective novel, *Write Me a Murder on Jules Verne's Island*.

<u>Can You Write Me a Review?</u>

I'd greatly appreciate an honest review on one or more of the following sites:

Reviews are the best way for readers to discover good books. My writer's motto is simple: "Readers Rule!" Thanks so much.

Always writing,

Austin Dragon

CONTINUE THE ADVENTURE

Get Your Next *Liquid Cool* Books!

These Mean Streets, Darkly (Liquid Cool Prequel Short)
Liquid Cool (Liquid Cool: The Cyberpunk Detective Series, Book 1)
Blade Gunner (Liquid Cool, Book 2)
NeuroDancer (Liquid Cool, Book 3)
The Electric Sheep Massacre (Liquid Cool, Book 4)
I, Alien Hunter (Liquid Cool, Book 5)
A.I. Confidential (Liquid Cool, Book 6)
Biopunk Blues (Liquid Cool, Book 7)
The Moon Is A Good Place to Die (Liquid Cool, Book 8)
Write Me a Murder on Jules Verne's Island: A Liquid Cool Cozy Murder Mystery (Book 9)

Liquid Cool Box Set (Liquid Cool Prequel and Books 1-3)
Liquid Cool Box Set 2 (Liquid Cool: Books 4-6)
Liquid Cool Box Set 3 (Liquid Cool: Books 7-9)

Liquid Cool: From the Crazy Maniac Files mini-series

Classic Cyborg (Book One)
Digital Samurai (Book Two)

Also by Austin Dragon
See all my books in science fiction, horror, and fantasy at:
http://www.austindragon.com/books

ABOUT THE AUTHOR

Austin Dragon is the author of the *After Eden* **Series**, including the *After Eden: Tek-Fall* mini-series, the classic *Sleepy Hollow Horrors*, the new epic fantasy adventure *Fabled Quest Chronicles*, and cyberpunk detective series, *Liquid Cool*. He is a native New Yorker, but has called Los Angeles, California home for the last twenty years. Words to describe him, in no particular order: U.S. Army, English teacher, one-time resident of Paris, political junkie, movie buff, Fortune 500 corporate recruiter, renaissance man, dreamer.

He is currently working on new books and series in science fiction, fantasy, and classic horror!

Connect with Austin on social media at:

Website and blog: http://www.austindragon.com

Pinterest: http://www.pinterest.com/austindragon

Goodreads: https://www.goodreads.com/ADragon

Other books by Austin:

See all my books at: http://www.austindragon.com/books

www.ingramcontent.com/pod-product-compliance
Lightning Source LLC
Chambersburg PA
CBHW020414260626
47156CB00007B/2388